THE GHOST
OF SECOND CHANCES

HAUNTING DANIELLE

The Ghost of Marlow House
The Ghost Who Loved Diamonds
The Ghost Who Wasn't
The Ghost Who Wanted Revenge
The Ghost of Halloween Past
The Ghost Who Came for Christmas
The Ghost of Valentine Past
The Ghost from the Sea
The Ghost and the Mystery Writer
The Ghost and the Muse
The Ghost Who Stayed Home
The Ghost and the Leprechaun
The Ghost Who Lied
The Ghost and the Bride
The Ghost and Little Marie
The Ghost and the Doppelganger
The Ghost of Second Chances
The Ghost Who Dream Hopped
The Ghost of Christmas Secrets

HAUNTING DANIELLE - BOOK 17

The Ghost
OF SECOND CHANCES

BOBBI HOLMES

The Ghost of Second Chances
(Haunting Danielle, Book 17)
A Novel
By Bobbi Holmes
Cover Design: Elizabeth Mackey

Copyright © 2018 Bobbi Holmes
Robeth Publishing, LLC
All Rights Reserved.

ROBETH PUBLISHING, LLC

This novel is a work of fiction.
Any resemblance to places or actual persons,
living or dead, is entirely coincidental.

www.robeth.net

ISBN-13: 978-1720577713
ISBN-10: 1720577714

Dedicated to my author friends. Thank you for all your support, encouragement, advice, and humor. This journey would not be half as fun—or as rewarding—without you.

ONE

Considering the spring break pedestrian traffic on the pier, Officer Brian Henderson wasn't surprised when he and his partner, Joe Morelli, stepped into Pier Café on Wednesday morning and found all the booths and tables occupied. Wearing their police uniforms and each carrying a hat in hand, the two men stepped all the way into the diner and glanced around. The door closed behind them. They looked for someplace to sit at the counter. Unfortunately, there was only one empty seat.

Before Carla could put their names on a waiting list, they heard a familiar voice call out from a nearby booth. "Brian, Joe, you're welcome to sit with me."

Turning to the person offering the invitation, they found Joanne Johnson, Marlow House's housekeeper and cook, and longtime Frederickport resident, smiling in their direction. She and Brian were about the same age, each in their fifties, while Joe was much younger. Each officer flashed Joanne a grin while walking to her booth.

"You're alone?" Brian asked as Joanne scooted over, making room for him to sit down.

"I just got off work. Thought I'd treat myself to breakfast out. You're welcome to join me. I'd like the company."

"Thanks," Joe said as he took a seat across from Joanne.

Brian glanced at his watch and then looked to Joanne as he sat down beside her. "A little early to get off work, isn't it? It's not even ten yet. With it being spring break, I'd think Marlow House would be hopping."

Before Joanne had a chance to respond, Carla stepped up to the table, turned the cups in front of Joe and Brian right side up, and filled them with coffee. She then took their orders.

After Carla left their table, Brian said, "That's right, I forgot Danielle told me she wasn't taking reservations for a few weeks."

"That was the plan," Joanne said with a shrug as she set her cup on the table. "Danielle figured we would need a break after having Clint's entourage stay with us for two weeks."

"I heard he was getting out of the hospital today." Brian picked up a sugar packet, tore it open, and dumped it into his coffee.

"That's why I was at work this morning. Got his room ready. We're putting him in the downstairs bedroom. No way he'd be able to maneuver the stairs with a cast on," Joanne explained.

"You don't seem too thrilled about it," Joe noted.

Joanne shrugged again. "I'm sorry, but he's an unpleasant man. Yet it's Danielle's call. Between you and me, that girl has too big a heart."

"How long do you think he's staying?" Brian stirred his coffee with a spoon while waiting for Joanne's answer.

"I've no idea. I asked Danielle, and she said nothing had been decided yet. Something about taking one day at a time. But really, it's not like we're a boardinghouse. So I have to assume it's temporary. It'd be rather expensive for him to stay very long."

"Knowing Danielle, she's probably giving him a discount," Joe suggested.

"I'm surprised they're releasing him so soon," Brian said. "When did he get out of the coma, like three days ago?"

"According to the doctors, there's nothing wrong with him—aside from the amnesia and broken leg. Nothing that requires hospitalization, anyway. They really don't have a reason to keep him, and from what I understand, he was adamant about getting out. He wanted the hospital to release him on Monday," Joanne explained. "But they wanted to keep him under observation for a few more days."

"For a guy who supposedly can't even remember who he is, I'm surprised he's so anxious to get out of the hospital. I'd think most people would be terrified and would want to stay somewhere safe," Joe said.

"Danielle claims he wants to stay at Marlow House because it's the last place he stayed before the accident, and he's hoping that will help jog his memory." Joanne reluctantly added, "I suppose I can understand that."

"Let's hope he gets his memory back quickly. I don't think Danielle needs to be looking after Clint Marlow for any longer than necessary," Brian said.

"She shouldn't be doing it at all," Joe grumbled.

"And did you know? He wants to be called Walt!" Joanne said.

Brian nodded. "Yes, the chief told us. He saw Marlow right after he came out of the coma. According to the chief, Marlow said he didn't feel like a Clint, so he decided to go by his first name."

"Technically his first name is Walter, not Walt," Joanne grumbled. "And I find it annoying he's using Walt Marlow's name. It isn't right."

"It is his name too," Brian reminded her.

"He's not at Marlow House yet, is he?" Joe asked.

Joanne shook her head. "No. Danielle is picking him up from the hospital this morning."

DANIELLE HAD PULLED up to the front door of the hospital several minutes earlier and now stood by the side of her Ford Flex, the passenger door wide open. She watched as a nurse pushed a wheelchair through the open doorway of the hospital and toward her vehicle. Its passenger, Walt Marlow, looked up and smiled at her, his blue eyes twinkling.

Walt the flesh and blood man looked much different from the last time she had seen Walt the spirit, and it wasn't the shorter hair. It was the fact he hadn't shaved for the last few days. It was more than a five o'clock shadow, yet not quite a beard. While she normally wasn't a fan of men's facial hair, she had to admit, Walt wore it well.

On his lap he held a plastic bag and a pair of crutches. She assumed the bag contained the meager items he had acquired while at the hospital. The previous day she had brought him a new pair of slacks, shirt, slippers, and undergarments to wear home. The tan slacks were a loose cotton-blend fabric, making it easy to pull on over his cast. She had found a white linen shirt to go with the slacks. They reminded her of a shirt Walt had worn in one of their dream hops. When selecting the clothes, she had thought of what suited Walt's style, not Clint's.

He seemed pleased with her selection, yet he had been apologetic over her having to go clothes shopping for him. She hadn't mentioned there were more clothes waiting at Marlow House. After all, she couldn't have Walt coming home and having nothing to wear. It wasn't like he still had the power to conjure up a new suit on demand.

Before helping Walt into the passenger side of the vehicle, the nurse handed Danielle the crutches and plastic bag. While the nurse carefully maneuvered Walt into the car, Danielle tossed the bag and crutches into the backseat and then walked around the Flex and got into the driver's side.

"You need to put on your seatbelt," the nurse instructed Walt. He looked at her with a confused expression, as if he didn't grasp her meaning.

Shutting her car door after sitting down, Danielle glanced over to Walt and frowned. She then realized what the problem was.

"I'll help him," Danielle told the nurse. "Sometimes that seatbelt sticks," she lied.

"Okay, but make sure he buckles up," the nurse said brightly. "You take care of yourself, Mr. Marlow."

"Thank you," Walt told her.

The nurse shut the passenger door and then turned from the vehicle and pushed the now empty wheelchair back toward the hospital.

"What was she talking about?" Walt asked.

"Your seatbelt, Walt." Danielle grabbed her own seatbelt and stretched it out to show him.

"What in the world?" He frowned.

"Your seatbelt, you put it on like this. Come on, you must have seen seatbelts in one of the shows you've watched on TV." She snapped the belt around her waist and looked over to Walt, waiting for him to do the same.

He shrugged. "I probably have, but I didn't really pay much attention to them. It doesn't matter; I don't want to wear it. I don't need to be belted in. It's not like I'm about to fall out of the car."

Danielle removed her seatbelt and turned to face Walt. "It's not really an option. It's the law."

"The law?"

Danielle nodded. "Yes. You have to wear a seatbelt in a moving vehicle."

Walt chuckled and leaned back in the seat, making no attempt to fasten his belt. "Considering the laws I've broken in the past; I'm not going to get too worked up over a seatbelt law."

"Walt, you have to wear your seatbelt. Anyway, if you don't, my car is going to make an annoying buzzing sound until you put it on."

Walt looked over to Danielle and noted her stern expression. "You're serious, aren't you?"

Danielle nodded. "Yes. Seatbelts save lives."

Walt considered Danielle's words a moment and then let out a sigh. "I suppose I shouldn't be careless with this life I've been given." He reached for his seatbelt. "Now, how do I do this?"

With a grin, Danielle leaned over Walt and helped him buckle up. When he was settled in his seat, she secured her own seatbelt. As she started to turn on the ignition, Walt reached for her hand, stopping her.

"Can we sit here a minute before we go?" Walt asked softly.

Danielle glanced out her back window and then looked back to Walt. "Just for a minute. But we're in a loading zone. If someone pulls up behind me, I need to move."

Walt nodded and then settled into his seat again, closing his eyes briefly. "I understand. But just a moment, please."

Danielle studied Walt. He opened his eyes and looked around the interior of the vehicle, as if seeing it for the first time.

"What is it?" she asked.

"Your car. It's so different from the last car I was in." He looked down to his feet briefly and then up to the dashboard.

"What was the last car you were in?" Danielle asked.

"My Packard Coupe."

Danielle grinned. "A Packard? What happened to it?"

Walt looked at Danielle and shrugged. "I don't know. I assume it was sold after I died. I don't imagine Brianna ever mentioned a Packard?"

Danielle shook her head. "Heck, Aunt Brianna didn't even mention Marlow House when she was alive. I suppose I could ask

Ben Smith what happened to it." Ben's father had been the court-appointed attorney of Danielle's great-aunt Brianna when she was a young orphaned child.

"I suppose it doesn't matter." Walt bounced gently up and down, his hands clinging to the outer edges of the seat.

Danielle chuckled. "What are you doing?"

"These seats. They feel different from what I remember."

Danielle turned on the ignition. "I imagine they do."

His attention now on the lit dashboard, Walt leaned forward and gingerly touched its control center. "You have a computer in the car?"

Danielle looked at the dash and shrugged. "Kinda, sorta. I suppose cars pretty much run by computers these days."

Walt let out a low whistle and shook his head. "I've seen car ads on television, but it's different actually sitting in one. You don't have any wood in here."

"Wood?" Danielle asked before hearing a honk. She glanced behind her out the back window. A car had pulled up. "I have to move."

Walt nodded. "That's fine. But do you think we could drive through town before we go home?"

"You want to see how it's changed?"

"I've only been out of Marlow House twice since I died. I didn't have the opportunity to look around either time. I'm curious to see what I'll recognize…how different everything is now."

"I'll give you the tour." Danielle steered the vehicle away from the curb and headed for the parking lot exit.

"I suppose you never have to climb a hill backwards in this, do you?" Walt asked as his hand stroked the door's interior and wiggled the controls. He jumped slightly when the window went down but quickly got the knack of how to roll it up again.

"What do you mean backwards?"

Still playing with the power window, making it go up and down, Walt said, "All the car ads I've seen on television show cars driving straight up mountain roads. None of them going backwards."

"Why would someone drive backwards up a mountain road?"

Walt stopped playing with the window and looked to Danielle. "Sometimes that was the only way you could get up the hill."

A few minutes later, as Danielle drove through the streets of Frederickport, Walt pointed to familiar landmarks and discussed the changes. He expressed relief that his hometown was still recognizable to him.

Danielle turned down one of the main sections of the business district. Walt spied an unfamiliar building up ahead with a large sign. It read *Frederickport Museum*.

"That's the museum?" Walt noted as they approached the building.

Hands firmly on the steering wheel, Danielle glanced briefly in that direction. "It is." As they drove by, a slender woman wearing a flower-print dress and straw hat was making her way to the front door of the building. In one hand she carried a purse, in the other a folded-up newspaper.

"So that's where they'll be putting my paintings," Walt said as they continued down the street, the museum now behind them.

TWO

Millie Samson was just ringing up several postcards for one customer in the museum store when a leggy blonde wearing a floral-print dress and straw hat entered the museum. Millie spied her from her place behind the counter, but it was Ben Smith, doing docent duty, who approached the woman in the front lobby adjacent to the museum store.

The Frederickport Museum was doing a brisk business for a Wednesday morning, due primarily to the influx of spring break visitors in the beach town. Vacationing families with young children often put the museum on their list of to-do activities, seeing it as an educational outing. The local children had had their spring holiday the previous week, so Millie assumed today's visitors with children were from out of town. However, the new arrival didn't have any children with her. She appeared to be alone.

IT TOOK Sonya Kozlov's eyes a moment to adjust to the interior lighting of the museum. To her right was an open archway leading to the museum store. An elderly woman stood behind the counter, now glancing her way as she handed a customer a small paper sack. Aside from the elderly woman and customer being waited on, there was a younger couple shopping in the gift store, along with several young children darting about while the man tried corralling them.

"Welcome to the Frederickport Museum," a man's voice greeted her.

Sonya looked toward the hallway leading to what she assumed was the main section of the museum and found an elderly man walking her way. On his shirt lapel he wore a name tag. It read *Ben Smith, Docent.*

"Hello, I assume there is a fee?" Sonya asked, her Russian accent noticeable.

After Ben told her the amount, she dug some bills out of her purse and handed them to Ben with the same hand holding the newspaper.

Ben took the money and when doing so, noticed the folded newspaper and the article in view. He nodded to the paper. "I assume you've read about the museum's newest acquisition."

"That's why I'm here. I would love to see the Bonnets," she told him.

"I'm really sorry, but we don't have them yet. If that's what you came to see, I'll be happy to refund your money." Ben handed Sonya her money back, but she waved it away.

"No, no. Keep it. I'd still like to look around. But I thought you already had one of his paintings here," she asked.

"It's in Portland right now. Would you like to see the display anyway? You can see the emerald."

"Emerald?" Sonya brightened up.

"This way." He then paused and added, "I'm Ben Smith, one of the docents."

A few moments later, Sonya stood with Ben in front of what had been Eva Thorndike's display. The easel and Eva's portrait were no longer there, but in their place was a framed photograph of the painting and written explanation that the portrait would be returning to the museum in the near future. It sat atop the glass display case. The Thorndike emerald, on loan from Danielle Boatman, remained locked in the display case.

"It's one of the original emeralds from Eva Thorndike's necklace, which is commonly referred to as the Missing Thorndike," Ben explained as Sonya leaned close to the display, peering at the emerald.

"Yes, I read about the necklace online." Sonya stood up straight and turned to Ben. She glanced down to the newspaper in her hand and its article on the museum. The article told how the museum would be displaying three paintings by the French artist Jacque Bonnet. "I was under the impression the paintings were already here. I was hoping to see them. Perhaps they are here, but not yet on display?" She craned her neck and looked toward the back of the museum, as if expecting the paintings to suddenly appear.

"Unfortunately, that newspaper article got a few facts wrong. When I was interviewed, I'm afraid they misunderstood me, and I didn't realize until the article came out."

She glanced briefly at the newspaper again and then smiled up at Ben. "You're the one interviewed in the article?"

Ben nodded. "I'm currently the president of the Historical Society."

"So where are the paintings now?"

"They've been taken to Portland to be authenticated. In the meantime, we have some renovations to do to the museum to make place for the new exhibit. That's supposed to start as soon as the paintings are officially authenticated, which I'm hearing now won't be until May. So I doubt the exhibit will be up until fall."

Sonya cocked her head slightly and studied Ben. "The paintings haven't been authenticated yet?"

Ben shook his head. "I'm pretty sure it's just a formality. But I can't blame the Glandon Foundation—who is actually the one purchasing the Bonnet from us, and the other two from another party—to make sure they are the real deal before paying all that money. It's really very exciting."

"The article made it sound like the paintings were being authenticated at the time the article was being written, and they would be displayed by now." She glanced briefly at the article again and then looked back to Ben.

"We expected to have it done this week, but the expert they're using had an unexpected family emergency. The earliest they could reschedule was the last week in May."

"Where are the paintings in the meantime? Shame we can't still enjoy them." Sonya let out a sigh and refolded the newspaper and then shoved it in her purse.

"I'm afraid they're locked up in a storage room in some Portland museum. I don't think anyone has even looked at them yet." Ben shrugged.

"What a shame." Sonya let out another sigh.

"You're a fan of Bonnet?" Ben asked. "I hate to admit, I wasn't even aware of the artist until we were informed our Eva Thorndike was probably one of his."

"I became familiar with his work when I visited France last year. I was quite taken with his distinct style. And when I read you had several of his paintings, I knew I had to come."

"Are you from around here?" Ben asked.

"No. I'm visiting friends in the area, and I happened to pick up their newspaper and saw the article on the paintings. I was so excited. I suppose I will just have to make a trip back to see them in the fall."

SONYA HURRIED down the steps of the museum, heading to her car. She was tempted to make the phone call now, but she didn't want anyone to overhear her. Curiosity alone had spurred this morning's impromptu visit to the museum. Never in her wildest dreams had she imagined what she would discover. She was almost giddy with excitement. Perhaps all was not lost.

Today's impromptu visit to the Frederickport Museum came about because of a series of events. It began when she had heard the disappointing fate of the Frederickport Bonnets. To make matters even more depressing, she learned there were actually three Bonnets in Frederickport, not just two. Three paintings that should now be in her possession, not sitting in some storage room.

After dealing with her disappointment, she had purchased a subscription to the local newspaper in hopes of keeping tabs on the paintings. In yesterday's mail came the newspaper article that seemed to imply the Bonnets were already on display at the museum. She could barely sleep last night, and when she woke up early this morning, she dressed quickly, jumped in her car, and drove from Maurice's home in Portland to Frederickport. If Maurice wasn't currently on a flight to London, she would have called him first.

What a surprise to discover that not only were the paintings not at the small museum—they hadn't been seen by the art expert. *They still don't know two of those paintings locked up in some Portland museum are fakes*, Sonya thought with delight.

Hastily unlocking her car, she slipped inside, closed the door behind her, and relocked it. Before tossing the purse on the passenger seat, she retrieved her cellphone. She still had his number in favorites. The phone rang twice before he answered.

"Why are you calling me?" came an angry male voice. "I told you not to call me again. We have nothing to talk about."

"If you wonder why you haven't heard anything about the paintings being fake, it's because the expert hasn't seen them yet." She leaned back in the car seat, holding the phone to her ear, and smiled. She had not felt so hopeful in days.

"I don't know what you're talking about. Sonya, please. It's over, and thank you for calling. It just reminds me I need to get another phone."

"No!" Sonya shouted, sitting up abruptly in the seat. "But it's not over, Mac. You can still get the paintings and get the money. Don't you want the money?"

"What are you talking about? I explained it. Any day now they're going to come looking for me, and I need to disappear for a while."

"No, Mac. You have until May. We've been given a reprieve. You're back in business. We're back in business. And I want my paintings."

THREE

"I suppose this street looks so familiar because I've been watching it from the attic window for almost a hundred years. I've watched it change—yet most of the time, I didn't understand the changes. Not until you came and helped me bring the world in focus," Walt mused as he looked out the car's passenger side window.

They had just turned down Beach Drive.

"That's Heather's house," Danielle pointed out as they drove by. A moment later, they pulled into the side drive of Marlow House.

"Danielle, would you mind if I sat outside for a while, under the trees?" Walt asked. "It feels like I've spent an eternity inside Marlow House, and I would just like to feel the air, listen to the birds. Maybe take a nap. You have no idea how good it feels to sleep."

Bringing the car to a stop, Danielle put it in park, turned off the ignition, and turned to Walt. "Are you saying you never slept when…when you…"

"When I was dead?" Walt turned to Danielle and smiled softly.

She nodded.

"Dead men don't sleep. Didn't I ever tell you that before?"

"Not really. I'm not sure we ever talked about it. And if we did, I don't think you ever said one way or another."

"One thing I remember, when on the other side, there are some things we aren't supposed to discuss with those on this side—it's against the rules."

"What about now? Can you break the rules?" Danielle grinned at the idea. She had always suspected Walt understood more about how it all worked on the other side than he had shared with her.

Walt chuckled. "I just said *one thing I remember*, because since I woke up in Clint's body, memories have been slipping away."

Danielle's grin vanished. "What do you mean memories have been slipping away?"

Walt shook his head and smiled wearily at Danielle. "Oh, I remember every conversation you and I have shared—every dream hop. The memories I'm referring to are from the other side. For example, I know there was a bargain I made that allowed me to stay at Marlow House—under specific conditions. But who did I make the bargain with? What were the conditions? Or where did this bargain take place? I have no idea."

"The condition was that you couldn't leave the house. And once you did, you couldn't return," Danielle told him.

"I remember that. Yes, it was part of it. But there was more. What exactly? I no longer remember; I just know there was more. It's out there, on the edges of my memory. Foggy and just beyond my grasp."

"I'd ask what else you've forgotten, but I suppose that's a silly question. If you've forgotten something, how would you know?"

Walt shrugged. "Perhaps. But it's the things that I do remember that make me aware of what I must have forgotten. For example, remember the Christmas dream hop, where your family was there? Or when Emma and her husband joined us in a dream hop to say goodbye to you?"

"Of course." No longer wearing her seatbelt, Danielle sat sideways in the driver's seat, facing Walt.

"I remember how to dream hop. Well, at least how I did it then. I don't imagine it's possible for me to do it now." Walt chuckled at the idea. "It was about focusing and thinking about who I wanted to bring into a dream. However, that didn't include someone like Emma or your family, who are already on the other side. I did something else that allowed them to join us. I know that—I can feel it. But what exactly? I have absolutely no idea."

"I just hope you don't forget anything else," Danielle said.

"I have a feeling I have already forgotten what I needed to forget."

"What does that even mean?" Danielle frowned.

Walt unbuckled his seatbelt. "To be honest, I have no idea. But it's something I feel…and there is something else."

"Something else?" Danielle asked.

"This all seems…surreal. Too good to be true, maybe? Like I'm dreaming and will wake up any moment and find out I'm still dead."

Danielle laughed. "I thought you just said dead men don't sleep, so how can they dream?"

Walt shrugged. "They don't."

"Then this can't be a dream? Can it?"

After getting out of the car a few minutes later, Danielle retrieved the crutches from the backseat. She helped Walt from the vehicle and was impressed at how well he was managing the crutches. With minimal assistance, he made his way to a patio rocker on the back porch.

"Thank you," Walt said when he sat down.

"Can I get you anything?" Danielle asked.

"No. I'd just like to sit out here for a while, maybe take a nap. I'm really very tired. Surprised how this morning's outing has exhausted me."

"Do you want me to make you something to eat?" While waiting for his answer, Danielle walked back to the car and retrieved her purse and keys.

"I'm not really hungry, thank you. I have to say, after almost a century without food, I'm wondering if my memories of how wonderful food tasted were exaggerated, or if hospital food is just horrible."

Danielle walked back toward Walt and laughed. "I suspect the latter. How about some chocolate cake in a little while? I made a double fudge chocolate cake last night in honor of your homecoming."

Walt's grin widened. "Your double fudge chocolate cake always looked amazing. Yes. I would love to try some. Maybe after I take a little nap?"

Danielle nodded. "Fine. And after you wake up, I'll see if you might be ready for some lunch before that cake."

"Sounds wonderful."

Danielle turned toward the house and started to walk away but paused. She turned back to Walt, stepped closer, and then leaned down and quickly kissed him on the cheek and whispered, "Welcome home, Walt."

In response, Walt reached up and grabbed hold of Danielle's left hand and held it tightly. Their gazes locked.

"I suppose we should take this slowly," Walt whispered, his gaze shifting briefly from her eyes to her lips.

"One day at a time, Walt," she whispered.

He gently squeezed her hand and then released it. Without premeditation, Danielle dropped a quick kiss on his lips and then turned and hurried to the back door leading into the kitchen.

WALT WASN'T sure how long he had been sleeping. He had drifted off peacefully while listening to the birds chirping in the nearby trees, soothed by the gentle sea breeze caressing his face. But there was no breeze now. No birds chirping. There were just voices. Women's voices. He knew those voices.

THE SPIRIT OF MARIE NICHOLS, an image of herself ten years prior to her death at age ninety-one, leaned toward Walt and studied his face. "Do you think he's dead…again? He looks dead."

"Marie, he doesn't look dead." Eva Thorndike—who even in death bore a striking resemblance to Charles Dana Gibson's illustrated Gibson girl—stepped up to Walt and took a closer look. Tilting her head to one side, she tapped one finger against her chin while studying his motionless features. "Although…he doesn't exactly look alive."

"And he's wearing a beard!" Marie clucked.

"It's not really much of a beard, but he does look rather dashing."

Walt's eyes flew open. Panicked, he looked from Eva to Marie and back to Eva before screaming, "Danielle!"

Danielle, who was just inside the back door in the kitchen, heard his frantic call, dropped what she was doing, and practically flew out the back door. As the door slammed shut behind her, she came to an abrupt halt upon seeing Walt—his eyes wide—staring up to Eva and Marie, who now hovered a few feet from him. What Danielle hadn't

THE GHOST OF SECOND CHANCES

seen was how the spirits had abruptly distanced themselves from Walt after being surprised by his unexpected outburst.

"What the…?" Danielle walked closer to Walt, her gaze shifting from him to the two spirits. It was obvious to Danielle that he could see Eva and Marie. Or at least, it certainly appeared that way.

"What's wrong?" Danielle finally asked.

Still in panic mode, Walt looked to Danielle and blurted, "I'm dead! Nerts! I knew it was too good to be true. I close my eyes for five minutes and this body up and dies on me!"

Danielle let out the breath she had inadvertently been holding and stepped closer to where Walt sat in the rocker. She flashed a sheepish smile to Eva and Marie, who seemed unsure as to the reason for Walt's peculiar behavior.

"You aren't dead, Walt. Why do you think you're dead?" Danielle asked, now standing next to his rocker.

Walt pointed an accusing finger at Eva and Marie. "That's why!"

Eva rolled her eyes and let out a sigh. "Seriously, Walt? Is that what this is about?"

Marie shook her head in confusion. "What just happened?"

"I can see them…hear them!" Walt exclaimed, his eyes wild.

"So can I. But I'm not dead," Danielle reminded him.

"But you can see ghosts. I can't!" Walt insisted.

"Notice how he freely calls us ghosts, but remember the hissy fit he'd throw if anyone dare call him one?" Eva told Marie.

"Walt, you are not dead," Danielle insisted.

"I'm dead. So what now? Do I have to go back?" Walt asked.

Joining Eva in an eye roll, Danielle leaned closer to Walt and pinched his arm. It wasn't a light pinch.

"Ouch!" Walt yelped as he grabbed the injured arm. He glared at Danielle. "What did you do that for?"

Danielle smiled down at Walt, looking not a bit remorseful for inflicting pain. "Because you can't pinch a ghost."

Rubbing his still-stinging arm, Walt considered what Danielle was saying.

"Plus, there is only one of you," Danielle said as she sat down in the chair next to him.

"One of me?" he asked.

"Exactly. I left alive-you sitting in that chair. Now, had you died, your body would still be sitting there, and your spirit—well, it wouldn't be sitting in the chair, unable to stand up without some assistance."

"Goodness, Walt, I would think you would be happy you could see and hear us," Marie grumbled. She took a seat on one of the empty patio chairs.

"I'm sorry, Marie...Eva...I...guess I overreacted," Walt apologized.

"You think?" Danielle chuckled.

"I wondered if this might happen," Eva said.

"What, that Walt would see spirits? Does this mean he'll see all spirits, or just you and Marie?" Danielle asked.

Eva shrugged. "I'm not really sure. You see, it's fairly common for babies or very young children to see spirits. Marie could see me when she was a baby."

"But I can't remember seeing ghosts as a child," Marie added.

"No, because children are taught such things are not real, so after a while they stop seeing them—stop remembering them," Eva explained. "They begin believing the lie."

"Except for me and Chris," Danielle noted.

"True. But there are always the exceptions—those disbelievers." Eva smiled.

"Disbelievers?" Danielle asked with a frown.

"You didn't quite believe what the adults in the world were telling you. Basically, you had more faith in yourself, which is why you never lost the ability to see and hear ghosts."

"And Heather?" Danielle asked.

"Heather is one of those people who believed because she wanted to please the adults in her world, but deep down, she didn't quite believe them. After a time, she learned to have faith in herself again and was able to see spirits, like she did when she was a child. As for Walt, he woke up in Clint's body already knowing about the existence of spirits—of Marie and myself. So there was nothing to stop him from seeing and hearing us. But will he see other spirits as you do? I assume so, yet I'm not positive."

"If all that's true, then why can't Lily see spirits? Oh, I know she saw Darlene, but why couldn't she see Walt when he was a spirit? She believed in him. And what about the others, like Ian and the Chief. They believed in Walt," Danielle asked.

Eva smiled at Danielle before answering. "Because some habits are simply too hard to break. They've spent a lifetime ignoring the spirit world. Simply believing now doesn't mean they can once again see spirits like when they were children. And it's entirely possible when they were young children they didn't see spirits. It happens, you know."

"I'm sorry I screamed like a dumb Dora a minute ago," Walt apologized. "I suppose I've been afraid none of this is real—or won't last. But I am pleased to know I'm able to see and hear both of you." He smiled at Marie and Eva.

Marie, who had been glaring at Walt, finally let out a sigh and smiled in his direction. "Can I ask you one thing?"

"Certainly," Walt told her.

"What's with the beard?"

Reaching up to briefly stroke his heavily stubbled chin, Walt grinned at Marie. "I forgot what a chore it is to shave every morning. After not picking up a razor for over ninety years, I find it might take me a little while to get back in the habit again."

FOUR

Chet Morrison pulled his car to a stop in front of Marlow House. With the engine still running, he sat in the driver's seat, his hands firmly planted on the steering wheel, and debated going up to the front door. There were no cars parked in front of the bed and breakfast, and all the front blinds were drawn. He wondered if perhaps no one was home.

Shifting his vehicle into reverse, Chet backed up so he could look down the driveway. With the car idling, he peered down the side of the house and spied Danielle's car. Backing up a little more so he could get a clearer view, movement caught his eye. If he wasn't mistaken, it was Danielle, and she wasn't alone. It was a man using crutches, and she was helping him make his way to the back door.

"She really did take the guy in," Chet said under his breath. With a grunt, he put his car back in drive and stepped on the gas.

Minutes later Chet pulled his car in front of Adam Nichols's property management office.

ADAM DIDN'T BOTHER STANDING up when Chet entered his office late Wednesday morning, but remained seated behind his desk. "What do you need?"

"My sister's giving me a hard time," Chet said as he flopped down in one of the two empty chairs facing Adam. "She says it's time I found a place of my own."

Adam leaned back in his desk chair while studying Chet. "So you're here looking for a rental? I have to tell you, most of my inventory is vacation rental. I don't think you want to pay what they're going for. Not full-time."

"Yeah. You gave me a flyer the last time I was in here. Prices are kind of steep. I was thinking maybe I could just rent a room someplace, not a house or apartment."

Adam shrugged. "Sorry, I can't help you there."

"I was thinking about a room at Marlow House. That's why I'm here. I know you're friends with Danielle Boatman."

"Marlow House? It's a bed and breakfast. Considering Danielle's rates, you'd be better off renting one of my houses." Adam sat up straighter in his chair, leaning over his desk while resting his elbows on the desktop.

"Boatman likes me. I could tell. She has a thing for me. If I work it right, I bet she'll let me stay there for practically nothing. After all, she doesn't need the money. From what I hear, she's loaded."

"Danielle doesn't have a thing for you. She doesn't even like you," Adam said with a snort.

"BS. She cut her freaking hair after I told her she should. Women don't do that unless they want to impress the guy. And I'm that guy."

Adam leaned back in his chair again. "So what do you need me for? Go on over to Marlow House and get yourself a free room. I would love to see how that works." Adam chuckled.

"She's still playing it cool with me. She's embarrassed. I don't want to spook her. I thought if you took me over there, make up some excuse why we're stopping by, and then you can mention I'm looking for a room."

"And you think she's just going to offer you one?"

"I won't make it easy for her." Chet chuckled. "I was rather thinking she'd end up begging me to take it when we're done with her."

"Oh really? And exactly what are '*we*' going to do to get her to be so accommodating?"

"You don't have to do anything. Just get me in the door with you. I'll do the rest," Chet smirked.

"While I'm tempted to take you over there just to see you make a fool of yourself, I don't think this is a good time. From what I understand, Danielle is picking up Clint Marlow from the hospital today." Adam then thought, *I don't think she needs two jerks on her hands.*

"Is he the one with the cast on his leg?" Chet asked.

Adam shrugged. "I heard he had a broken leg."

"He's the one who was in the car accident, and his fiancée was killed?"

"Yes. They were staying at Marlow House before the accident."

"I heard from Carla at the diner that he has amnesia," Chet said.

"That's what I heard."

"Carla also said he's a major tool."

Adam chuckled. "Again true. I feel a little guilty; I'm the one who sent him Danielle's B and B website. He looks just like Walt Marlow's portrait."

"Yeah. I heard about all that. He's at Marlow House now. Which is one reason I need to get over there and stake my claim."

"You're on your own, Chet. Danielle is a friend of mine."

"I thought I was a friend too?" Chet asked. "If it weren't for me, you would have gotten your ass busted for breaking into the gym back in our senior year."

"That was a million years ago. And as I remember, if it weren't for you, I wouldn't have broken into the gym. You and those damn Bandoni brothers!" Adam grumbled.

"They're okay. In fact, I'm heading out to see them after I leave here."

"I thought they would be dead or in prison by now."

"No, still kicking and living in their grandma's house. She died a couple of years ago."

"Yeah, I've run into them a few times when I've been in Astoria. Didn't know they were back at their grandmother's house."

Chet nodded. "To be honest, I don't think they ever moved out. I can't say I blame them. The house might be old, but it's not far from the beach, and I bet it would be worth a fortune now."

"I can't believe you're still friends with those guys. Back in high

THE GHOST OF SECOND CHANCES

school, I remember them coming to town and causing trouble just about every weekend."

"That's because their grandma would have given them hell if she found out they were causing trouble in Astoria. Small town."

"Frederickport's a small town," Adam reminded him.

"True. But their grandma didn't live here, and they didn't go to school here."

"So what, you kept in touch with them all these years?" Adam asked.

"Nah. But when I came back to Frederickport, I drove over to Astoria and ran into them. They needed an extra hand for a job they were doing, so they hired me. I can always use the money."

"What kind of work?" Adam asked.

Chet shrugged. "Just handyman stuff."

"Handyman stuff?" Adam said with a snort. "Didn't you flunk woodshop?"

"Shut up." Chet stood. "If you aren't going to help me with Danielle, I'll get going."

"Leave her alone, Chet. Seriously. You're wasting your time. Trust me. All you're going to do is piss her off, and you really don't want to piss off Danielle."

Chet laughed. "You just worry about your Melony. I've got Danielle Boatman under control. Just wait and see. Before you know it, I'll be living rent-free in Marlow House, and I wouldn't be surprised if Danielle insists on buying me a new car. She can afford it."

"Yeah, right," Adam said under his breath as he stood up to see Chet out.

STANDING at his office window looking outside, Adam watched as Chet got into a dilapidated car parked by the sidewalk in front of his building. The vehicle was in serious need of painting—first the dents would need to be hammered out. But considering the amount of rust Adam could see from where he stood, he doubted that would be possible.

"Yeah, right, Danielle is going to buy you a car. Dream on, buddy," Adam said under his breath. Turning from the window, he sat back down at his desk and picked up his phone to call Danielle.

"Hey, Adam, what's going on?" Danielle asked when she answered her phone a moment later.

"I wanted to give you a heads-up. Chet might be stopping by Marlow House."

"Chet?"

"The guy you have a thing for. Remember, he's the reason you cut your hair," Adam teased.

"Eww, gross. Why is he stopping by Marlow House?"

"Sounds like his sister is tired of his freeloading and wants him out. He can't really afford to rent much. He has this crazy idea about staying in a room at Marlow House."

"First of all, I am not a boardinghouse. Second, if he's having a problem coming up with rent money, I seriously doubt he could afford one of my rooms."

"But, Danielle, he's not planning to pay," Adam said sweetly, trying his best not to break out in laughter. "At least not much."

"Excuse me?"

"He figures with a little sweet-talking he can get you to let him stay there for practically nothing. Maybe even free."

"Sweet-talking? Umm, his idea of sweet-talking is pretty warped. And stay for free? Are you serious?"

"I'm afraid I am. Also, he thinks he'll get you to buy him a car. Not right away, of course. And I have to say, he could use a new car. He's driving a pile of crap right now."

"This guy is delusional!"

"I always thought he was missing a few fries from his Happy Meal." Adam let out a laugh and then added, "Who am I kidding? He's missing the entire burger patty."

"I don't need this aggravation," Danielle grumbled.

"That's why I wanted to give you a heads-up. Chet isn't dangerous. Well, at least I don't think so. But he's always been persistent and somewhat annoying."

"Annoying I will agree with." Danielle let out a sigh. "Thanks for warning me. You think he's going to show up today?"

"He said something about heading to Astoria to see some friends there. So hopefully he won't show up on your doorstep today. But when he does, I just wanted you to be prepared."

"Thanks, Adam. I do appreciate it. I rather wish I hadn't cut my hair now."

"WHY DO you wish you hadn't cut your hair?" Walt asked Danielle after she got off the phone. He sat on the parlor sofa, his cast propped up on the coffee table.

Adam had called Danielle's cellphone just as she had walked into the parlor, carrying a plated slice of chocolate cake for Walt. When answering the phone several minutes earlier, she had set the plate on the small parlor desk while Walt waited patiently.

Now off the phone, she set it on the desk and picked up the plate of cake, carrying it to Walt.

"Remember I told you about the guy who tried that lame pickup technique called negging on me?" Danielle asked as she handed him the cake.

"Yes." Walt's attention shifted from what Danielle was saying to the plate of chocolate cake now in his hand. Just as Danielle started to further explain the call, Walt took a bite of the cake. Before finishing her sentence, Walt abruptly held up his hand to stop her from talking. He closed his eyes and moaned.

Startled by his sudden change of demeanor, she asked, "What is it?"

Shaking his head, Walt waved her away and then took a second bite. After a moment, he looked up into her eyes and said, "This. Is. Heaven."

FIVE

Police Chief MacDonald's youngest son, Evan, was taller than other second graders. Lean and lanky, with a sweet face, enormous brown eyes, and thick long lashes women would pay a fortune to have—and he had a secret. Like Danielle Boatman, he could see ghosts.

On Wednesday afternoon Evan didn't eat lunch with his classmates, as he normally did. Instead, he stayed in the classroom with his teacher, Lily Bartley. The two sat at the reading table together, Evan eating a ham and cheese sandwich while Lily munched on baby carrots, celery, and chunks of cheddar cheese. They were alone in the room.

"I can't believe Walt is coming home today. Do you think it's really him?" Evan asked.

Lily glanced at the wall clock and then picked up another carrot. "He should be there by now. And Danielle seems to think it's him."

"How come you didn't visit him in the hospital? I asked my dad to take me to see him, but he said I had to wait until he came home."

"I didn't see him for probably the same reason your dad didn't want to take you to the hospital." Lily bit off half of the carrot and chewed it up.

Evan frowned. "What's that?"

"Clint was nothing but a stranger to you. So why would you be visiting him? Your dad knows all kinds of people at the hospital. They'd think it strange if he took you to see him."

"But I thought you knew Walt's cousin?"

Lily chuckled. "Barely. Plus, it's common knowledge I thought he was a jerk. I ran into him once at Pier Café, and he was so rude to me. It was embarrassing."

"Oh." Evan finished half his sandwich. He then looked at Lily, his brows drawn into a frown, and asked, "What are people going to say when you're friends with Walt now? Aren't they still gunna think it's strange?"

Lily let out a sigh. "You have a point. But I figure people will think I'm going over to Marlow House to see Dani and, well, people's opinions can change. And after a while people will forget how Clint acted when he first arrived and start to like him."

"What if they don't?" Evan asked.

"What do you mean?"

"Maybe they won't forget. Jody Pepper barfed in Miss Anne's kindergarten class. All over the wooden blocks. They had to throw the blocks away. She still gets teased about it. No one forgot."

Lily let out another sigh. Evan had a point. Jody was also in her class, and just yesterday she had to tell two of her students to stop calling the girl Jody Barfy Block.

"And what if it isn't Walt?" Evan asked.

"It is. I'm sure of it," Lily insisted.

"How do you know? You haven't seen him yet," Evan reminded her.

Lily absently twisted the end of her red braid as she considered the question. *How did she know?* Lily had been the optimistic cheerleader through the ordeal, telling Danielle to stop fretting when Walt initially took over Clint's body and was still in the coma. But since he had woken up and she hadn't seen him for herself, doubt had managed to creep into her subconscious. She couldn't wait until school was out, and she could see Walt for herself and assuage her fears. Glancing at the clock again, she counted the hours until she could go home. Ian had taken Sadie to Salem that morning and had promised to be back in time to pick her up at school, after which they both planned to go to Marlow House and see Walt. She hoped it really was Walt.

THEY SAY cats sleep thirteen to sixteen hours a day. Max's daily average tended to be on the high end, especially during the last few days. Evenings at Marlow House had been rather lonely without Walt to hang out with. Marie stopped by regularly, yet hers were not nocturnal visits. She had other haunts after sunset, and they didn't include chatting with a contrary feline.

The black cat had been napping on the attic sleeper sofa since before Danielle had left to pick up Walt at the hospital, when a bird hit the window. Jolted awake, Max lifted his head and yawned. He looked to the source of the sound. Blinking his eyes, he quickly leapt from the sofa to the windowsill and peered outside. Looking down, he caught a glimpse of the stunned bird lying on the ground below the parlor window. His white-tipped ears twitched.

Jumping down to the floor, with the intention of going downstairs and having a closer look at the bird, he started for the open door. What he failed to see as he made his way down the attic stairs a few moments later was the stunned bird regaining consciousness and flying away.

WALT SAT ALONE in the parlor, contemplating making his way to the backyard so he could sit outside again. Unfortunately, his crutches were sitting on the other side of the room, and he figured the only way to get them would be to hop. For a moment he missed his ghostly powers—it would have been a snap to float the crutches across the room. Of course, that would also mean he would not need the crutches in the first place.

Absently, Walt waved his right hand and looked at it. There was no lit cigar between two of his fingers. He didn't expect there would be. The wave was more a habit—not much different from the habit of smoking. Danielle had asked him that morning if he missed his cigars. The truth was, smoking as a spirit provided no real sensory stimulation—aside from an olfactory stimulation—something that even those around him also experienced when they could smell the cigar smoke. He didn't quite understand it, considering a bodiless spirit had no nose, no olfactory nerve. Yet he could also smell the ocean when Danielle would leave the windows open.

In spite of his spirit-self having the ability to observe smells, the sense of taste had been lost on him. Had he tried mimicking eating

THE GHOST OF SECOND CHANCES

cake as he had smoked a cigar, he knew there would have been no heavenly flavor—no flavor at all, just like smoking was different for him when he had been alive the first time as opposed to smoking while a spirit.

While the sense of taste had been lost on him, he could recall smelling Danielle's cakes baking in the oven, which had been maddening. Something in the back of his mind told him that had he moved on after death, he could have enjoyed cake again—as he was doing now with his second chance at life. But he didn't know for certain. It was all speculation.

He glanced at the coffee table. Sitting next to his cast-encased leg was a cellphone. Danielle had given it to him earlier, after he had finished his piece of chocolate cake. Walt closed his eyes for a moment, once again remembering the heavenly taste of Danielle's chocolate cake.

Walt opened his eyes and let out a sigh. "If I'm not careful, I'm going to get fat." He leaned forward and picked up the cellphone from the table and looked at it. Danielle had told him she had purchased the phone for him the day before. She said it wasn't like hers—but to Walt, it looked like hers. According to her, it was a phone that you load minutes on, whatever that meant. While she had given him a quick tutorial on how to use it and had told him to use it to call her if he needed help when she was somewhere else in the house, Walt didn't want to do that. He felt he was enough of a burden without calling her every five minutes when he needed something.

After giving the phone another look, he tossed it back on the coffee table and then gingerly pulled his broken leg from the table, setting his foot on the floor as he prepared to stand up. Scooting to the end of the sofa, to allow him to use one of the sofa's arms for leverage, he was distracted when he heard a loud meow coming from the open doorway leading to the hall.

Looking up, his gaze met Max's. The two stared at each other as Max walked slowly—panther-like—in his direction—the cat's black tail waving like a flag behind him.

"Max?" Walt asked, his unspoken question understood.

A moment later Max jumped onto the coffee table and sat down, staring at Walt.

"You understand me? Don't you?" Walt said in awe.

Max meowed.

"Yes. It's really me. No, Max. Even if I could, which I can't, I promised. Remember?"

"What are you doing?" Danielle asked from the doorway. She looked inquisitively from her cat—who continued to sit on the parlor coffee table—to Walt, who sat on the sofa.

Walt turned to Danielle, a silly grin on his face. "I didn't lose it!"

Danielle walked all the way into the room. "You didn't lose what?"

"He understands me, Danielle—I understand him!" Walt said excitedly.

Danielle shook her head in disbelief. "No. You have to be imagining things. That's not possible. You just think you understand what he's thinking."

Walt didn't have time to argue with Danielle. The next moment they heard Lily shouting, "Hello!" from the entry hall.

Danielle quickly made her way to the open doorway and looked out to the entry. "We're in here."

"Ian wanted to park the car in the garage, and then he and Sadie are coming right over. But I couldn't wait, so he let me out," Lily explained as she came running into the parlor. She stopped the moment she spied Walt sitting on the sofa, looking at her.

"Is it you? Is it really you?" Lily whispered, walking closer to Walt. She had removed her braid on her way home from school, and now her rusty-colored hair fell wavy past her shoulders.

"Hello, Lily," Walt said softly.

Just as Lily reached the sofa, she stopped. Nervously, she chewed her lower lip and studied Walt, who continued to smile up at her.

"What is it, Lily?" Walt asked.

"What were Ian and I sitting on in the dream hop?" Lily blurted out.

Walt frowned. "Excuse me?"

"When you brought us into the dream hop, what were we sitting on?"

Walt's smile widened. "As I recall, we were sitting in the middle of the ocean—on surfboards."

Lily let out a shout and then flew to Walt, giving him a hug. "It really is you, Walt!"

Danielle, who stood by the small parlor desk observing the greeting, asked with a smile, "I thought you had no doubts?"

Lily released Walt from her hug and sat on the sofa next to him. "I didn't think I did. But…well…"

Danielle smiled at her friend and then walked to one of the chairs across from the sofa to sit down. "I understand."

The next moment they were interrupted again when Ian and Sadie walked in the front door. Like his wife had done, Ian gave a shout upon entering. A moment later he was in the parlor, shaking hands with Walt while Lily prattled on about their shared dream hop and surfboards.

Sadie, however, was not acting like Sadie. Instead of running into the room, tail wagging, she remained at the open doorway, sitting quietly while observing the room's occupants. It didn't take Walt long to notice Sadie sitting quietly, staring at him.

"Sadie?" Walt asked. Again, the unspoken question was understood. "Yes. It's really me."

Sadie let out a bark and then came charging to the sofa, her tail wagging, and without pause jumped onto Walt's lap.

Walt let out a grunt and hugged the dog. While laughing, he said, "I had no idea you were this heavy!"

"Sadie, down," Ian snapped. He then told Walt, "I'm sorry… Sadie, I said down! You're going to hurt him!"

Walt laughed and said, "It's okay, Ian. I told Sadie she could get on my lap." The next moment Sadie jumped off the sofa and sat by Walt's side, eagerly looking up at him, her tail still wagging.

"Sadie, would you mind getting me one of my crutches," Walt said aloud.

To everyone's surprise, Sadie calmly turned from Walt, walked to the crutches, and grabbed one in her mouth. The next moment she dragged it to Walt.

Eyes wide, Danielle stared at Sadie and stammered, "Walt, you weren't imagining it."

SIX

"Are we done yet?" Heather Donovan groaned. She sat at her computer at the Glandon Foundation headquarters while Chris sat in a chair next to her, a thick three-ring binder open on his lap. The two had been working side by side for the entire day, only taking a quick break to eat sandwiches Chris had ordered in from the local deli and to periodically let Chris's pit bull, Hunny, out in the yard to do her business and run around.

Heather had worn her long dark hair down that morning, yet now it was twisted into a careless knot atop her head and held in place with a makeshift clip she had fashioned from a large paperclip.

Chris slammed the binder closed and said, "I think so."

"Do we have to do this every year for the accountant?" Heather asked.

"Unfortunately, yes." Chris stood up, set the binder on the desk, and stretched, extending his arms overhead while twisting his body at the waist from side to side. "I'm starved."

Hunny, who had been napping nearby, lifted her head and looked at her human, wondering if it was time to go home.

"Me too." Heather turned off her computer and picked up her purse from where it was tucked under her desk.

"I tell you what, for all your hard work, why don't you let me treat you to dinner at Pearl Cove?"

"That sounds tempting, but I thought you'd be heading over to

Marlow House. Aren't you curious to see if it's really Walt? I know I am."

Chris leaned back against the desk and looked down at Heather, his arms crossed over his chest. "You don't think it is?"

"I hope it is." Heather set her purse on her lap, absently hugging it. "But I suspect a part of you is kind of hoping it's not."

Chris shook his head. "No. Not at all."

"You and Danielle might have a chance of working it out," Heather suggested.

"I've come to realize, if Danielle and I were really meant to be together, I don't think a ghost would keep us apart."

Heather grinned at his use of *ghost*. "If it is Walt, I wonder if he's still going to have an issue with that word."

Chris shrugged. "If it is Walt, I imagine he'll have other things to worry about now."

"True." Heather stood up, purse in hand. "But you sure you don't want to go over there now?"

"Not tonight. Let them get settled in. It's going to be strange for them. This...new Walt."

"Okay, then I'll take you up on your dinner invite."

Uncrossing his arms and no longer leaning back against the desk, Chris said, while waving a finger at Heather, "Umm, before we go, do you think you could..."

Heather frowned. "Could what?"

"Maybe do something with your hair?"

It took Heather a moment to understand what he was saying. But when she did, she reached up to the top of her head and pulled out the misformed paperclip. Tossing the clip on the desk, she rolled her eyes at Chris.

IT WAS her first night on the job. She had just moved to Frederickport days earlier. Before moving to the beach community, she had already been promised the position. Pearl Cove's owner had met her at the restaurant she had worked at in Portland, and had been impressed with her work, after which he had offered her a job. Of course, one of her girlfriends had crudely asked, "Are you sure it's your work he was so impressed with and not how you look?" Either way, she had jumped at the offer. Who didn't want to live in a beach town?

She suspected it wasn't always this busy on a Wednesday and attributed it to the fact they were still in the middle of spring break. Thirty minutes earlier a man had called in asking for a reservation, and she had managed to work him in. When he initially placed the reservation, he used the name Johnson, but she already had a Johnson on the waiting list, so he gave his full name, Chris Johnson.

When he arrived with his date, she thought they were the oddest, most mismatched couple she had ever seen. He was a hottie. The kind of guy depicted on the covers of racy romance novels, and she loved the way he dressed—simple, yet classy.

But his date, she looked as if she were auditioning for a part in *The Addams Family*. It wasn't that she was unattractive—but her raven-colored hair was woven into a simple braid with straight-cut bangs covering her eyebrows, and it was a little overdone on the eye makeup and lipstick closer to black than red. The woman wore dark leggings and an oversized shirt that could have doubled as a dress, considering its length, in a busy pattern of purples and black.

She showed them to their table, and considering their body language, she doubted they would be waking up together in the morning.

"I'VE NEVER SEEN her in here before," Heather noted when the hostess left their table. She opened the menu that had been handed to her.

"She's new," Chris said as he looked over his menu.

"Looks like she'd be more at home at Hooters," Heather quipped, her eyes still on the menu.

Chris let out a snort. "Is that nice?"

Heather shrugged. "Don't tell me you didn't notice?"

"Kinda hard not to. So, what do you want?" Chris asked.

"I'm starved. You're rich. And you made me work twelve hours today. So, steak and lobster."

Chris closed his menu and chuckled. "Fine. Steak and lobster it is."

Twenty minutes later after the waiter took their orders and

served them their cocktails, Heather asked, "So when are you going over to Marlow House?"

"Probably tomorrow." Chris picked up his drink and took a sip.

"You really think it's Walt?" she asked.

Chris leaned back in his seat while one hand absently fiddled with the rim of his cocktail glass. "Danielle seems to believe it's him. And I was thinking about it. If Clint had changed his mind at the last minute and Walt was forced to move on, I think Walt would have come back to let Danielle know."

Heather frowned. "Come back how?"

"A dream hop. We know it's possible for those who have moved over to the other side to visit us in a dream."

"I know. But I always understood it's more difficult. Not something they can do all the time, or our deceased loved ones would be constantly popping in our dreams."

Chris looked up to Heather. "Would they really?"

"What do you mean?" Heather frowned.

"We always assumed it was more difficult. But I wonder—maybe the truth is our loved ones who have moved on want us to live our lives, and they know it's hard to do if they're constantly popping in and out of our dreams. I think we're supposed to live this life that was given to us to its fullest and not be preoccupied with what comes after. And who knows, maybe there are things they have to attend to on the other side, so they don't really have the time."

"You think it might not be as difficult for someone who has moved over to the other side to dream hop?"

"I'm thinking maybe we have jumped to an assumption that may not be wholly true. I've heard people talk about having dreams of their loved ones when they really needed it. Maybe spirits tend to do it more when they feel they are truly needed. And if Walt was forced to move over to the other side, I don't believe he would want Danielle to think Clint was him—or to be unsure. I think he'd visit her—or one of us—and let us know."

"Sounds like you're pretty sure it's Walt." Heather sipped her cocktail.

"Yeah, I'll be surprised if it isn't."

"And you are okay with all this?" Heather asked in a low voice.

"I like Walt."

"I know. But I know how you feel about Danielle."

"When this all started, Walt asked me practically the same thing," Chris told her. "At the time I told Walt I figured this would level the playing field. After all, hard to compete against a ghost. That whole forbidden-love thing."

"And now?" she asked.

"Now, I think I was fooling myself. Danielle's a good friend. I've come to accept that's all she will ever be. Maybe one reason I wanted Walt to do this was that I knew it would close that door for me once and for all and force me to move on." Chris picked up his glass and took a long drink.

"I have to say, you seem to be taking it all well."

Chris shrugged.

"Maybe you should start dating again," Heather suggested. "I think the hostess might be available."

"The hostess?" Chris frowned.

"Yeah. Didn't you see the way she was looking at you? And she kept looking at me as if asking, *how in the world are you with him?*" Heather laughed.

"No, the hostess is all wrong for him!" Eva argued when she appeared the next moment, sitting in the empty seat next to Chris. The next moment, Marie appeared in the other empty chair.

"Hi, Eva, Marie," Heather greeted them. "Have you seen Walt yet?"

"Yes. We saw him, and he saw us," Marie answered.

"What do you mean?" Chris asked.

"It means Marie and I could have visited Walt in the hospital these last few days. We didn't bother dropping by since we assumed he wouldn't be able to see or hear us—which apparently we were wrong about."

"Are you saying Walt can see you both?" Chris asked.

"Yes. Poor boy, when he first saw us, he thought he had died again," Marie said with a chuckle.

"That's interesting," Chris mused.

"I'm not completely surprised," Eva told him. She then went on to give them the same explanation she had given Walt and Danielle when the subject had been broached that morning at Marlow House.

Chris arched his brow. "I have to wonder, will there be any other surprises?"

SEVEN

Walt sat on the edge of the mattress in the downstairs bedroom and watched as Danielle opened and closed the dresser drawers and closet doors to show him the shirts, slacks and other garments she had purchased for him. Max perched next to Walt on the bed, also watching Danielle, his black tail swishing back and forth.

"Everything has already been laundered, so it's all ready to wear," Danielle explained. "I think it should all fit. I went by the sizes of the clothes Clint had on at the time of the accident."

"You've really done too much. But I sincerely appreciate it," he told her.

"Don't be silly. Anyway, I only bought about half a dozen shirts and pairs of slacks. Just enough to get you by until you're up to going shopping yourself. But until you get that cast off, I don't imagine you'll feel like trying on clothes at the store."

"To be honest, the idea of shopping exhausts me." Walt yawned. "I forgot what it felt like to be physically exhausted." He yawned again.

"Oh, and I hope you don't mind, I threw them away."

Walt frowned. "Threw what away?"

"Clint's clothes. Well, the ones he had on at the time of the accident. They were in that plastic bag you brought home with you from the hospital."

"No, that's fine. I certainly don't want them."

Danielle pointed to the top of the dresser, where a stack of miscellaneous items sat, including a wallet, cellphone and some folded sheets of paper. "Clint's cellphone and wallet were also in that bag. And some release papers from the hospital. I left them there. I figure you'll probably need Clint's wallet—at least his identification."

"I suppose I need to go through his wallet. But what happened to the rest of his things? It's not that I particularly want to wear Clint's clothes, but where are his suitcases—the ones he had here?"

"According to the chief, all of Clint's belongings were removed from the vehicle after the accident. The van was pretty smashed up, but it didn't belong to Clint anyway. They put his things in storage —including the portraits."

"Ahh yes, the reproductions. I forgot all about those. What are you going to do with them?" Walt asked.

Danielle smiled at him. "Me? Well, it's not really up to me. They belong to you now. Well, at least they belonged to Clint."

"When I was a spirit, I didn't mind having my portrait in the library. I suppose I saw it as a way of exerting my presence. Yet now, it feels a little bit like it did when Angela gave them to me—too much. No one needs a life-sized portrait of himself."

"We don't need to decide what to do with them now. I don't have a problem with putting them in the library where the originals were. I will confess, I find I rather miss the portraits, even Angela's."

Walt shrugged. "It's up to you, Danielle. Whatever you want to do with them is fine with me."

"For now, I think it best they stay in storage, at least until the portraits Chris purchased are officially deemed authentic Bonnets. I don't need Macbeth or any of his cronies breaking into Marlow House for the paintings. Then I suppose we can have Clint's things delivered here, and you can go through his suitcase and see what you want to keep."

Walt cringed. "No. Sounds ghoulish. I'd rather we just donate his belongings to some charity."

"Are you sure?"

"Most definitely." Walt yawned.

"I guess you probably want to get to bed?" Danielle asked.

"I'd like to take a shower first." Walt glanced to the adjoining bathroom.

"I assume the nurses at the hospital showed you how to do that with a cast on?" she asked.

"Yes. I'm going to have to bother you for a few things."

"Just so you know, I already purchased an assortment of toiletry items for you. I put everything in your bathroom. I wasn't sure what you liked, so in some cases—like with razors—I bought you several different kinds." She paused a moment and eyed his emerging beard. "Although, not sure you'll need those."

Walt reached up and stroked his chin while smiling at Danielle. "You don't like my beard?"

"I'm not much for beards, but I have to say that looks rather nice on you."

Walt let out a sigh. "To be honest, it was not a style choice on my part. I forgot how tedious it was to shave my face every morning. And then one slip with the razor? After decades of not feeling pain, it's amazing how excruciating a razor cut can feel."

"Are you saying you don't want to shave because you're afraid you might cut yourself again?" Danielle grinned mischievously.

"No." Walt sounded insulted. "The mention of the cut was more a side note. I'm not confessing to being afraid of a razor—I'm confessing to being lazy."

Danielle laughed. "So tell me, Walt, we haven't really had a chance to discuss it. Certainly not with that busybody roommate you had in the hospital always listening to our conversation. What's it like for you now—being in a body again? Is it what you expected?"

Walt considered her question a moment and waved his hand. If he expected a cigar to appear, he was sorely disappointed. He stared at his empty hand and said, "For one thing, I can't do that anymore."

"You said you didn't miss smoking."

Walt shook his head. "I don't. Not in the way a smoker misses it. This body is not addicted to nicotine, so I haven't any physical desire to smoke. I suppose it's more a habit, something I was used to doing with my hands. Although, when I think about it, I didn't really have hands, did I? Just an illusion of hands." He grinned at her.

"So nothing else?"

"Oh no, there are many things I never considered. The itching, for instance."

"Itching?"

Walt glanced at his broken leg and then leaned down and patted the cast. "This itches, a sensation I haven't experienced in ninety years. While annoying, I have to admit, it's also a reminder of how my physical sensory perception switch has been turned on again."

"Like when I pinched you?"

"No. That just hurt." Walt flashed Danielle an unconvincing scowl.

"Sorry about that." Her apology was no more convincing than his scowl.

"Getting used to my physical being has been a bit of an adjustment. I recall the first day awake, I felt so—grungy. This body hadn't been bathed for several days, aside from a sponge bath, and I found the sensation of unclean skin unpleasant."

"I always heard that back in your day people weren't into bathing."

"I suppose that might have been true for some people, but I rather looked forward to my daily shower."

"When I first moved into Marlow House, I didn't think much about the showers in the bathrooms. I later learned they wouldn't have been common back when you were alive."

"True." Walt nodded. "I added them about a year before my death. I wanted to modernize the house."

Danielle glanced around the bedroom. "Didn't you tell me this room was your grandparents'?"

"Yes. When my grandfather had the plans for this house drawn up, it included two master suites, this one and the one you're in now. When they first moved into the house, my grandparents used your room, which became my room in later years. They moved to the downstairs bedroom when it became difficult for them to use the stairs, which had always been the plan."

"And I appreciate his foresight—and yours." Danielle grinned.

"An interesting story my grandfather once told me. When he had the house built, he wanted a private staircase from one of the upstairs bedrooms to the attic."

Danielle frowned. "Why?"

"I'm not really sure. But apparently my grandmother didn't like the idea, so they boarded it up."

"You mean there's a hidden staircase in this house that leads to the attic?" Danielle asked incredulously.

"To be honest, I was never sure if the stairs were scrapped while drawing up the house plans or after the house was under construction. My grandfather was never clear on the subject, and I didn't pursue it."

"Which bedroom?" Danielle asked.

Walt shrugged. "I'm not really sure. I always assumed it was from your room."

"I suppose I shouldn't be surprised."

"Why is that?" Walt asked.

"Haunted houses and hidden staircases, they sort of go together."

Walt chuckled. "Technically speaking, Marlow House is no longer haunted."

"I don't know about that, considering how often Marie and Eva drop by."

"True."

"So is there anything else you've been more aware of since taking over Clint's body? Maybe something that you had forgotten about?"

There was, but Walt certainly had no intention of sharing it with Danielle. After ninety years of never having to use the bathroom, it was something he realized he certainly hadn't missed. Instead he shared, "Being tired—and sleeping. I forgot what that felt like." Walt yawned.

Danielle stood up. "I guess that's my cue to let you get ready for bed. Do you need me to get anything for you?"

"If you don't mind, I'll need two large plastic trash bags, a hand towel, masking tape, an Ace bandage, and a rubber band. Do we even have all that? I'm sorry, I should have said something earlier."

"Whatever do you need all that for?" Danielle frowned.

"The nurse showed me how to cover my cast to take a shower. That's what I need. But if we don't have all that here, I suppose I could take a sponge bath tonight." Walt didn't look happy at the prospect.

"Oh, you don't need all that stuff," Danielle chirped. She walked to the adjoining bathroom and returned with a package. She handed it to Walt.

"What's this?" he asked.

"I ordered it online. It's better than a plastic bag. You slip it on your leg, and it seals on top so your cast stays dry. It got great reviews."

Holding the package in hand, Walt smiled up at Danielle. "You thought of everything, didn't you?"

Danielle shrugged. "I just wanted to make the transition as easy as possible for you."

"Thank you, Danielle. Thanks for everything."

She glanced from him to the door leading to the front hall and then to the bathroom door and back to Walt. "Umm…do you need any help…umm…taking a shower?"

Walt grinned up at her. "I appreciate the offer. But I think I have this under control."

"Do you want me to help you with that thing?" Danielle nodded to the package in his hand.

He shook his head. "No. It looks like it has directions. I'm sure I can manage."

"Okay. Well, if you need anything…"

"I have the cellphone you gave me. And I have Max here. He's agreed to stay with me tonight. If I forget how to use the cellphone, I can always send him up to get you."

Danielle glanced down at Max and chuckled. "I just hope he lets you sleep."

Before leaving the room, Danielle dropped a quick kiss on Walt's cheek and whispered, "Goodnight, Walt." Just as she started to turn away, he grabbed her right hand and pulled her back to him. Without a word, their lips met for a brief yet intimate kiss. When the kiss ended, Danielle smiled down at Walt and silently left the bedroom.

WITHOUT INCIDENT, Walt managed to undress and slip the plastic cast protector over his broken leg. Waiting for him in the shower was a bench Danielle had obviously placed there for him yet had failed to mention earlier. It was similar to the one he had used at the hospital. Walt smiled at all she had done for him.

Max stood guard at the bathroom door, prepared to run upstairs for help should Walt slip and fall in the shower. Fortunately, Walt managed to bathe without falling. After his shower, he dried off and removed the plastic protector and set it over a towel bar to air out.

Glancing down at the cat, he said, "Max, I'm not up to making my rounds. Can you check out the rooms on the lower floor, then the upstairs? Make sure everything is how it should be, and then come back here?" It wasn't the spoken words Max understood, it was the mental telepathy projected from Walt. The cat let out a meow and then turned and ran from the room.

Hopping toward the bathroom sink, Walt looked into the mirror. He still hadn't gotten used to seeing his reflection. Or was it Clint's? He leaned closer to the mirror and inspected the faint scar along his forehead. They had removed the stitches before he had left the hospital, and the nurse had noted how well the injury seemed to be healing.

Rubbing the tip of one finger over the faint scar, Walt studied it in the mirror.

"I can't even see where the stitches were," he muttered under his breath. "Amazing."

EIGHT

Chet wasn't in a hurry to get back to Frederickport on Wednesday evening. He knew his sister, Laverne, would just start griping at him again about how he had to do more around the house and start paying rent or, better yet, move out. It wasn't as if she was using her extra bedroom anyway. She didn't have any kids, and no one ever visited her. If anything, she should be happy to have the company, especially since her husband had left her. But she didn't appreciate him. Just that morning he had reminded her how lonely she would be if he left. She had countered with one of her typically snarky remarks, something about getting a dog if she needed company.

Instead of going back to his sister's tonight, Chet figured he would crash at the Bandoni brothers' house in Astoria. *That would teach her a lesson*, he thought. He would let her spend a night alone, wondering where he was and worrying about him. In the morning, when he went back home, she would be relieved to see he was all right, and then she would shut up for a while about him finding an apartment.

"I'm out," Chet said as he tossed his playing cards on the table. He sat with the Bandoni brothers at their well-worn pine dining room table off their small kitchen, playing poker. On the kitchen counter was a stack of empty pizza boxes. They had finished off the pizza an hour earlier. The boxes wouldn't fit in the trash can; it was brimming with empty beer bottles.

A few minutes later Arlo Bandoni, the middle brother, started shuffling the deck for a new hand when his older brother, Franco, told Chet, "I've only seen Boatman's picture. But she looked hot. And you say she has a thing for you?"

"Yeah, right," Arlo muttered under his breath as he started dealing the cards. Arlo, who was a year younger than Franco and a year older than their baby brother, Angelo, was the tallest of the siblings, yet only by a quarter inch. They were all big men, in height and breadth—intimidatingly so.

"Laugh if you want, Arlo," Chet snapped. "Like I said, right after I told her she would look better with short hair, she ran out and cut it. The very next day. When I saw her again, she was so freaking embarrassed; it was hilarious."

"Not sure how that means she has a thing for you," Angelo said as he picked up the cards his brother had dealt him and began arranging them in his hand.

"He's right, Angelo." Franco spoke up. "Women, they like a man who tells them what to do."

"Not the women I know," Angelo grumbled.

"That's because you're too soft on them!" Franco scolded.

"I agree with Angelo. It's all this feminist crap they're feeding women. Makes them think they don't need a man," Arlo countered.

"It's a lie they tell themselves," Franco told his brother. "These days, women don't know what they want. It's up to us to tell them. And sometimes when they don't listen, you need to remind them who's boss. Sounds to me like this Boatman was embarrassed when she saw Chet again because she had been fed all that women's lib crap. She doesn't know what to think." Franco turned to Chet. "This is when you need to take a firm hand. Let her know who's boss and who she belongs to. That's what she's waiting for."

"You think so?" Arlo asked.

"Damn right!" Franco insisted.

"I like making them twist and turn a little," Chet said with a laugh. "I don't want her to feel too confident about me."

"Well, I wouldn't wait too long. That woman has money," Franco said.

"No kidding," Angelo agreed.

"If it were me, I'd already be making myself at home at Marlow

House. And once you get married, then you take over managing the money. A woman has no business managing all that money," Franco said.

"Marriage?" Chet squeaked. "Who said anything about marriage?"

"What good is a hot woman with a crap load of money if you don't marry her? You just date her, and then she calls the shots. No way!" Franco said.

"Yeah, she is hot. And she is loaded. But I don't think I want to settle down with just one woman," Chet whined.

The brothers laughed.

Chet frowned. "What's so funny?"

"You're hilarious, Chet," Angelo said with a grin. "Who ever said marriage meant you can't see other women? If anything, it makes it better because then your other women know their place and you avoid all the BS of them trying to get you to walk down the aisle."

"Being faithful to a spouse is the wife's job. A real woman expects her man to have something on the side," Franco said.

Chet was about to ask how they all knew so much about women since none of them had ever been married, and as far as he knew, none of them was seeing anyone, when someone started pounding loudly on the front door.

"It's after midnight. Who's that?" Franco grumbled as he stood and tossed his cards, facedown, on the table. No one else bothered getting up, but all turned toward the front door and watched as Franco went to answer it.

"Mac!" Franco exclaimed after opening the door.

As Macbeth Bandoni walked into the house, Angelo and Arlo stood up, while Chet remained seated.

"What are you doing here?" the cousins asked in unison.

"I've been driving all day," Mac grumbled as he tossed the duffle bag he had been carrying to the corner. "We've got a job to finish." The next moment Mac spied Chet sitting at the table, watching him.

"Hello, Mac," Chet greeted him coolly.

"What's he doing here?" Mac asked his cousins.

"We didn't know you were coming," Angelo said lamely.

"You need to go. I have to talk to my cousins," Mac told Chet.

"We're playing poker," Chet told him.

THE GHOST OF SECOND CHANCES

"The game's over," Mac said.

Chet glanced from Franco to the other two brothers. They just shrugged, and no one contradicted Mac.

"It is kind of late," Franco said. "Maybe we should call it quits." In response, Arlo leaned over and started gathering all the cards into one pile.

"I was hoping I could crash here tonight," Chet said.

"Not tonight," Mac told him.

Chet looked to Franco.

With another shrug Franco said, "Some other night, Chet. This is family business."

LAVERNE MORRISON HAD TAKEN back her maiden name. When doing that, she had never intended to revert back to her premarriage self—specifically that of looking after her younger brother, Chet. Yet after his troubles in Missouri, she didn't feel she could turn him away.

However, Laverne Morrison was a different person from who she had been in her youth. If she wouldn't put up with a deadbeat husband, why would she allow her brother to continue taking advantage of her? She had given him plenty of chances—more than he deserved.

She glanced at the clock in her kitchen. It was after midnight. The dirty dishes filling the sink weren't hers. Well, technically, the pots, pans, dishes, glasses, and silverware belonged to her. She just hadn't used them. Chet had.

From the kitchen she walked to the guest bathroom. Standing in the doorway, hands on hips, she looked into the room and surveyed the damp towels littering the floor and counter, and the pile of dirty clothes shoved in the corner. They were Chet's clothes.

Laverne moved to the guest bedroom. Chet had had the audacity to lock the door, but it wasn't going to keep her out. She didn't even need a key; a small screwdriver would work. Unlocking the door, she threw it open and shook her head at the mess that was her guest room. It was obvious he hadn't laundered the bedsheets since his arrival. They looked utterly disgusting. Laverne didn't think she would bother washing them. Better to throw them away—or perhaps use them to wrap up Chet's belongings.

Fuming over the mess her brother had made, she stomped back to the kitchen and grabbed several large trash bags from the cabinet under the kitchen sink. Returning to the bathroom, she scooped up all his dirty clothes from the floor and shoved them into a bag. She then marched to the guest bedroom.

In the bedroom she removed his suitcases from the closet and began hastily packing them. What she couldn't fit into a suitcase, she intended to shove in one of the plastic bags. Afraid Chet might show up before she was finished, she hastily packed, carelessly folding his clean clothes.

One by one she opened the dresser drawers, dumping their contents onto the bed before shoving it into a suitcase. What came tumbling out of the sock drawer gave her pause. Laverne stood at the side of the unmade bed, looking down at the pile of socks. Nestled atop it was a small handgun.

"Chet has a gun?" Laverne muttered. "I thought he couldn't have a gun?"

Warily, Laverne picked up the pistol and inspected it. Familiar with handguns, she looked to see if it was loaded. It was. *Chet has no business having a gun*, she thought. Should he be found with it in his possession, he could get sent to jail—again.

CHET PULLED up to the front of his sister's house. All the lights were off. He was still annoyed at having to drive all the way back to Frederickport—especially considering the number of beers he had consumed. The last thing he needed was to get busted for drinking and driving. Fortunately, he managed to drive from Astoria to Frederickport without getting pulled over. Now, all he wanted to do was fall into bed.

He didn't see the suitcases and filled trash bags as he walked up to the front of the house, because it was too dark. It wasn't until he tripped over them did he realized they were there. The motion light installed by the front door flashed on just as he stumbled over the pile. Once the light turned on, he recognized the suitcases.

"What the…" he grumbled, snatching up the envelope taped to one of the bags. He tore it open.

The letter inside read: *Chet, you can't stay here anymore. You refuse to abide by any of the house rules or contribute to the household expenses. I want my house back. I am done taking care of you. Don't bother trying to come back. I am having the locks changed in the morning.*

Chet tossed the letter to the ground. "Seriously?"

Bending over, he pulled open one of the black trash bags to see what was inside. He immediately recognized some of his clothing. Shoving the bag aside, he marched up to the front door and unlocked it. Yet when he tried pushing the door open, the chain inside stopped it from opening all the way.

"Laverne!" Chet shouted, pounding on the door.

There was no answer

He pounded again. "Laverne!"

Still no answer from his sister's house, but next door the lights turned on.

When he shouted again, he heard the neighbor yell, "I'm calling the police!"

NINE

Simple pleasures had eluded Walt for the last ninety years. Pleasures he had either overlooked or underestimated during his first lifetime. One was the comfort of a good bed. He had to give Brianna O'Malley Boatman credit, she had done an excellent job when replacing the beds in Marlow House.

Reluctant to leave the comfort of the mattress, he stared up at the ceiling and wondered if Danielle was awake. Glancing over to the alarm clock on the nightstand, he saw that it was almost 9:30 a.m. He didn't imagine she was still sleeping. Danielle was normally awake, up, and dressed by this time in the morning.

With a yawn, he stretched and sat up in the bed, a task made more difficult because of the cast on his left leg. Now sitting up, he glanced around the room. Max was nowhere to be seen, and the bedroom door was shut. He suspected Danielle had closed his door sometime this morning, after Max had left his room.

With another yawn and stretch, Walt tossed the covers off himself and shifted his body, preparing to get out of bed. Awkwardly moving his feet to the floor, Walt sat on the edge of the mattress, wearing only a pair of boxer shorts. He glanced down and smiled. Danielle had bought him a pair of pajamas, but the thought of pulling the pajama bottoms up and over his cast seemed exhausting to him last night, so he'd decided to wear the boxers.

He didn't tell Danielle he had never worn boxers before. They hadn't been a thing when he had been alive. In fact, they didn't discuss the undergarments she had purchased for him. She had only said, "I wasn't sure what kind you wore, so I bought both."

Fact was, neither type had been around when he had been alive. Men's undergarments during the 1920s had included flannel, tight-fitting, knee-length drawers. Fortunately for Walt, he had watched enough television since Danielle's arrival that he was aware of the underwear options now available, and he was spared such a personal discussion with her. It was bad enough she had to buy them for him. He wasn't sure boxers would be comfortable attire under his pants, but he liked them for sleeping.

"Am I a tighty-whitey man?" Walt chuckled as he managed to get up and hobble toward the bathroom. The first time he had heard that expression on television, he'd had absolutely no idea what it meant. Had he known it referred to a type of men's undergarments, he would never have asked Lily during a dream hop to explain its meaning. Lily tried to contain her laughter at the question but was unable to, which meant she woke up from the dream before giving her answer.

The next time Lily found herself alone with Walt, she broke into a detailed explanation of men's underwear, including the debate over boxers versus briefs. If not already dead, Walt might have died from embarrassment at her candor. His only saving grace, Lily could neither see nor hear Walt at the time of her telling, so she never had to see his discomfort over the topic.

Sufficient time had passed since Lily's dissertation on tighty-whities, and he now found humor in the long-ago conversation. There was just one thing he wasn't sure about. The briefs Danielle had purchased were not white.

"So do I call them tighty-bluey? Tighty-grayie?" He shook his head and thought, *No, that doesn't have the right ring to it.*

NOW DRESSED in baggy gray slacks and a button-up blue and gray cotton shirt, his right foot in a slipper, Walt stood before the bathroom mirror, combing his hair and debating whether he should shave or not. His beard was filling in nicely, yet it was still relatively short. The hair on his head was now much longer than it had been when he had first woken up in the hospital; in fact, it was closer to the length he normally wore. Walt frowned. He couldn't recall his hair ever growing this fast before. However, he also hadn't remembered what a pain it had been to shave each day.

Leaning closer to the mirror, he looked at his forehead and frowned.

Where is it?

He stepped closer, running his finger over the side of his forehead that had been stitched after the accident. Nothing was there. There was no sign of the injury.

"They must have some really great medicine," he muttered.

Setting his comb on the bathroom counter, he started to button his shirt sleeve when something caught his attention. He paused a moment and then rolled up his left shirt sleeve, examining his wrist.

WHEN WALT CAME out of his room fifteen minutes later, he stood out in the hallway for a moment, listening. He heard sound coming from the direction of the kitchen and started that way. Halfway down the hall, he remembered the cellphone Danielle had given him. She had told him to use it when he needed to contact her.

"It's going to take me a while to get used to carrying that thing," Walt muttered as he continued to the kitchen, making no attempt to return to the bedroom for the phone.

To Walt's surprise, he found Joanne Johnson in the kitchen, not Danielle. He stood at the open doorway a moment and watched as Joanne emptied the dishwasher. He couldn't believe she hadn't heard him coming. He wasn't exactly quiet when using the crutches. She would have to be deaf not to have heard him, and he knew she had excellent hearing.

After a few moments he cleared his throat and said, "Good morning."

Joanne stopped what she was doing and turned to face Walt, her expression unsmiling.

"Danielle is not here," she said curtly and then turned back to what she was doing.

Walt watched her a few moments and then said, "I assume you are Joanne Johnson?"

"I see you remember my name." Joanne closed the dishwasher, her back to Walt.

"Danielle told me about you. I'm afraid I don't remember you," Walt lied.

Joanne turned to Walt with a hostile expression. "Yes, she said you had amnesia. Do you need something, Mr. Marlow? If not, I am busy and need to get back to work."

"First, you can call me Walt," he said with a friendly smile.

"I'm not sure I can do that," she snapped.

"Why not?" He frowned.

"For me Walt Marlow will always be…well, our Walt."

"Your Walt?" he couldn't help but smile. "You mean my cousin?"

"I'd rather call you Mr. Marlow."

"Whatever you feel comfortable with," Walt said. "But do you think you could spare me five minutes? I really would like to talk to you."

Joanne stared at Walt a moment before answering. Finally, she said, "I suppose you're hungry."

He arched his brows. "Hungry?"

"I know you haven't eaten yet. Danielle told me you were still sleeping. That you needed your rest and not to wake you up."

"Where is Danielle?" he asked.

"She had to go out and run some errands." Joanne took a deep breath and said, "Go ahead and sit down. I'll bring you some coffee and something to eat."

Walt smiled at Joanne. "Thank you." He hobbled to the kitchen table as Joanne poured him a cup of coffee. Just as he sat down, she set a full cup before him and slid the creamer and sugar closer to him. A moment later, she set a clean spoon on the table.

He watched as Joanne grabbed a pan from the oven and set it on the stove.

"I hope you like quiche," she said as she cut a slice of ham and cheese quiche from the pan she had pulled from the oven.

"I've never had it."

Joanne paused and turned to Walt. "I thought you had amnesia?"

Walt shrugged and flashed Joanne a smile. "At least, I can't recall having it."

Joanne picked up the plate of quiche and then grabbed a fork from a drawer.

"Would you please sit with me while I eat so we can talk?" Walt asked kindly.

Narrowing her eyes, Joanne studied Walt as she dropped the plate of quiche before him on the table.

"I suppose I could take a coffee break," she said begrudgingly.

A few moments later, Joanne sat at the table with Walt, coffee cup in hand.

"This is amazing," Walt purred after taking his first bite of quiche. He looked at Joanne. "Did Danielle make this?"

"Yes. She's an excellent baker."

"I had her chocolate cake yesterday. It was a slice of heaven. But this, I can't describe it." Walt took another bite and groaned.

"I don't recall you being so impressed with Danielle's cooking before," Joanne noted. She sipped her coffee and eyed Walt suspiciously.

He shrugged. "It seems like almost a hundred years since I've had anything this good."

"I suppose it's that hospital food," Joanne suggested.

"Maybe." Walt smiled and took another bite.

"So what did you want to talk to me about?" she asked.

Walt set his fork on his plate and looked across the table to Joanne. "I wanted to apologize."

"Apologize for what?" she asked.

"For how I treated you."

"I thought you have amnesia?"

"Danielle told me. She said I was a real ass."

Joanne stared at Walt a moment. Whatever she had imagined he wanted to say, it wasn't this. "She told you that?"

"Since I don't remember anything about my life—about who I was—I asked Danielle to tell me everything she knew about me."

"And she told you, you were an ass?" Joanne sputtered, trying not to choke on the coffee she had just sipped.

Walt nodded. "Pretty much. She told me I was horribly rude to her friend Lily—who I met last night. And to her friend Adam, who I haven't yet met. At least, not since the accident. And she told me how I tried to get you fired. I'm so sorry about that. I have no idea why I would have done something like that."

"You really can't remember anything?" Joanne asked.

Walt shook his head. "No. Sorry."

"Why don't you go by Clint now? That's what you were called."

Walt shrugged. "Clint is my middle name. When I was told that's what I went by, well, it just didn't sound right to me. I didn't feel like a Clint."

"You felt more like a Walt?" Joanne asked.

"It seemed more natural."

"How about Walter? It's your real name."

"True. But I don't feel like a Walter either. I'm a Walt."

"No, you aren't," she snapped.

"You don't like me, do you?" Walt asked, his tone sounding more teasing than accusatory.

"I didn't like Clint."

"I didn't particularly like him either." Walt grinned.

"You didn't like yourself?"

Walt chuckled and took another bite of the quiche. A moment later he grabbed a napkin from a stack on the table and wiped his mouth. Eyes twinkling, he looked up to Joanne. "By the way Danielle described him, he didn't seem like a very likable fellow."

"Then why do you think Danielle invited you to stay here?" she asked.

Setting his fork on his plate again, he looked up at Joanne and said, "I asked her if I could stay. I thought perhaps it might help me regain my memory. And I'll be paying her rent. I suspect Danielle is just a nice person, which is why she said yes."

"How long do you intend to stay?"

Walt shifted uncomfortably in the seat. "I don't know. You're anxious for me to leave, aren't you?"

Joanne shrugged. "It really is not my business what Danielle does. Or who she lets stay here."

"Yet you would rather I not stay, because I was so rude before. Is that correct?"

Joanne nodded. "I suppose."

"I can understand that, Joanne. Having to endure rude people at your place of work is unpleasant. But I promise I will be on my best behavior. Please give me a chance."

Joanne sipped her coffee and considered his words. After a moment she set her cup on the table and looked up at Walt. "I am sorry about Stephanie. I should have told you that."

Walt smiled sadly. "One of the things I can't remember is Stephanie. But I am also sorry about that. Especially for her father. I met him when I was in the hospital, and he seemed like a very nice man."

"So you really don't remember anything about her? Knowing she's dead…you feel nothing?"

"Nothing personally. She's a stranger to me."

Joanne considered his words and took another sip of coffee.

"How about it, Joanne. Can we have a truce?"

"Truce?" Joanne frowned.

"Or better yet, maybe start all over again?"

She stared at him a moment, considering his offer.

Walt smiled and held out his right hand to her. "Hello. My name is Walt Marlow. Nice to meet you, Joanne Johnson."

TEN

The morning sun had woken Chet several hours earlier, but he had nowhere to go, so he remained in the backseat of his car, trying to catch a few hours of sleep before people started showing up at the beach parking lot where he had spent the last night. But now his back was killing him, so he rolled out of his car and stretched, trying to decide what he was going to do now.

Returning to his sister's was not an option. He knew her well enough that when she was in one of these moods, it was best to give her time to settle down. In a week or so she would be welcoming him back, he was sure of it. But, in the meantime, he needed to find someplace else to stay.

Chet walked to the back of his vehicle and opened his trunk. After rummaging through his suitcases, he found something clean to put on, yet cursed his sister, because now it was wrinkled. Grabbing his shaving kit, he took it and his fresh change of clothes and stumbled to the public bathroom.

After shaving and changing his clothes, Chet returned to his car with a plan.

"I'll go to Marlow House. To hell with Adam, I don't need him," Chet muttered while climbing into the driver's seat. "Maybe Laverne did me a favor." Before turning on the ignition, he readjusted the rear-view mirror and looked at his reflection. With the back of his hand he removed a dab of shaving cream he had missed and then ran his fingers through his hair. Once satisfied with his appearance, he readjusted the mirror and turned on the ignition.

WALT HAD JUST finished breakfast when it started raining outside. He had intended to spend the rest of the morning on the side patio and wait for Danielle to come home, but he changed his plans and headed to the parlor instead. Normally rain would not discourage him, yet he had a cast to consider, and he didn't want to get it wet.

Once in the parlor, he found a book his spirit-self had left sitting on the coffee table. He hadn't finished it. Making himself comfortable on a chair, his cast propped up on a footstool, he started to read. A few minutes later, Joanne walked into the room.

"Can I get you anything before I go upstairs?" Joanne asked.

"No, thank you," Walt said. "But I appreciate you asking."

Joanne chuckled and walked all the way into the parlor. She glanced at the book Walt was reading.

"What's funny?" Walt asked, looking over the book he held.

"I have to give you credit. You certainly are making an effort to be cordial."

"I suspect it takes as much effort being friendly as rude, and I don't see the point in being rude for no reason," Walt told her.

"I wonder if you felt you had a reason to be rude to me." Joanne's question wasn't asked in a snarky manner but delivered with sincere curiosity.

"The reason being I was an ass?" Walt asked with a chuckle.

Joanne laughed. She then paused and glanced at the book. "I see you found something to read."

"It looks interesting."

"From what I recall, you didn't enjoy reading."

Walt smiled at Joanne. "I think we should be open to new experiences. If I didn't enjoy reading before, perhaps it's time I learned."

"If you enjoy the book and decide you want to finish it, you might want to tell Danielle you're reading it, before she puts it away and you can't find it again."

"I'll be sure to do that."

"Danielle always keeps a book on the coffee table in here. But she regularly rotates them, and when she sets a new one out, the last

THE GHOST OF SECOND CHANCES

one goes back in the bookshelf in the library. I remember once when I first started working for her, I asked her if she or Lily was reading the book sitting on the parlor table, and when she said no, I started to put it back in the library. But she stopped me and said she liked to keep a book sitting out on the parlor table—liked the way it looks." Joanne paused a moment and then chuckled before saying, "But then I noticed the next week it was a different book. Since then, each week it always seems to be a new book."

That's because I was the one who used to leave the books in here when I was reading them, Walt thought to himself.

"Although, if I'm not mistaken, I believe that one is from the public library, not one of ours. So perhaps Danielle is reading it."

Walt flipped to the front cover of the book and looked inside. He smiled up at Joanne. "Yes, you're right."

"I have to say Danielle does love her books." Joanne then took a deep breath and glanced around, a frown furrowing her brows.

"Is something wrong?" Walt asked.

She shook her head, still frowning. "Wrong? Not really. But I just realized I haven't smelled it in days."

"Smelled what?"

Joanne shrugged. "Old houses have their own peculiar smell. Every once in a while, I get a whiff of cigar. At least, that's what it reminded me of. It would come and go. No room in particular…odd…"

Before Walt had a chance to respond, the doorbell rang.

"If you will excuse me, I'd better get that," Joanne said before hurrying off to answer the front door.

WHEN JOANNE ANSWERED the door a few minutes later, she came face-to-face with a forty-something man who looked vaguely familiar.

"I'm here to see Danielle Boatman," he announced.

"I'm afraid Danielle is out right now," Joanne explained, not asking him into the house.

"Oh, really?" He looked disappointed. "I'm a very good friend of Danielle's. Do you know when she's going to be back?"

Joanne glanced at her watch and then looked back at the man, her hand clutching the edge of the door. "And your name?"

"My name is Chet Morrison."

"Chet Morrison! Yes, that's why you look so familiar. You're Laverne's brother. I'm Joanne Johnson."

Chet smiled. "Yes. I remember you now. Nice to see you again. I remember you used to clean this house. You stayed when Danielle took over the place?"

"She didn't tell you?" Joanne asked.

"No, she didn't mention it."

Joanne opened the door wider. "Danielle should be home soon. Would you like to wait for her?"

"Thank you. Yes, I would."

"Come, you can wait in the parlor."

After Chet walked into the house, Joanne closed the door behind him and showed him to the parlor. When the pair walked into the small room, Walt looked up from the book he was reading.

"Chet, this is one of our guests, Walt Marlow," Joanne introduced. "Mr. Mar…Walt…this is a good friend of Danielle's, Chet Morrison."

Walt closed the book and set it on his lap. He arched his brow and said, "Really?"

Chet walked to Walt and extended his hand in greeting. Curious, Walt accepted the handshake and studied the man.

"Chet is going to wait in here for Danielle, while I get back to work. She shouldn't be long. You two can keep each other company."

"Any chance I could get a cup of coffee?" Chet asked as Joanne was about to leave the room.

She paused and looked back at him. "Certainly. I have some quiche. Would you like a piece with your coffee?"

"Quiche?" Chet scowled. His stomach growled. "Uhh, yeah. Quiche would be great."

After Joanne left to get the quiche and coffee, Chet took a seat and grumbled, "Damn, I hate quiche. Wussy food."

"If you don't like quiche, why did you tell her you want some?" Walt asked.

Chet shrugged. "I didn't get a chance to have breakfast this morning. I'm starved."

"Why is quiche…what did you call it…wussy food?" Walt asked.

Chet frowned. "Seriously? *Real men don't eat quiche.*"

Walt had no idea what Chet was talking about. He didn't

respond, but instead he opened his book and lifted it up, pretending to read while he periodically peered over the cover to watch Chet, who was busy glancing around the room, checking everything out. A few minutes later, Joanne returned with the quiche and coffee and then left the room.

As Chet devoured the quiche, Walt closed his book and set it on his lap. "Does this mean you aren't a real man?"

Chet glanced up to Walt and rolled his eyes. "Ha-ha." He then picked up his coffee and took a sip, almost burning his mouth. It was piping hot. He set it back on the table to cool off.

"So tell me, how is it you know Danielle?" Walt asked.

Chet shrugged. "Danielle and I...we hang out sometimes."

"Hang out?"

Chet smiled over at Walt. "To be honest, she sort of has a thing for me."

"She does? I didn't realize Danielle was seeing anyone."

Now finished with the quiche, Chet sat back on the sofa and crossed one leg over the opposing knee, taking up a good portion of the sofa. "I like to keep things casual, but, well, she wants more."

"She does?"

"When a woman makes drastic changes to please a man, it's usually a sign they want more than friendship from him. But frankly, I'm not sure I'm ready for that."

"What kind of changes?" Walt asked.

Chet grinned. "She used to have really long hair. I told her she should cut it, and the next day, she did."

So that's who you are, Walt thought. *The man who thinks a way to a woman's heart is through insult.*

Their conversation was interrupted by a loud meow at the door. Chet turned to the meow and watched as Max sauntered into the room.

"A cat?" Chet said.

Max sat down in the middle of the parlor, between Chet and Walt. He glanced from man to man.

"He's Danielle's cat. I'm surprised you don't know him. She absolutely adores Max. In fact, from what I understand, she's broken up with fellows who didn't get along with her cat," Walt told him.

Chet shrugged. "Yeah? Well, cats love me." Chet leaned down and put out his hand, wiggling his fingers. "Here, kitty, kitty."

Sitting still, his tail swishing back and forth, Max looked to Walt; their eyes met.

"Here, kitty, kitty…" Chet repeated.

Max looked from Walt to Chet and then back to Walt. He meowed and then turned toward Chet and leapt up onto the sofa.

"See, cats like me," Chet boasted.

Just as Chet picked up his cup of hot coffee to take a sip, Max stepped into his lap and settled down, as if preparing to take a nap. He started to purr.

Chet laughed. "See, the cat loves me."

Just as Chet was about to sip his coffee, a purring cat nestled on his lap, Max looked over to Walt, their eyes again meeting.

Suddenly Chet let out a tortured shriek, throwing his cup and sending some of the hot coffee into his own face. He tried to stand up, but the cat remained firmly attached—back and front claws digging painfully into the thighs of his denims, refusing to let go.

"Get this cat off me!" he shouted. Reluctant to grab at the cat, afraid he would then find razor-sharp feline teeth in his hands, Chet wailed pitifully.

I think that's enough, Max.

Max released his hold and flew from the sofa, heading out of the parlor.

ELEVEN

Walt set the book he had been holding on the end table. Leaning down, he picked up the crutches he had set next to the chair and awkwardly stood up. Chet had hurried to the downstairs bathroom after his encounter with the cat. Walt assumed it was to assess the damage. Considering the thick denims Chet wore, Walt didn't believe Max had done any real harm, just mild discomfort.

After hobbling to the open doorway, Walt looked down the entry hall to the bathroom. Its door was closed, and Max stood nearby, looking from Walt to the door.

Walt stared at Max.

You'd better make yourself scarce when he comes out. I don't want him kicking you. And don't go outside when he's in his car. I don't want him sending you to the other side. Don't be alone with him.

Max resisted the temptation to meow in response. He turned, disappearing down the hall. He hadn't survived this long by being overly foolish.

DANIELLE WAS ABOUT to turn into her driveway when she spied an unfamiliar vehicle parked behind Joanne's car in front of Marlow House. She pulled behind the strange car and parked.

"Who's here?" Danielle muttered as she stepped onto the sidewalk and made her way toward the unfamiliar vehicle. Checking out the car, she noted it had Missouri license plates. Considering its condition, she was surprised it had made it all the way from Missouri to Oregon.

A few moments later she was sprinting up to her house and unlocking the front door. When she opened it, she found Walt standing alone in the entry hall, just outside the parlor.

"Hey, Walt," Danielle greeted him. "I'm surprised you're inside. It's beautiful outside right now."

"The last time I looked, it was raining," Walt told her as he glanced from Danielle to the closed door of the powder room.

"It stopped raining about fifteen minutes ago." Danielle shut the door behind her. "Do you know whose car is parked in front of the house?"

Walt motioned to the bathroom. "You have company."

"Someone's here? Who?"

Before Walt had a chance to explain, Chet came walking out of the bathroom. Looking down, Chet stepped gingerly, wincing uncomfortably with each step. However, the moment he spied Danielle, his gait instantly changed, reminding Walt of one of those saddle-sore cowboys trying to tough it out after a prolong time on a horse.

"You?" Danielle stammered.

Chet flashed her a grin and walked toward her, masking the flashes of pain he experienced with each step as denim rubbed against his scratched skin. Silently, he told himself to just be thankful the stupid cat hadn't sunk his claws in a little higher. He felt ill at that possibility and forced a smile.

"I was hoping I could talk to you a moment." Chet glanced over at Walt and then back to Danielle. "Alone."

"What do we have to talk about?" Danielle asked.

Max, who had been peeking out from around a plant, caught Walt's attention.

Okay, Max, Danielle is here, and you don't need to hide. In fact, I think it might be a good time to keep her company—if you know what I mean.

Max let out a loud meow. Chet, who had been walking toward Danielle, stopped abruptly and stared down at the cat, who was running toward his human.

"Aw, Max, did you miss me?" Danielle cooed. She leaned down

THE GHOST OF SECOND CHANCES

and scooped Max up in her arms. He settled down and began to purr.

Walt resisted his temptation to laugh at Chet, who he was certain had turned green at the sight of the black cat now snuggling in Danielle's arms.

"I'll give you privacy. I know no one's in the living room," Walt told them.

Danielle flashed Walt a glare yet wondered what his bemused expression was all about.

Stay with her, Max. If she needs me, you know where I am.

Reluctantly, Danielle led Chet into the living room. She took a seat on one of the chairs while he sat on the sofa, facing her and eyeing the cat nervously.

"I really am busy. What is it you wanted to talk to me about?" Danielle asked.

"This is strictly business," Chet told her.

"Business?"

Chet started to cross one leg over the opposing knee, but winced and changed his mind, setting both feet on the floor in front of the sofa, his man-spread wide.

"I need to find somewhere to stay, but considering how busy I am, it seems foolish to rent a house or even an apartment. And then I remembered Adam mentioned you rent rooms here."

"We're a bed and breakfast, not a boardinghouse." Danielle absently stroked Max's back. The cat's eyes remained locked on Chet.

"I understand Mr. Marlow is renting a room here."

"Mr. Marlow is a guest of the B and B," Danielle explained.

"Boardinghouse or B and B, what's it matter what you call it?" Chet laughed. "You still rent rooms, and I would like to rent one."

"For one thing, the B and B is not currently accepting any new guests. We're taking a little vacation."

"But Marlow is staying here."

Danielle smiled sweetly. "Mr. Marlow is an exception because of his tragic accident. But like I said, we aren't taking any new guests for a while."

"Since you already have someone staying here, I don't see what it will matter if you take one more," Chet argued. "You have empty bedrooms, and I would like to rent one."

"I'm sure you can get a room at the Sea Horse Motel. It's very nice over there."

"I doubt there'll be anything available at the Sea Horse right now, not with spring break going on. Plus, it's a motel."

"So? What's wrong with a motel?" Danielle asked. "You said you just wanted a room, and that's pretty much what a motel is—they rent rooms."

"It would cost a fortune staying at a motel," Chet grumbled. "Surely you can take pity on me."

"I'm not sure what you imagined our rates are, but I can assure you they are higher than what the Sea Horse Motel charges."

Chet flashed Danielle a broader smile. "Aw, come on, Danielle, stop being mad at me."

"Mad at you? I don't even know you."

"I know I embarrassed you about your haircut. I'm sorry about that. But I was right. You look really great in short hair. Maybe if you work a little on the makeup like I suggested, you could really be a knockout."

Danielle groaned. Max, who continued to sit in her lap, could feel her body tense.

"I'm sure we can work out some reasonable price for a monthly rate, and then you won't have to worry about renting one of your rooms when you decide to open up again," Chet told her.

Before Danielle could reply, Max leapt down from her lap and strolled toward Chet. Chet, who was just hitting his stride, froze a moment and watched as the cat made his way to the sofa.

"Umm...maybe you can keep your cat away from me?" Chet stammered.

The next moment Max jumped onto the sofa. Chet stood abruptly and moved away from the cat, who continued to walk in his direction.

"I'm not renting you a room," Danielle announced as she stood up. "You need to leave now."

Eyeing the cat nervously, Chet accepted Danielle's pronouncement and fled from the room with a hasty goodbye.

A few moments later Danielle stood at the window by the front door. She looked out and watched Chet rush toward the street. "I think he's afraid of cats," she muttered.

"Danielle, I see you're back. Did you see Chet?" Joanne asked after she came downstairs a minute later.

"Chet, that's right. I was trying to remember what his name was," Danielle said aloud, speaking more to herself.

"I thought he was a good friend of yours?" Joanne asked.

"Chet seems to have a problem grasping the true nature of relationships," Danielle said.

Joanne frowned. "I don't understand."

Danielle glanced briefly to the closed front door. "I don't know him well. I've met him a couple of times. Not someone I consider a friend."

"I'm sorry I let him in," Joanne apologized. "He said you were good friends, and he isn't exactly a stranger to me; I know his sister."

"No problem." Danielle flashed Joanne a smile.

"I've just always liked his sister, Laverne. I always felt sorry for her."

"Why was that?" Danielle resisted the temptation to ask if it was because she had a jerky brother.

"Their parents died in a house fire a number of years ago—tragic, really. I always felt especially sorry for Laverne. A sweet girl, although she could have a bit of a temper, as I recall. But who could really blame her? She took care of her parents for years—they had serious medical issues, both of them. And she practically raised her brother."

"You mean Chet?" Danielle asked.

Joanne nodded. "Yes. It was just the two of them; Laverne was the oldest. She's just a few years younger than me. I don't remember much about Chet. Although, I believe when he was younger, he used to hang out with Adam Nichols. And Adam, well, he was a bit wild as a teen."

"If you ladies will excuse me," Walt interrupted. He hobbled out of the parlor on his crutches. "I think I'm going out front to see some of that sunshine Danielle was telling me about. Maybe try out the front swing."

"I should probably get you a towel to wipe down the swing. I imagine it's wet from the rain," Danielle suggested.

"I can get it myself. Should I take one from the bathroom?" Walt used one crutch to point to the bathroom Chet had used.

"That would work." Danielle grinned.

Joanne and Danielle watched as Walt made his way to the bathroom, where he retrieved a hand towel before heading to the front door.

After Walt stepped outside and closed the door, Joanne said, "He apologized to me."

"Walt?" Danielle glanced from Joanne to the door and back to Joanne.

"Yes. And I have to admit, it sounded sincere and nothing at all like Clint."

"Well, he does have amnesia."

"This is horrible to say, but I think that man would be better off if he never regained his memory."

"Why do you say that?" Danielle asked.

"I have to admit there is something very charming about him now. There was nothing charming about him before. But it is a little odd calling him Walt. I'm working on that."

"I suspect he'll just appreciate you giving him a second chance."

"But what happens if he regains his memory and goes back to acting like he used to?"

Danielle reached out and gently touched Joanne's hand. "Then that will be on him, won't it? If we give him a second chance and he decides to resume his bad behavior, well, he's the one who is the loser, not us. Let's just see how he does, and give him a second chance."

TWELVE

Walt sat alone on the front swing. He glanced down at his cast with a wry smile. During his first life, he would have cursed the broken leg, especially at a time like this when he was as anxious as a six-year-old on Christmas morning. Yet he wasn't excited to open presents, it was a life he wished to explore—a romantic relationship with Danielle he wanted to pursue. But he refused to bemoan a broken leg, which according to the doctor meant eight weeks in a cast. How could he complain when he had a second chance at life? Perhaps, he wondered, this was the Universe's plan. With a broken leg he was forced to slow down—allowing him to ease into his new reality.

A meow interrupted his thoughts. Walt glanced to his left and spied Max strolling in his direction from the side yard. Walt assumed the cat must have made his exit out the pet door in the kitchen after fleeing the living room. He was curious to learn what had happened between Chet and Danielle.

"So what went on in there, Max?" Walt asked when the cat leapt up on the swing and sat next to him.

Max stared up at Walt, his black tail swishing back and forth.

"I know you didn't understand what they were saying. Oh... Danielle seemed tense? So you...oh...you just walked toward him?" Walt laughed. "I think you spooked him. But like I said before, if you run into him again, avoid him. He might hold a grudge."

Max looked from Walt to the street and let out a loud meow.

"Hunny?" Walt frowned. He then looked out to the street and spied what Max was telling him. Walking down the street toward Marlow House was Chris and his pit bull, Hunny. Hunny, a young brindle pit with a white chest, walked next to Chris off the leash, as his human casually held a rolled-up leash in one hand.

Max meowed again and then jumped down off the swing and made his way to the side yard.

"You were a lot braver when Hunny was a pup," Walt called after the cat.

A moment later, Hunny came racing up the front walk with Chris trailing behind her. She wasn't in pursuit of the cat; her attention was on the man sitting in the swing.

Walt focused his attention on Hunny and smiled. Just before the dog reached the swing, she came to an abrupt stop and sat down. Still focused on Walt, she tilted her head from side to side.

"Yes, it's really me, Hunny," Walt said gently. "But please be careful, my leg's broken."

Tail wagging, Hunny stood up and wiggled her way to Walt. When Chris reached them, the pit was nuzzling her nose in Walt's hands and covering them with sloppy kisses.

"I see she recognizes you."

Walt smiled up at Chris. "She does."

"Welcome home, Walt," Chris said, putting out his hand.

Walt accepted the handshake. "Thanks, Chris."

A moment later the two men sat side by side on the porch swing as Hunny curled up on the ground nearby.

"Eva and Marie told Heather and me you can see them like before, and Danielle told me you can still communicate with Max and Sadie. I wasn't particularly surprised about being able to see spirits, but I was about the other. Wasn't sure I quite believed her until I saw you with Hunny just now."

At the mention of her name, Hunny lifted her head a moment and looked at the two men.

"They were both a surprise to me," Walt told him.

Chris turned toward Walt, studying his face. "How does it feel, being alive? You got a nice beard going on there, by the way."

Walt absently stroked his beard. "I forgot what a pain it was."

Chris chuckled. "You mean shaving?"

THE GHOST OF SECOND CHANCES

Walt nodded and moved his hand from his beard back to the side rail of the swing. He clutched it.

"How is the leg doing?" Chris asked.

Walt shrugged. "It doesn't hurt. Gets a little itchy. But I have to say, it is an adjustment getting used to—well, sensory sensations. Even standing in the shower and feeling the water on my skin—it's —I can't explain it."

"Is it uncomfortable for you?" Chris asked.

"No. Just the opposite. It feels amazing—like Danielle's chocolate cake."

"Her chocolate cake?"

Walt smiled. "Tasting food—good food—it's something I never truly appreciated before."

"I thought Danielle said you had stitches in your forehead. I don't see anything."

Walt let out a sigh. "It's the strangest thing. I don't remember a cut ever healing so fast. And from what they told me, it was a pretty big gash."

Chris leaned forward and looked at Walt's forehead. "I thought Danielle said you had something like ten stitches. I don't see anything."

Walt pressed his right foot on the ground, stopping the swing from its gentle back and forth motion. He pointed to where the stitches had been. "That's where it was."

"Wow, I don't see anything," Chris noted before settling back in the swing. "Clint's body must be in good shape if it heals that quickly."

Walt gazed off across the street and was quiet a moment. Finally, he took a deep breath, exhaled, and said in a sober voice, "When I was about ten, I fell off a horse. Left a scar on my left wrist, shaped like a horseshoe, which I used to find ironic considering the circumstances of the injury. I got several stitches, and that scar never left me."

"I suspect it has something to do with medical advances—doctors are more skilled today. Equipment used, even for stitching up wounds, I would imagine is better today," Chris suggested.

With his right hand, Walt unbuttoned his left cuff and folded it up, revealing his wrist. He showed it to Chris.

Chris looked at Walt's wrist and frowned. "Wow. Your cousin had a horseshoe scar on his left wrist too? Now that is bizarre."

71

Walt shook his head and re-buttoned his shirt sleeve. "No, he didn't."

"What do you mean? That wasn't a scar you just showed me?"

Walt let out a deep breath and settled back in the swing. His right toe pushed on the ground, sending the swing back in motion. "Chris, if you woke up in another man's body, what would be the first thing you would do?"

"What do you mean?"

"I'm serious. Think about it. Put yourself in my place. What's one of the first things you would do—or would want to do as soon as you were able to? Before doing anything else."

Chris thought about it a moment and then chuckled. "I suspect I would want to check out the body I got myself into."

"Exactly. The moment I was alone, I looked over every inch of this body. Well, any inch that was possible to see. When I looked at my new wrists—the scar wasn't there. I know it wasn't because I thought, *Well, at least you don't have that scar anymore*."

Chris reached out and grabbed Walt's left wrist. Walt did not resist as Chris quickly unbuttoned his cuff and examined the horseshoe-shaped scar. "How did you get this? It's clearly a scar."

Walt shook his head and after a moment took his wrist back. "I first noticed it yesterday morning when getting ready for Danielle to pick me up. It wasn't as prominent as it is now. Strangely, as quickly as the scar on my head disappeared, the one on my wrist emerged."

"That's freaking bizarre."

"You're telling me!"

A woman from the sidewalk shouted, "Walt!" Both men looked up and found Heather, dressed in a purple jogging suit and carrying her calico cat in her arms, rushing toward them, her black braids bouncing up and down.

Hunny immediately jumped up upon seeing Heather approach. But it wasn't Heather that concerned Hunny, it was the calico cat maliciously eyeing her. Hunny quickly moved behind the swing, cowering.

"Oh, Hunny, stop looking like sweet little Bella is going to eat you up," Heather said when she reached the swing. She then looked at Walt and grinned. "You're looking great, Walt. Nice to see you alive. Welcome home."

Walt grinned at Heather. "Thanks. Nice to see you and Bella."

"I thought you weren't convinced it was really Walt?" Chris

teased.

Heather shrugged. "I talked to Danielle this morning, and since she's convinced, I figure it had to be Walt. But just in case..." Heather set Bella on Walt's lap.

Walt glanced down at the small cat and smiled. "What exactly am I supposed to do?"

Bella paced back and forth on Walt's lap several times and then nestled down and began to purr.

"Danielle said you're still able to communicate with our fur babies, so I figured you can prove it. Then it'll alleviate any doubt about your true identity."

"Umm...and how am I supposed to do that?" Walt asked.

"Tell me what Bella is thinking."

Walt chuckled yet did as she asked. He picked up Bella and looked her in the eyes. After a moment he said, "Stop, Bella, that's not nice."

"What did she say?" Heather asked excitedly.

"Bella is trying to think of ways to torment poor Hunny," Walt told her.

"It really is you!" Heather exclaimed as she scooped Bella up in her arms.

Chris stared at Heather and shook his head.

Heather frowned down at Chris. "What?"

"You are one weird girl, Heather."

"I'm not a girl. I'm a woman."

Chris shrugged. "Then you are one weird woman."

"Why do you say that?" Heather asked.

"Hell, I could have claimed Bella was thinking of ways to torment Hunny, and that wouldn't make me some sort of dog whisperer. We all know your cat is constantly batting at poor Hunny."

Heather shrugged. "So you don't think Walt can still communicate with them?"

"I didn't say that," Chris said, now sounding more frustrated than amused. "I'm just saying what he just said wouldn't by itself convince me."

"You're just being perverse, Chris Johnson."

"And you two work with each other?" Walt chuckled.

"He pays well," Heather chirped.

"Why aren't you two at work today?" Walt asked. "It's not the weekend."

"Taking the day off. We put in a lot of hours yesterday," Chris explained.

"Hi, guys," Danielle said a moment later when she joined her friends on the front porch.

"Hello, Danielle. We were just welcoming Walt home." Heather then went on to tell her about what Walt had said about Bella, while Chris sat silently, rolling his eyes at her train of thought.

"There is one thing I wonder about," Danielle said after Heather finished her telling.

"What's that?" Walt asked.

"Both Max and Bella seemed to enjoy tormenting poor Hunny when she was a pup. But these days I've noticed Max tends to take off more when Hunny comes around, whereas Bella still enjoys tormenting Hunny."

"That's easy to explain," Walt said.

"It is?" Chris asked.

"Sure. Max lived on the street for a number of years before coming here. He's more keenly aware of dangers than Bella, who has been with Heather since she was a kitten. Bella isn't aware of the damage Hunny could do if she decided she's had enough of Bella's teasing, whereas Max is a little concerned Hunny might decide to settle the score."

"They've told you all that?" Chris asked.

"Basically. I've tried to reason with Bella, told her she may be pushing the envelope with Hunny. But she is young. Won't listen. Kind of like a teenager."

"That's it, Walt!" Heather said excitedly.

Everyone turned to Heather. "What's it?" Danielle asked.

"Chris said Walt was concerned about what he would do for a living—"

"Walt doesn't need to do anything," Danielle interrupted.

"I have to do something," Walt said.

"Exactly," Heather said with a nod. "Walt can be a pet whisperer."

Walt frowned. "A pet what?"

"You know, when people are having a problem with their pet, they can bring it to you. You can help them work it out, talk to the pet, explain things. Sort of like a translator," Heather explained.

Chris stared at Heather, his expression blank. He shook his head and muttered, "You are one weird woman."

THIRTEEN

Chet pulled up in front of his sister's house and parked his car. He had been driving around since leaving Marlow House, trying to figure out what to do next. Laverne's car was not in the driveway where she normally parked, and he assumed she was at work. Putting his car back in gear, he pulled into the driveway, put the car in park, and turned off the ignition. He couldn't believe Laverne had actually changed her locks. No way did she have time to do that before going to work this morning. She was bluffing, of that he was certain.

Sitting in the car, he studied the house for a few minutes. After his parents' death during his junior year of high school, the estate had been divided between Laverne and himself. With her share she had purchased this house, which they had both lived in until Chet finally left Frederickport the first time. He had come into his half of the inheritance after he turned twenty-one and soon learned a hundred thousand dollars really wasn't that much money. It was gone within six months. When Laverne's brief marriage ended, she managed to keep the house. Chet assumed it had something to do with the fact she had owned it before the marriage.

Taking the keys out of the ignition, Chet got out of his car and sprinted up to the front door. Laverne would settle down when she came home from work and found he had cleaned the house and had dinner on. That would keep her happy for a few more weeks, it always did.

Chet fumbled with his key ring a moment, looking for his sister's house key. When he found it, he tried unlocking the door. It didn't work.

"She did it! She really did it!" Chet cursed. Not quite believing it, he tried forcing the key into the lock. It still would not work.

Just as Chet turned from the house, he spied his sister's car driving up the street. He walked to his car and stood by the driver's side, its door still open. He watched as Laverne stopped by the entrance to the driveway and rolled her window down.

"You're in my parking space!" she yelled up to him, her engine still running.

"I can't believe you really changed the locks!" he shouted back.

"I told you I would! You need to move your car!"

"Not until we talk!" he yelled.

Laverne let out a curse and then parked her car in front of her house. Slamming the car door shut after exiting the vehicle, she stomped up the driveway to her brother.

"Do you want me to apologize, Laverne? Is that what you want me to do?"

"No, you lazy fool. I want you to find someplace else to live. I'm tired of carrying your sorry butt."

"If I remember, you're the one who begged me to come back to Frederickport. *Stay with me*, you said. *A fresh start in Frederickport, I will help*, you said."

"Stupid me, I thought you would actually try this time."

"What makes you think I haven't been trying? It's not easy finding full-time work when you have a record. It's not my fault."

Crossing her arms over her chest, Laverne arched her brow. "Not your fault? I don't seem to recall anyone forcing you to rob that market."

"You don't know what it was like. I'd lost my job. You don't know how it feels to be hungry," he said angrily.

"What, you couldn't have called me and asked for help?"

"You think so?" Chet spat. "You're turning me away now. Refusing to help me. Why should I believe you would have helped me then?"

Dropping her arms to her sides, Laverne clenched her hands into fists. "So now you're blaming this on me?"

THE GHOST OF SECOND CHANCES

"It's not like I had parents to call for help. You saw to that."

Laverne gasped, clenching her fists tighter. "Don't go there, Chet. I'm serious."

Their argument was interrupted when Chet's cellphone rang. He pulled the flip phone out of his back pocket and answered it while his sister stood glaring at him.

"Hello?" Chet answered.

"Chet, it's Franco. Are you in Frederickport?"

Holding the cellphone to his ear, Chet met his sister's glare yet continued talking to Franco. "Did I have a choice? You guys practically threw me out the door."

"Hey, sorry about that. But you know how Mac is," Franco said.

"Right. Mac is a peach. So what do you want?"

"Remember that thing you said you could get for us?" Franco asked.

"Yeah, what about it?"

"We need it now. Do you have it?"

Chet glanced to his car. "Yeah. And you have the money?"

"Yes. But we need you to do something else."

"What?" Chet asked.

"I don't want to talk about it on the phone. Can you come here?"

"You want me to drive back to Astoria? Now?"

Upon hearing her brother say Astoria, Laverne frowned. "Who are you talking to? Mac who?"

"Yeah. We need you as soon as you can get here." Franco told him.

"I'm busy. Trying to find a place to stay. My sister kicked me out."

"Who are you talking to?" Laverne asked again.

"You can crash here for a few days. And if this works out, you won't have a problem finding a place to stay. Hell, you can buy your own house," Franco said.

"Sounds interesting," Chet muttered.

"Just one thing," Franco added.

"What's that?"

"You can't tell anyone about this," Franco insisted.

Chet laughed. "Seriously? You think I'm stupid enough to tell anyone what I'm getting for you?"

"Just keep our business between us."

77

Chet studied his sister a moment and then said, "No problem."

"Good. When can you get here?"

"I'm leaving now." Chet closed the flip phone a few moments later and shoved it in his back pocket. He started to get in his car when his sister grabbed him by the forearm, trying to stop him.

"Where are you going?" Laverne demanded.

Shrugging off his sister's hold, Chet climbed into his car and said, "What do you care? You told me to leave."

"Are you hanging out with those Bandoni brothers again?" she demanded.

Chet looked up at his sister as he sat in his car. "Hanging out? You make it sound like I'm still in high school." Before slipping his car key in the ignition, he removed his sister's house key from the key ring and flipped it at her. Surprised by the key toss, she fumbled for a moment yet managed to catch the key.

"I figured you would want that back."

"It doesn't work anymore anyway," she snapped, blocking him from closing the car door.

"Move, Laverne. You wanted me gone, I'm going. Move."

"Answer me, Chet. Why are you going to Astoria?"

Chet smiled up at Laverne. "Guess who's in Astoria. Mac. I saw him last night. Same ugly mug. Never could understand what you saw in that short little puke."

"You need to stay away from his cousins. They're bad news. You're going to get yourself locked up again if you aren't careful."

"You're one to talk, Laverne, considering you and Mac." The next moment he turned on his ignition and jerked the car in reverse. Laverne stepped away from the vehicle as he raced backwards out of her driveway and then jammed the car in drive and sped away.

Watching her brother's car disappear down the street, Laverne muttered, "You fool."

THE BANDONI BROTHERS sat with their cousin Macbeth at what used to be their grandmother's kitchen table. Franco had just gotten off the phone with Chet.

"Is he coming?" Mac asked.

"Yeah. But you need to be nicer to him if we want this to work out," Franco told him.

Mac laughed. "So he really fancies himself a contender for Danielle Boatman's affection?"

"That's what he told us," Franco said.

"What did he say when you warned him not to say anything to anyone?" Mac asked.

"He said he hasn't. Said he won't," Franco said.

"What about his sister?" Arlo asked. He's been staying with her."

Franco frowned and slumped back in the chair. "I can't imagine he would tell anyone about his little side business. And I know his sister kicked him out; he told me. But I think she was there when I was talking to him. I kept hearing someone in the background asking him who he was talking to. It was a woman. I'm pretty sure it was his sister."

"I can handle her," Mac told them.

"You know she's divorced now," Arlo said.

Mac chuckled. "Yeah, I heard that. When I was staying at Marlow House, I was tempted to stop by her place for old times' sake. But I knew Chet was staying there, and he's too dumb to keep a story straight. I didn't need him screwing up things for us."

"It's kind of a shame we didn't know about the Bonnets back then," Franco mused. "Back then no one was even living in Marlow House. How easy it would have been to break in and take them. I bet no one would have even noticed."

"For one thing, I wasn't familiar with Bonnet's work when you were in high school," Mac reminded them. "But you have a point. We could have also snagged the Thorndike one. It was stored in some basement in one of the city buildings back then."

"Missed opportunities," Arlo grumbled.

Mac stood up. "We're going to rectify that. I don't want to be here when Chet shows up. You guys take care of him."

"Where are you going?" Arlo asked.

"I'm going to head back to Frederickport and have a little chat with Clint."

"Clint? What for?" Franco asked.

"Nothing for you to worry about. You boys just focus on what you need to do. I'll call you this evening."

"Don't we need to know what you're planning to do?" Angelo asked.

Mac glared at his youngest cousin. "No, you don't. I don't think your little brain can handle more than one task at a time. Focus on what you need to do and wait for me to tell you what to do next."

The brothers sat silently at the kitchen table as Mac left the house. They remained quiet and seated at the table until they could hear Mac's car drive away.

"I hate when he treats us like idiots," Angelo grumbled.

"You know Mac. He's always been like that," Arlo reminded him.

FOURTEEN

Adam Nichols stopped at the mini-mart down the street from his office to grab a soda on Thursday afternoon. What he really wanted was a beer, but he had an appointment with a new client in an hour, and he didn't think that would be a smart thing to do with beer breath.

By the line at the front register, Adam wondered if this were some sort of mini-mart rush hour. Holding his unopen can of soda in one hand, he stood behind an average-height woman with mousey brown hair. There were six people ahead of her in line.

"I don't remember ever seeing this place so crowded," Adam grumbled under his breath. He considered putting the soda back and leaving, but he figured he was already here, and he was thirsty.

The woman with the mousey brown hair heard his comment and turned to face him.

"Laverne?" Adam said in surprise.

Laverne Morrison looked a great deal like her younger brother. Not unattractive, but plain—the type of face that was easy to forget. However, Adam remembered another Laverne, back when he was in high school, and she was his friend's much older sister. Back then she had bleached her hair blond and wore a good deal of makeup. Nothing like her freshly scrubbed face today, without even a hint of lipstick. She also wore her clothes tighter back then, and as he could recall, her figure played a prominent role in many of his teenage fantasies. But she had changed after her parents' death. No longer bleaching her hair, she stopped wearing makeup, and even her clothing style became ultraconservative.

"Hi, Adam. I thought that was you behind me." She flashed him a smile.

"How are you doing? I saw Chet yesterday. Said he might be moving out."

"He already has. I saw to that last night."

Adam chuckled. "You kicked him out, did you?"

"You know what they say about houseguests. They start smelling like fish."

"He mentioned looking for a room to rent. Did he find something yet?"

"He told me he was going to stay with the Bandoni brothers in Astoria."

"Seriously? He mentioned doing some work for them. But I didn't realize he would consider staying with them."

"Those boys were nothing but trouble back when they were in high school. Coming to Frederickport for no other reason than to cause trouble. I don't believe they've changed. And I can't imagine what kind of work they have for Chet."

"Not sure I would call them boys. Have you seen how big they are?" Adam chuckled.

"They were big boys back then," Laverne reminded him.

"Yeah, well, now they're even larger. I've seen them a few times when I've been in Astoria. I sure wouldn't want to run into any of them in a dark alley. At least, not when they're in a bad mood."

WALT STOOD ALONE at the dresser in the downstairs bedroom. Reluctantly, he picked up Clint's wallet and opened it.

With a sigh he said, "I suppose it's time I learn more about this life I've taken over."

"Who are you talking to?" Danielle asked from the open doorway.

Walt shrugged. "To myself, I guess." Wallet in hand, he hopped over to the bed and sat down on the edge of the mattress.

"Interesting conversation?" Danielle asked as she walked all the way into the room.

"I figured it was about time I go through Clint's wallet."

Danielle scrunched up her nose. "Yeah, I guess you'll need to use his driver's license and other IDs, like his Social Security number." She walked to the bed and sat down with Walt. She watched as he removed all the cards from the wallet and spread them on the bedspread between the two of them.

Glancing over the cards, Walt reached down and picked up Clint's Social Security card and looked at it a moment before handing it to Danielle. "I assume that's Clint's Social Security number?"

She looked at the card a moment and then handed it back to Walt. "It's yours now."

Walt shrugged and tossed the card back on the bed. "I remember when I first saw a commercial about Social Security on television, and I had no idea what it was talking about. You explained it all to me."

"I remember. I Googled it for you and learned the first Social Security numbers were issued about eleven years after you died."

Walt nodded and then picked up Clint's driver's license. "I suspect I'll need to get a new one of these. Clint's was issued in California. I'll need an Oregon driver's license."

"Yeah. But you should wait a while. After you make it common knowledge you intend to stay here."

With a snort Walt said, "That's going to be interesting."

"Those closest to us already know the truth," Danielle reminded him.

Walt started to toss the license back on the bed when Danielle snatched it from him. "How about driver's licenses? Did you have to get a license back when you were alive?"

"Yes. About five years before I died, Oregon started requiring them. I remember it cost me twenty-five cents and was good for life. Since I died, I imagine that one is no longer valid, and I'll have to get a new one," he said with a chuckle.

"Did you have to take a driver's test?"

"Driver's test?" Walt frowned.

Danielle nodded. "Yeah, to make sure you knew the rules."

Walt shrugged. "I don't recall taking a test. From what I remember, you had to have something like five days' driving experience."

"I'm afraid you'll have to take a written test before you get an Oregon driver's license this time. I know I did. But I'll pick up the pamphlet on the driving laws for you to study, so you shouldn't have a problem passing."

"I imagine a great deal has changed in the last ninety years," Walt said with a sigh.

"Hey, you are officially older than me!" Danielle blurted, her attention on the birthdate listed on Clint's driver's license.

"What are you talking about?"

"You're always saying you're just twenty-six. But your cousin was thirty-six."

"I seem to recall knowing he was that age," Walt told her. "In fact, I think you told me."

"Now it's you. You're officially thirty-six."

"You sound entirely too cheerful over the fact I've lost a decade."

"Considering it took about ninety years to lose a decade to become older than me, not such a bad deal."

"True."

Danielle dropped the driver's license on the bed and then started gathering up the credit cards. "You'll probably want to take care of these."

"What are they?" Walt asked.

"Credit cards. This is definitely something that wasn't around when you were alive."

"Two things. First, there were stores that offered credit cards, so to speak, not like what you have today. And second, you need to stop saying when you *were alive*. If you'll notice, I'm alive now."

"Sorry. You know what I mean."

Walt pointed to the credit cards in Danielle's hand. "What do you think I should do with those?"

"We need to find out which ones have a balance. You need to get Clint's debts paid off. If you ignore them, they'll just keep racking up fees and interest."

"How do I go about that?" he asked.

"We can start with these cards. But there might be some debts that aren't associated with anything Clint had in his wallet. I know Ian found some financial information on Clint. I'll check with him. Also, it might be a good idea to run a credit report on Clint, see what pops up."

"How do we do that?" Walt asked.

Danielle considered the question a moment. Finally, she said, "Adam."

Walt frowned. "Adam? You mean Marie's Adam?"

Danielle nodded. "He runs credit reports on his renters. He must be signed up with some company that does that. I'll see if he'll do it for me. After all, we already have your license and Social Security numbers." Danielle picked the license and Social Security card back up and put them in a neat stack with the credit cards.

"Thank you, Danielle. I'd appreciate it. I need to get these loose ends tied up with Clint. But I'm not sure where to start."

"It's not like there's a handbook that lists what you need to do when you take over someone else's body." Danielle glanced over at the cellphone on the dresser. "And then there's Clint's cellphone."

"What about it?" Walt asked.

"I know the battery is probably dead. The phone hasn't been charged since before the car accident. But even if it was charged, I've no idea what the password is."

"It's not like I need Clint's phone. You bought me my own," Walt reminded her.

"True. But I imagine there's some information on the phone—contacts—that might be useful. Plus, we should probably find out who he had his phone service with. There's probably a phone bill out there for you to pay." Danielle stood up and walked to the phone, still carrying the stack of cards.

"What are you doing?" Walt asked.

"No reason to put this off." She picked up the cellphone. "I have a cord that'll work on this. Let me charge the phone. Maybe we can figure out the password. Sometimes people use familiar numbers, like birthdates. And I'll run over to Adam's office before he closes up. See if he'll run the credit report for me."

NO ONE WAS SITTING in the front office of Frederickport Vacation Properties when Danielle entered the building. But as soon as she stepped inside, she heard Adam shout from his back office, "Come on in!"

"Real professional," Danielle said with a chuckle a few moments later when she entered Adam's office. "Do you always yell out at your clients?"

Adam leaned back in his desk chair and smiled. "I knew it was you. Saw you coming through the window."

"Where's Leslie?" Danielle took a seat facing the desk.

"She had to run to the post office. And I'm just sitting here debating if I should call her and have her pick me up some beer on her way back."

Danielle frowned. "Beer?"

Adam shrugged and sat up straight at his desk, scooting closer to it. "A client just called, cancelled his appointment."

"So that means you need beer?"

Adam waved his hand dismissively. "Never mind, you wouldn't understand."

"I guess not," Danielle muttered under her breath.

Adam folded his hands together on his desk and asked, "So what can I do for you?"

"I have a favor to ask."

His hands still folded together on his desk, Adam shook his head and made a tsk-tsk sound. "Sorry, you used up all your favors for this week."

Danielle smiled. "I did?"

"Yeah, I gave you a heads-up about Chet. Did he show up asking for a room?"

Danielle let out a groan and rolled her eyes. "He did."

Adam chuckled. "Apparently you didn't cave to his irresistible charms. I ran into his sister this afternoon, and she told me he was going to be staying in Astoria with the Bandoni brothers. I wondered if he had stopped by Marlow House first."

Danielle bolted upright, her expression blank. "Did you say Bandoni brothers?"

"Yeah. So what did Chet say when he stopped by?"

"You know the Bandoni brothers?"

Adam shrugged. "Yeah. Do you?"

"Umm…in a way. How do you know them?"

"From high school. We didn't go to the same school, but we would see them at football games, and they would come to town to party. Chet used to hang out with them. I did a few times, but they were trouble. Aside from occasionally running into one of them when I go to Astoria, I haven't really talked to them in years."

"Did you know their cousin Macbeth?" Danielle asked.

Adam frowned. "Macbeth?"

"He might have gone by Mac."

"Wait a minute, you said Macbeth? Didn't Lily say that was the artist's real name? The one Marlow hired to reproduce your paintings?"

Danielle nodded. "His real name is Macbeth Bandoni, and the Bandoni brothers are his cousins."

"Holy crap. I remember Mac Bandoni. He'd come and stay with them sometimes." Adam paused a moment and then added, "He dated Laverne for a while."

"Laverne?" Danielle frowned.

"Chet's older sister. The one he was living with. But that was years ago. I certainly didn't recognize him. Old Mac didn't hold up very well."

FIFTEEN

When Danielle returned to Marlow House late Thursday afternoon, she found Walt sitting on the back porch, reading a book, while Max napped nearby on a patio lounger. She had stopped at Beach Taco on the way home to grab something for an early dinner. With all that was going on, she didn't feel like cooking, and Joanne had already gone home.

"What do you have there?" Walt asked when she got out of her car and started walking toward him.

Danielle held up the bag briefly as she said, "I stopped and grabbed something for us to eat. Do you like tamales?"

"Did you buy some oysters too?" Walt asked.

Danielle frowned. "Oysters?"

Walt gazed off for a moment recalling a long-ago memory. "When I was a boy and would visit Portland, we'd stop at one of my grandfather's favorite oyster bars. It served tamales. I always liked the tamales, but to be honest, I didn't develop a taste for oysters until I was older."

Danielle sat down in the empty chair next to Walt and opened the paper sack. "Sounds like an odd combination."

Walt shrugged. "Oyster bars with tamales were common."

"I guess they really didn't have regular Mexican restaurants back then."

Walt shook his head. "No, not really."

"I wasn't sure what you'd like, so I picked up an assortment. They make really good tacos and tamales. I also picked up some taquitos." Danielle pulled the plastic soufflé cups filled with hot sauce, salsa, and guacamole out of the sack and set them on the table between her and Walt, and she then pulled out the wrapped food. After setting the food on the table, she stood up and folded the now empty paper sack.

"Let me go inside and grab something for us to drink. Maybe get some plates. Looks like they forgot to give me napkins, so I'll get some of those too."

Several minutes later, Danielle was back outside with Walt as he curiously unwrapped some of the food, inspecting it.

"I've seen you and Lily eat this before. I was always curious to try it." Holding a partially wrapped taco in his hand, Walt studied it.

"Surely you've had a taco before?"

Walt shook his head. "No, can't say I have. I've had tamales, but never a taco." Cautiously, Walt took a bite of the taco. Some of the crispy shell broke off, but he managed to catch it before it fell onto his lap.

Danielle watched as Walt chewed up his bite of taco. "So how do you like it?"

Still chewing, Walt nodded. Finally, he said, "It's good."

Glancing down at the table, Danielle spied the plastic soufflé cup of homemade hot sauce. She grabbed it and pulled off its lid. "Here, try it with hot sauce."

Walt waved away the sauce and smiled. "No. I think I need to take this one step at a time." He took a second bite.

After Walt had finished his taco and started eating his tamale, he asked, "Was Adam of any help?"

"He ran a report on Clint. It didn't have much. Nothing we didn't already know. I think I'll ask the chief for help."

"Did Adam ask why you wanted my credit report run?"

"I told him because you were staying here indefinitely. Said I thought it might be a good idea to run one."

"Indefinitely?" Walt arched his brow. "How did Adam take that?"

"I didn't say indefinitely exactly, more like you weren't a typical B and B guest, and I figure most rental places run reports before they take someone month to month."

Walt nodded and started to take another bite of the tamale. Just before he did, he paused and said, "This is much better than the tamales I remember eating when I was a kid."

Danielle smiled at Walt and then remembered she hadn't told him everything she had learned from Adam. Her expression grew serious, and she said, "I also found out Adam knows the Bandoni brothers. And he's even met Macbeth."

"I suppose that doesn't surprise me, they do live in Astoria, and I know Adam has connections there. But Macbeth, didn't he meet him here when he was doing the portraits?"

Danielle nodded. "I don't think they ever really talked when he was doing the paintings, but he saw him a few times when he was here. Of course, he wasn't using his real name. Last time Adam saw him was when he was in high school—Adam, not Macbeth. Macbeth is older than Adam."

"He didn't recognize him?"

"I guess not. He never knew him that well. The main reason he remembered him was because the Bandonis loved to talk about their cool cousin who traveled the world. Adam never knew him as Macbeth—but as Mac. He also dated Chet's sister that summer."

"Chet? You mean that palooka who was trying to get you to rent him a room?"

Danielle nodded. "I guess he's staying in Astoria with the Bandoni brothers now."

Walt frowned. "That's interesting."

MACBETH BANDONI PULLED into the pier parking lot and parked his car. After getting out of the vehicle, he fitted a straw beach hat on his head and pulled it down to obscure his face. Wearing jeans and a white T-shirt, he tossed a beach towel over one shoulder and slammed his car door shut.

Slipping on a pair of oversized sunglasses, he looked at his reflection in his car window. He smiled and said under his breath, "I look like another tourist."

Instead of walking down the pier to the beach, he went in the opposite direction, making his way to the next street after Beach Drive. He then cut back, moving through yards, until he was along the fence to the side yard of Marlow House. Spying an opening along one section of fencing, he slipped into the yard, taking refuge behind several leafy bushes.

To his surprise he spotted Danielle Boatman sitting outside with his old partner Clint Marlow. They were eating and talking, but he couldn't hear what they were saying. Careful not to move and risk rustling the leaves, he waited and watched.

Finally, Danielle stood up and began gathering up the dishes and paper debris from whatever they had been eating. He watched as she carried the trash and dishes into the house and then held the door open for Clint, who hopped his way into the kitchen.

Leaving the beach towel in the bushes and removing his sunglasses, Macbeth crept to the back door, passing a sleeping cat on a patio lounger. Crouching down, he sat next to the door leading into the house. He could clearly hear voices coming through the swinging pet door.

Using the tip of one finger, Macbeth gingerly nudged the pet door outward an inch and managed to peer into the house. Both Danielle and Clint sat at the kitchen table, their backs to the door. Macbeth smiled and eased the pet door closed again. He sat and listened.

"I imagine Clint's phone is about charged," Danielle said.

"If we can't figure out what Clint's password is, do you think whatever phone company he used might be able to help us?" Macbeth heard Clint say.

Macbeth leaned closer to the door and silently asked, *Since when did you start speaking in third person?*

"I don't think they can help you retrieve whatever information Clint had on the phone," Danielle said. "But they could probably reset the phone so you can use it. Like a new phone. But that's just a guess."

"I only care about how the information on Clint's phone might help me get his life settled. Pay off his outstanding bills. It would be nice if he had enough in his bank account to do that."

What is going on? Macbeth wondered.

"Even if he doesn't, Walt, it's no big deal. I'll simply write a check, and it will be done."

"But that's your money, Danielle."

"Stop saying that, Walt. It was your money first."

Macbeth pulled away slightly from the house and stared at the pet door. *Your money first? What does that mean?*

"I still have to do something. Find my way in this new life I've been given."

"One day at a time. For now, I suppose you just need to get used to being in Clint's body. Adjusting to being alive again."

Macbeth drew his brow into a frown. *What are they talking about?*

"It would have been nice had Clint not broken his leg in the crash." The man Macbeth knew as Clint said before he chuckled and added, "There is so much I want to do."

"I suppose eight weeks in a cast will go by quickly."

"As opposed to ninety years as a ghost?"

"Walt!" Danielle laughed. "Did you just call yourself a ghost?"

"I don't seem to mind it as much now that I'm on this side."

It went silent, and after a few moments, Macbeth began wondering if one of them had left the room. If so, he imagined it would have been Danielle, since he assumed Clint would make considerable noise using his crutches. Again using one finger, he pulled the pet door outward and peered inside. To his shock, the two were kissing.

Letting the pet door close again, Macbeth felt his head spinning. *What is going on?* he asked himself again.

A loud meow interrupted Macbeth's thoughts. Jerking his head to face the source of the sound, he found himself staring into the golden eyes of a black cat, who stood just inches from him. He swallowed nervously and then glanced to the pet door. Macbeth recognized the cat from when he had stayed at Marlow House. It was obvious the animal wanted to go through the pet door.

Moving quickly and trying to be as quiet as possible, Macbeth crawled away from the house and then broke into a sprint, keeping his head down as he dashed into the bushes.

The cat, who continued to stand by the back door, watched him run away, and then he turned back to the house and moved through the pet door opening, shoving the flapping door inward as he did.

DANIELLE AND WALT turned abruptly to the pet door when they heard it swinging back and forth. They watched as Max strolled toward them.

"Hey, Max. I see you finally woke up," Danielle greeted him.

Max looked to Walt. Their eyes met. After a moment, Walt said in a low voice, "I want you to lock the door, Danielle."

Noting the serious tone in Walt's voice, Danielle did as he instructed and then turned to him.

"Now you need to call the chief. Max tells me a man was sitting by the back door right before he came into the house. According to Max, it appeared he was listening to us."

Danielle let out a gasp and glanced to the now closed door.

"Max says he ran off into the bushes. I think you need to call the chief."

SIXTEEN

Police Chief MacDonald walked into the kitchen carrying a beach towel. He tossed it on the kitchen table where Walt and Danielle sat. "I found this in the bushes near the fence on the south side of the house. Part of the fence is broken there, and it must be where he got in."

"The neighbors on that side don't live here full-time. No one's there right now," Danielle told him. Sitting on Danielle's lap was her cat, Max, who peered over the kitchen table at the chief with curious golden eyes.

MacDonald took out his notepad and asked, "Did Max describe the guy?" As soon as he spoke the words, the chief closed his eyes, shook his head, and muttered, "I can't believe I just asked that question."

Ignoring MacDonald's last comment, Walt said, "The intruder looks familiar to Max, but basically we all look the same to him. He said he was wearing some sort of hat—like the kind they wear on the beach."

MacDonald groaned, tossed the notepad on the table, and sat down. "I can't believe I'm trying to get information from a cat."

As if he knew he was the subject of the conversation, Max let out a meow.

"I'm sorry I had to call you, Chief," Danielle apologized. "But if I had just called the station about a trespasser, and one of your officers came over to take the report, how could I tell them we didn't actually see the guy, my cat did."

MacDonald sighed and flashed Danielle a weak smile. "I understand. This just never gets—*normal*." He chuckled and then looked over to Walt and asked, "How are you doing? Getting along okay with that leg?"

"I've discovered I'm fairly good at hopping. But if I didn't have the cast on, I probably wouldn't have asked Danielle to call you. I could have handled it myself."

"No, you did the right thing." The chief picked up his notepad from the table. "We need to know when trespassers are peeping in houses. We had a report the other night about some guys poking around on the houses over on Sunset Drive. The only thing that was reported missing was some beer out of Jim Bellow's extra refrigerator in his garage. It's not that they can't afford to buy their own beer—or find someone to buy it for them if they're underage—but they seem to find lurking around houses and stealing beer more of a game. Won't be such a fun game when one of the neighbors decides to pull out a gun and shoot someone."

In the next moment Lily and Ian came walking into the house from the side yard.

"Did you find anyone?" Lily asked.

"The chief seems to think it's some out-of-control spring break visitors," Danielle told them.

The chief stood up. "I don't recall saying that, exactly. It could also be someone checking out houses to break into. I'll write up a report. I'll leave off the part about Max being the witness."

Ian laughed. "That might be a good idea."

"We'll have an extra patrol swing by this street tonight," the chief added.

"Are you sure you understood what Max was trying to tell you?" Lily asked Walt. "If you guys didn't actually see anyone yourselves, are you sure anyone was really here?"

The chief picked up the beach towel off the table and showed Lily. "I found this along the fence, behind the bushes. Plus, that section of the fence had an opening, and it looked like someone had recently gone through it."

"Oh…" Lily gulped. "I was rather hoping this was nothing more than a cat's overactive imagination."

"I wouldn't get too upset, Lily. Burglars out casing houses rarely take along their beach towel. Unless, of course, it's to wrap up their loot," Ian said with a grin.

Lily elbowed Ian. "Stop. Now I'm not going to be able to sleep tonight."

"We have Sadie. She'll let us know if anyone is trying to break in."

"And we have Max," Walt said with a chuckle.

Lily looked over to Walt and cocked her head slightly. "You know, when I used to live here, I always felt very safe knowing you were around."

Walt let out a sigh and glanced down at his broken leg. "But now I'm fairly useless."

"Hey, I will take useless alive you over spiritual security guard any day," Danielle said.

Walt smiled at Danielle and reached over and patted her hand.

"THIS IS ALL SO FREAKING BIZARRE," Ian said when he and Lily walked into their house forty minutes later. Sadie eagerly greeted them, tail wagging.

"I think you have only said that maybe one million times already," Lily said as she closed the door behind them.

"Walt sitting at that table in Clint's body. Walt talking to a cat."

"People talk to animals all the time. You talk to Sadie."

"Ha-ha," Ian said dryly. "You know what I mean."

"I know. But you need to stop obsessing about how weird this all is. This is our new normal."

Together Ian and Lily walked into the living room, Sadie trailing behind them.

"I talked to Kelly this afternoon, and she asked me how long I thought Clint would be staying at Marlow House." As Ian sat down on the sofa, he reached out and grabbed Lily, pulling her on his lap.

"Your sister is going to freak when she realizes he's not going anywhere." Lily made herself comfortable on Ian's lap.

"No. Joe is going to freak. And that will freak my sister."

MACBETH HID in the bushes as a patrol car moved slowly down

THE GHOST OF SECOND CHANCES

Beach Drive. It was past midnight, technically Friday morning, and Macbeth hadn't yet returned to Astoria. Instead, he had been watching Marlow House. The house had been dark for two hours now, and he was fairly confident everyone inside was asleep.

He knew there were no guests staying at Marlow House aside from Clint. After witnessing that kiss earlier, he wondered where Danielle Boatman would be sleeping. Macbeth doubted Clint would be able to make it up the stairs in his cast. Yet, considering that kiss, he knew something was going on.

After watching the windows at Marlow House a little longer, he was certain Danielle had retired to her room upstairs—and Clint had gone to his room downstairs.

MOONLIGHT STREAMED through the downstairs bedroom window. A rattling sound jolted Walt awake. He bolted upright in his bed and looked to the bedroom door. It was ajar, and he could hear rattling—it sounded like it was coming from the front door.

Glancing around, he looked for Max. "A cat is never here when you need him," Walt grumbled under his breath.

He heard the distinct squeaking of the front door hinges. Someone had entered the house.

Walt's only thought—*I need to tell Danielle to lock her bedroom door and call the police.* He looked to his nightstand for his cellphone so he could call Danielle. But it wasn't on the nightstand. Walt then remembered he had left it sitting on the dresser across the room.

Scooting to the side of the bed, he awkwardly moved his left foot off the mattress, followed by the right foot. He stepped on his crutches. When going to bed, he had set the crutches against the nightstand, but they had since fallen to the floor.

The footsteps continued to come in his direction.

Leaning down, he tried to grab a crutch but in doing so almost slipped off the mattress. He caught himself and remained seated on the side of the bed. His bedroom door flew open.

There, standing in his open doorway, was Macbeth Bandoni.

Without thought, Walt blurted, "Mac—" He caught himself and didn't finish saying the man's name, but it was too late. Walt cursed himself.

Macbeth chuckled. "I see you got your memory back," Macbeth

said as he walked into the room, closing the door behind him. The moonlight lit up the room, making it unnecessary to turn on the overhead light.

"What are you doing here?" Walt asked.

"I thought it was time we conclude our little business deal. And I see you have a new scam going on." Macbeth chuckled again. "I have to give you credit. I never saw that one coming."

Walt eyed Macbeth nervously. "I don't know what you're talking about."

"I heard you today and your little fantasy you've got going on with Danielle Boatman. I knew she had something for that guy in the portrait, but how you managed to con her into believing you're that guy now. Wow. I have to give it to you. How you pulled that off—I can't even imagine."

Macbeth walked over to the bed and picked up the crutches off the floor, moving them to the other side of the room. He then sat down on a chair facing Walt.

Walt took a deep breath and said, "I'm afraid I really don't know what you're talking about. You see, I have amnesia. I can't remember anything from before my accident."

"Right, amnesia." Macbeth laughed. "I forgot. I think you forgot too, since you just called me by my name."

"What do you want?" Walt asked.

"To begin with, I want the portraits. The fakes are still waiting to be authenticated, and once they find out we switched the paintings, I have to disappear. You, on the other hand, might be okay, as long as you can continue to push this amnesia scam while seducing the not too bright but very rich Danielle Boatman. As for me, I want the paintings before I disappear."

"I don't even know where the portraits are," Walt said.

"The police have them. They belong to you. So you need to have them delivered here and then give them to me. You do that, and I'll leave you to your new scam."

"I don't know what you're talking about."

"Stop already, Clint. I saw you kissing her. I have to say, you had me fooled. I really did believe you were crazy for Stephanie, but you managed to get over her quick enough. Not sure how long you'll be able to pull off this charade, and considering how chummy Boatman is with the local cops, I think you might want to get what you can from her and then disappear, like I intend to do. Just some friendly advice."

Macbeth stood up. "You call the police station tomorrow and tell them you want your things delivered here, including the paintings. I'll contact you, and we can make arrangements to pick them up. We need to get this done this week before the fakes are discovered. And if you don't do this, I'll make sure everyone in Danielle Boatman's life knows about the con you're trying to pull on her."

SEVENTEEN

Walt heard the front door close at the same time Max strolled into his bedroom. Still sitting on the edge of the mattress, he stared down at the cat.

"Now you show up. Is he gone?" Walt asked.

Max walked to the bed, his eyes fixed on Walt.

"He is? That doesn't surprise me. After what he said, I assumed it was him."

Max was about to jump on the bed when Walt said, "I need to make sure he's gone before we wake Danielle."

Max turned and ran from the room. A few minutes later, Walt could hear the faint sound of the pet door swinging in the kitchen door.

Bracing his hands against the edge of the mattress, Walt stood on his right foot, keeping his left leg with the cast slightly bent. Standing on one foot, he hopped to the dresser and grabbed his phone. He then hopped to the chair Macbeth had been sitting on minutes earlier and sat down. He called Danielle.

"Walt?" she answered in a groggy voice a few moments later. "Is something wrong?"

"I want you to lock your bedroom door, now. And then I'll tell you the rest," Walt ordered.

"Walt? What's wrong?"

"Danielle, please. Do what I ask, now!"

THE GHOST OF SECOND CHANCES

A moment later Danielle said, "Okay, it's locked. Are you okay? What's wrong?"

"Macbeth was here a minute ago. I heard him leave out the front door. But Max is checking to see if he's still hanging around the house."

"Macbeth? How did he get in? I'm sure I locked the door, and I changed that lock, he doesn't have a key."

"He got in some way. Picked the lock perhaps?" Walt suggested.

"Well, *that* doesn't make me feel very safe," Danielle grumbled. "I should probably call the police."

"Danielle, if he's gone, we need to talk to the chief about this, but I don't think we need to drag him out of bed right now. He's got his boys to consider, and trust me, we don't want to share with Joe or Brian what Macbeth told me tonight."

"What did he tell you?"

MAX FOLLOWED Macbeth to his car at the pier and watched him get in and drive away. The cat then returned to Marlow House and conveyed the information to Walt. Confident Macbeth would not be returning that night, Walt told Danielle it was safe to come downstairs. Before she did, she slipped on her floor-length robe over her pajama bottoms and T-shirt. Since she already had socks on her feet, she didn't bother looking for her slippers, but she did manage to run a brush through her hair before leaving her bedroom.

Almost forty minutes after Macbeth had left Marlow House, Walt and Danielle sat in the library on the sofa, with Max curled up on Danielle's lap. She stroked the cat's head as he purred and drooled, his overbite reminding her of a vampire bat. Intermittently she would stop stroking his head and gently rub his white-tipped black ears.

"So Macbeth was the one Max saw sitting outside the kitchen door?" Danielle asked.

"Yes. And I'm the sap that called him by name." Walt groaned.

"It happens, Walt. He caught you off guard. I say you keep pushing the amnesia story. Most of our friends knew Jim Hill's name was Macbeth. I could have told you, and you can say you guessed who he was by how I described him. And if Macbeth starts repeating what he overheard—which will mean he'll have to admit to eavesdropping at our back door—I'll deny any of it happened."

"You are rather good at lying." Walt chuckled.

Danielle shrugged. "And who would believe I'd let you—*Clint Marlow*—kiss me."

"As I recall," Walt said, his blue eyes twinkling, "you initiated that kiss in the kitchen."

WHEN MACBETH RETURNED TO ASTORIA, he found Chet's car parked in front of his cousins' house and Chet sleeping on the living room sofa. Careful not to wake Chet, he made his way to Franco's bedroom. Without knocking, he opened the door and went inside, gently closing the door behind him. He could hear Franco snoring.

Sitting on the side of his cousin's bed, he shook him awake.

"What the—" Franco sputtered as he found himself startled awake.

"Keep quiet," Macbeth admonished. "I don't want to wake anyone else."

"Wonderful, you just want to wake me," Franco grumbled while sitting up and rubbing his eyes.

"Did you get it?" Macbeth asked.

"Seriously? That's why you woke me up?" Squinting his eyes, he glanced over to the alarm clock on his nightstand.

"I need to know. Did he give it to you?"

"No. Not yet. He said he would get it for me in the morning."

"I want it now," Macbeth said. "But I don't want him to know you took it."

"I don't get it?" Franco frowned.

"I saw Clint tonight. He no more has amnesia than I do. He's pulling another scam on Danielle Boatman."

"What kind of scam?"

"This time he's going for all her money."

Franco scratched his head. "How so?"

"I saw them kissing."

"Kissing? I thought Chet said she had a thing for him."

"Chet has always been full of crap," Macbeth said with a snort. "But that will work in our favor."

"How so?"

"Because when I kill Clint Marlow, I intend to frame Chet."

"You're going to kill Clint? Why?"

"It's none of your freaking business. You just get me that gun, and when you do, don't get any of your prints on it. When I use it to kill Clint, I want to make sure the only prints on the gun are Chet's. If we wait for Chet to hand it over, he's liable to wipe it down first. At least, if he has any brains, he will."

"What about the paintings?" Franco asked.

"I screwed up when I went to the police the first time. With Clint still alive, there was no way they were going to hand the paintings over to me. I should have known better."

"So what do you plan to do now?"

"I made sure Clint is going to have the paintings delivered to Marlow House. After he's murdered, and everyone is at his funeral, we can break into the house and get the paintings."

"Funeral? Why would he have the funeral here?"

"Seriously? Clint doesn't have any money, no ties anywhere. Anywhere but here. He's conned Danielle Boatman, and you bet she'll have him buried here with the rest of the Marlows."

"But when they find the portraits gone, won't they realize you killed Clint?"

"Why? They'll have the murder weapon, the fingerprints, the motive. He had a thing for Boatman. And when I disappear with the paintings, I'd rather they not connect the murder to the missing art."

"But Chet will tell them about you—about us."

"Not if he's dead, he won't." Macbeth laughed.

"What about us?"

"You'll get what I originally promised."

"But now that you don't have to split with Clint, you can afford to increase our share."

Macbeth laughed. "Yeah, right. That isn't happening. Anyway, you boys would end up throwing all that money around, and before you know it, they would start thinking you had something to do with the heist. It's better for you this way. You'll have a little extra spending money without having to disappear. You'll thank me for this. Just go get that gun."

CHET SAT at the kitchen table devouring toast, cereal, and coffee that he had pilfered from the Bandoni brothers' pantry.

"Morning, Chet," Franco greeted him when he walked into the kitchen. Glancing over to the open box of cereal and carton of milk Chet had left sitting out on the counter, he added, "I see you found something to eat."

Chet let out a grunt in response and continued eating, milk dripping from his chin.

Macbeth stepped into the kitchen and said, "Franco, I need to talk to you." He then stepped back into the other room.

The moment Franco left the kitchen and joined his cousin, Macbeth asked, "Did you get it?"

"I started to look last night. But Chet must have heard you come in, and it woke him up. He almost caught me looking through his car."

Macbeth cursed.

"Don't worry, Angelo is out there right now looking while Chet is filling his gut. He'll get it."

"You did tell him not to get his fingerprints on it?" Macbeth asked.

"Yes. He's not stupid."

"You got that money?" Chet asked when he burst into the room a moment later, interrupting Macbeth and Franco's hushed conversation.

"Yeah, but you don't need to get it now." Franco's eyes darted toward the front door.

"No reason to wait." Chet turned abruptly and headed for the door, Franco and Macbeth behind him.

When they got outside, they found Angelo standing in the street by Chet's car. Angelo quickly grabbed the trash can that had been placed by the curb the night before and started dragging it up to the house.

"I just threw my stuff in the car. It'll take a minute to find it," Chet said before sprinting down the driveway.

"Do you think Angelo found it?" Macbeth whispered to Franco.

"If he did, my bet, he put it in the trash can."

"Just hope he wrapped it in something. Carefully," Macbeth grumbled.

Together Macbeth and Franco walked down the driveway and stood by Chet's car, watching him search through his belongings.

After a moment, Franco glanced up to the house and spied his youngest brother disappearing into the garage with the trash can.

Fifteen minutes later Chet cursed. "Laverne, you didn't!"

"What are you talking about?" Macbeth asked.

"It's not here. Laverne must have taken it!" Chet cursed again. "But I'll get it back. I'll make her give it to me."

"I don't want the gun now. Not if Laverne knows about it," Macbeth insisted.

"Don't worry. I won't tell her I'm selling it to you," Chet promised.

Macbeth stubbornly shook his head. "No. I don't want it now."

"But we agreed on the price!" Chet fairly whined.

"Don't worry, Chet," Franco said in a soothing voice. "We'll figure out something else. We still need you for what we have planned. It will be more than enough money. And you can crash here for as long as you want."

Chet looked from Franco to Macbeth. "You haven't told me what else you need me to do."

"Don't worry about it now. Mac never likes to tell us more than we need to know about a job. It's safer for everyone that way."

"But aren't you going to need the gun?" Chet asked.

"I know somewhere else we can get one," Franco said. "And Mac is right. We don't want to use a gun that might be traced back to one of us in case it's found. Let your sister keep it. We'll get another one."

"It can't be traced back to any of us. I stole that gun."

"Where?" Macbeth asked.

Chet frowned. "Why do you care?"

"Did you steal it when you were in Missouri?" Macbeth asked.

"So?"

"If they trace the gun to one stolen from Missouri and you've got that Missouri license plate on your car, not to mention you have a record, you know the cops are going to ask your sister if she has ever seen you with a gun. It could lead them back to you and to us," Macbeth said.

"Oh…" Chet grumbled. "I see what you mean."

EIGHTEEN

The patio thermometer registered in the fifties on Friday morning, an average for April in Frederickport. The morning chill didn't deter Danielle and Walt from sitting on the back patio and enjoying their coffee. It had been unseasonably warm the past week, with record highs in the seventies. But Danielle knew that was not going to last. She might have opted to take coffee inside this morning, where it was warmer and less damp, but Walt seemed to crave the outdoors. When she had mentioned the temperature earlier, his comment had been something along the lines of "Nothing a jacket won't cure." Fortunately, a jacket had been one of the clothing items Danielle had picked up for Walt while he was still in the hospital.

"You said Joanne won't be back until next week?" Walt asked as he sipped his coffee. His first cup of coffee since taking over Clint's body had been in the hospital. It had been sorely disappointing, nothing like how he had remembered. He might have skipped the morning ritual if he hadn't tried Danielle's coffee the day before. Hers was not bitter and stale like what he had tasted in the hospital. As a spirit, he had enjoyed the rich aroma of Danielle's coffee—but he found drinking it even better, something he had been unable to do without a body. When on the other side, he had been able to enjoy scents without the benefit of an olfactory nerve, while the sense of taste eluded him.

THE GHOST OF SECOND CHANCES

"She's visiting some friends in Vancouver. I was afraid she was going to cancel." Instead of wearing a jacket, Danielle sat on the patio chair curled up in an oversized fleece blanket.

"Why?" Walt wrapped his hands around his cup, warming his fingers.

Danielle flashed Walt a lopsided grin. "Why, you, of course. She didn't think it was a great idea leaving me alone with you."

"I thought she was giving me a second chance?"

Danielle shrugged. "She is. But still…anyway I reminded her you had a cast on your leg, so I didn't think you were much of a threat."

Walt frowned. "I know my cousin was a schmuck, but I don't believe Clint would have been a threat to you—at least not in the way Joanne seems to imagine."

Danielle grinned. "According to Joanne, you look at me funny now."

Walt arched his brows. "Funny?"

She nodded. "Yes."

"Are you guys trying to freeze out here?" Lily called out as she and Ian entered the side yard with Sadie. The golden retriever rushed ahead of them, running for Walt.

"Morning, Lily, Ian," Danielle greeted them when they got closer. "After almost a hundred years stuck inside, Walt likes sitting out here."

"He likes freezing his butt off?" Ian asked with a shiver.

"It makes me feel alive," Walt said as he scratched Sadie's right ear. The dog stood before him, her chin resting on his right knee, and her tail wagging.

"If you aren't careful, you're going to catch pneumonia, which might mess up that alive thing," Lily said.

Before Walt could respond, he felt raindrops.

"THIS IS MUCH BETTER," Lily said twenty minutes later. She sat in the living room at Marlow House with Danielle and Walt. Ian stacked kindling and logs in the fireplace. Sadie settled by Walt's feet, while Max—who had been in the living room when Ian and Lily had first arrived—remained on the windowsill looking outside, his black tail swishing back and forth.

"I don't imagine the spring breakers are going to be thrilled with this turn in the weather," Ian noted as he lit the fire.

"They knew what to expect when they came here at this time of year," Lily said. "This is more normal for Frederickport. Anyway, we had rain earlier this week."

"Yes, we had a little rain, but it was a good twenty degrees warmer. Yesterday, the beach was fairly crowded down by the pier." Ian brushed his hands off on the sides of his jeans and watched as the flames in the fireplace flickered, growing in intensity.

"This will probably push most of the visitors inside, which will be good for the local restaurants and bars," Danielle said.

Lily turned to Walt and Danielle, who sat together on the sofa, Walt's broken leg propped up on the table, and Sadie napping on the floor below it. "So the peeper was Macbeth?"

"That's what it looks like," Walt said.

"What are you going to do?" Ian asked as he took a chair next to Lily and sat down.

"I called the chief this morning. Told him what happened. He's going to stop over in a little while so we can figure out what to do now," Danielle explained.

"If Chris's guy could have authenticated the portraits by now, would that have prevented all this?" Lily asked.

"I'd love to blame Chris," Walt said with a chuckle. "But I have a feeling Macbeth might have shown up as soon as he heard those paintings had been authenticated and realized the ones in the crate were the ones he painted."

"Then he would have known someone had switched the paintings back," Ian said.

Walt nodded. "That's what I figure. Naturally, he would suspect Clint, thinking maybe he had double-crossed him. But I can't imagine he thought Clint planned the accident."

"So what now?" Lily asked.

Danielle glanced at her watch. "I guess wait to see what the chief thinks."

"How about a fire?" Lily blurted.

Ian looked at the now blazing fire in the nearby fireplace. "What do you mean?"

"Not that fire," Lily said with a laugh. "What if we stage a fire and burn the crate. Get rid of the paintings. Then they won't have any reason to bother Walt."

"While I don't imagine the chief would be on board with staging a fire in the storage facility they use—unless you mean a fire here after the crate is delivered—I'm not sure exactly how is that going to help?" Danielle asked.

"Then Macbeth will leave you alone," Lily explained.

"Think about what you just said, Lily," Ian told her. "I'm sure you can figure out the flaw in that plan."

Lily frowned at Ian. "What do you mean…oh…the originals…"

Ian nodded. "Unless Chris wants his expert to say the originals are fakes, which I don't think would be a great solution, it won't solve anything."

Lily slumped back in her chair. "True. Lame suggestion."

"The only thing I can think of, we let Macbeth steal the portraits," Ian suggested.

"What good will that do? It's no different than burning them," Lily asked. "Once he steals them and tries to pawn them off as originals, he'll find out they're fakes. It'll just piss him off, and he might come after Walt, which I thought was what we're trying to avoid."

"I didn't say we let him actually get away with it," Ian said.

"You mean let him steal the paintings and make sure he gets caught making his getaway?" Danielle asked.

"Sure. Once he's in jail, he won't be breaking in here anymore," Ian said.

"Have you seen his cousins?" Danielle asked.

Ian frowned at Danielle. "You think they might be a problem?"

"I'm just saying Macbeth isn't in this alone," Danielle reminded him.

POLICE CHIEF MACDONALD arrived at Marlow House twenty minutes later. After hearing Walt's account of Macbeth's visit, Lily asked, "Can't you just arrest the guy? After all, he did break in here."

"Sure, I could. But I imagine he'll deny breaking in, and it'll be Walt's word against Macbeth's," the chief told her. "And what was the motive for the break in? Even if we could prove he was here, he would probably be out in a few hours. After all, he didn't take anything, and he could say he just came to visit his friend."

"You have a point," Danielle said with a sigh. "Plus, if it went to court, Walt can't very well sit on the witness stand and recount what Macbeth said to him. It will only make him look bad."

"And without that, there is no motive for Macbeth breaking in, aside from him wanting to see his friend," the chief said.

"Yeah, but breaking in to see him in the middle of the night?" Lily asked.

The chief shrugged. "He can say Walt let him in. As for the time of the visit, I'm not sure that's going to sway any jury. After all, Macbeth can play the eccentric artist role. Even using an alias is something he can easily explain away."

"What about Ian's suggestion? Let Macbeth steal the portraits, and then you'll have something to arrest him for," Lily asked.

The chief sat down in one of the chairs in the living room. "I don't like the idea of using the portraits as bait to get him to break in again just so we have cause to arrest him and send him to jail. After all, it's not like Walt can take care of things like he used to."

"Why does he have to break in?" Walt asked. "He expects me to just give him the portraits, and the more I think about it, that might be the solution."

Danielle looked at Walt. "But what happens when he figures out they're the fakes? He might be back. I thought that's what we're trying to prevent."

"I'm sure we can get Marie and Eva to help us out," Walt said.

"How? The only thing Eva knows how to toss around is glitter," Danielle asked. "I know Marie mentioned something about knocking out Adam's electricity at his office, but I'm not sure how that's going to help."

The chief turned to Danielle and asked, "Why would Marie knock out her grandson's electricity?"

Danielle shrugged. "Who knows why ghosts do some things?"

"Walt, what can Eva and Marie do?" Lily asked.

"We'll make sure Eva and Marie are here when Macbeth picks up the portraits, and then they can follow him. After Macbeth learns the paintings are fake, Eva and Marie can see what he plans to do next. If he is going to retaliate in some way, they can let us know, and we can be prepared. Who knows, maybe Macbeth will write off his losses and move on to his next scam."

"I would rather see the man arrested," the chief grumbled. "After all, he did break into your house, not to mention attempted grand larceny."

"I agree, Chief," Danielle told him. "But like you said, if you arrested him now, he would probably be out in a few hours. Maybe Walt has a good idea. It would be safer if Walt just turned the paintings over to Macbeth, providing Eva or Marie can keep an eye on him and let us know what he plans after he realizes they aren't the originals."

NINETEEN

Laverne had been working at Fuller Hardware for over a decade. She had been there before her engagement, during her marriage, and remained after her divorce. She had been one of the first employees hired by the store's founder and owner, Ray Fuller. Ray was a good ten years older than Laverne and a decent boss. He trusted Laverne to do her job, and he maintained a respectful distance between himself and his employees. As Laverne's coworker, Jillian, liked to say, "Ray is all business." To which Laverne would agree while speculating if Ray was even aware of their marital status.

"I knew the warm weather wasn't going to last," Jillian grumbled as she unboxed the batteries and hung them on the rack by the register.

"It's Frederickport, what did you expect?" Laverne asked. The two women were alone in the front of the store while their boss was back in the storage room. One customer browsed through the selection of paints three aisles over.

"So tell me, did you really do it?" Jillian asked.

Laverne glanced up from the receipts she was sorting and looked at Jillian. "Did I do what?"

"Did you kick your brother out? You said you were going to do it if he didn't move out by the end of the week."

THE GHOST OF SECOND CHANCES

Laverne gave Jillian a half smile and shrugged. "Yes. But I have to admit, I'm feeling a little guilty about it now."

"Come on, Laverne, don't you dare let him suck you into guilt! I watched as you tried to hold your marriage together with that… well, you know what I think of your ex. And I watched as you got your life back only to have your brother move in and take advantage of you. I'm glad you're sticking up for yourself. You have to stop letting these guys—be it a husband or brother—take advantage of you. Your problem, you're way too nice."

Looking downward, her eyes seemingly focused on the receipts, Laverne shook her head. "No. I'm not that nice. Trust me."

"Yes, you are." Jillian reached over and patted Laverne's hand. "So where is Chet staying?"

Laverne shrugged. "That's the problem. I think he's staying with some guys he knew back in high school. Not a good bunch. Certainly not anyone he should be hanging out with. Not now."

"If it's a problem, it's Chet's problem. Not yours."

Laverne let out a sigh and looked up at Jillian. "But he's my baby brother. I shouldn't have kicked him out."

Jillian groaned. But before she could say anything, Ray called out for Laverne. The two women looked in his direction. Walking from the storage room, he carried a sealed cardboard box in his arms.

"Laverne, I need you to drive to Astoria," Ray said when he reached the women. He set the box before Laverne on the counter.

"Astoria?" Laverne asked.

Ray nodded. "I need you to deliver this for me."

Laverne's job description included deliveries, yet normally not to Astoria. They were typically local deliveries to Frederickport addresses. Yet she didn't mind driving to Astoria; it would get her out of the store for the rest of her shift and away from Jillian. While she knew Jillian only had her best interest at heart, she didn't want to justify her feelings regarding her brother. They were complicated. It was something Jillian would never understand. Laverne regretted venting to Jillian earlier about Chet, yet at the time she had needed someone to talk to.

Twenty minutes later, Laverne sat in the driver's seat of the Fuller Hardware van, en route to Astoria. The rain stopped just as she headed out of town.

Driving down the road, Laverne found herself relieved that she hadn't told Jillian where those high school friends of Chet's—the ones he was staying with—lived. She wondered if this unexpected delivery was a sign—an opportunity to see her brother. She wasn't sure she was going to ask him to come back to Frederickport, but she did want to see if he was okay. Plus, it was better this way. If Chet thought she had made the trip just to see him, he would assume he could continue taking advantage of her. When asked why she was in town, she could convincingly tell her brother the main reason she was in Astoria was to make a delivery for work. The fact she was driving the company van would substantiate her story.

Once in Astoria, Laverne drove first to the address her boss had given her. She knew Ray was waiting for her phone call to confirm the package had been safely delivered. After making the call, she headed over to the Bandoni house. After all these years, she had no difficulty finding it.

When she arrived in front of the house, she didn't see her brother's car parked outside. She drove down the street, made a U-turn, and then parked on the other side of the road. With the motor still running, she sat in the van and looked at the house, wondering if her brother had parked in the garage. However, there didn't seem to be anyone home.

She remembered the house as a cheerful well-maintained beach cottage. But that had been years ago. The coastal climate had long since stripped most of the paint from the clapboard siding. Mac's grandmother had prided herself on growing prizewinning rosebushes, but those bushes were now gone. The only landscaping included a lawn that needed mowing and trees in need of grooming.

MACBETH BANDONI TURNED the corner to his cousin's house. He immediately noted the van parked across the street. He was able to read the sign painted on the side of the van just as he pulled into the driveway. It said *Fuller Hardware*. Parking his car, he glanced in his rearview mirror to look at the van again. It was then he remembered. Chet had said something about his sister working at Fuller Hardware. A woman sat in the driver's seat of the van, looking in his direction.

Curious, Macbeth got out of his car and turned to face the woman. Their gazes locked.

"I'll be…" Macbeth muttered under his breath. "It's Laverne." He suspected she'd seen him when the van sped away the next moment, disappearing down the street.

"What is she up to?" Macbeth grumbled as he got back into his vehicle. Slamming the car door shut, he quickly put on his seatbelt and then turned on his ignition. The next moment his car backed out of the driveway and then sped down the street, in search of the Fuller Hardware van.

LAVERNE PULLED into a restaurant parking lot, feeling flustered. She parked the van and sat there a moment, considering her brief encounter at the Bandoni house. "Was that really Mac?" she asked herself. Had Chet not mentioned Mac was back in town, she would never have recognized him. Age had not been kind to Mac, yet she was fairly certain that had been him standing in his cousins' driveway. Turning off the engine, she removed the key from the ignition. Still rattled over seeing Mac, she got out of the van and made her way to the restaurant without calling her brother.

Five minutes later, Laverne sat alone in a booth. Instead of looking at the menu, she pulled her cellphone out of her purse, intending to ask Chet to meet her at the restaurant.

"Hello, Laverne," a male's voice said.

Laverne, who had been looking down at her cellphone, glanced up into the face of Mac Bandoni. He stood beside her table. Absently licking her lips, she set the phone down without making her call. "Hello, Mac. It has been a long time."

"I heard you got a divorce," he said as he sat down in the seat across from her.

"I'm waiting for someone," she blurted. "You can't sit here!"

Macbeth laughed. "Is that any way to treat an old friend? I saw you parked across the street from my cousins' house. Are you looking for your brother?"

Laverne swallowed and nodded. "Where is he? I wanted to meet him for lunch."

"If that's who you're waiting for, it'll be a long wait. I know he went somewhere with my cousins and won't be back until this evening."

Before she could respond, the waitress appeared at the table and asked if they were ready to order.

Laverne slipped her phone back in her purse and stood up. "I don't think I'll be having anything to eat now."

Mac reached out and grabbed hold of Laverne's wrist, forcing her to sit back down. "No, stay, Laverne. We need to catch up." He looked at the server and said, "You can bring us a couple of coffees, and then we'll be ready to order."

"I don't want to have lunch with you," Laverne hissed after the server left the table.

"Come on, Laverne, we have a history. Me and you. I know your deepest secrets," he whispered.

"What do you want from me?" she asked.

Macbeth leaned back in the seat and crossed his arms over his chest. "I have to say, I'm curious why you're so jumpy with me. After all, I just did what you wanted."

"I don't want to talk about it. I never wanted you to do it."

"Really? I don't believe that. People are usually pretty honest when they have too much to drink. I remember you said you had never had alcohol before. You didn't even want to taste it. But once you did, you couldn't stop. Do you remember what we were drinking?"

"Just leave me alone," she trembled. "I could have had you arrested. I should have."

"Kind of hard now. That ship has sailed. And you'd end up in the cell next to me—that's if they had coed prisons." Macbeth grinned.

"Are you just here to torment me?" she asked.

The next moment the server arrived with the coffee. Macbeth told her to bring them both a hamburger and fries, and when the server left the table, he leaned forward, setting his elbows on the tabletop.

"No. I don't want to torment you, Laverne. There was a time I was quite crazy for you. I thought you felt the same way."

She closed her eyes a moment and took a deep breath. "Then what is it?"

"It's about your brother."

She frowned. "Chet? What about him?"

"He's staying with my cousins."

THE GHOST OF SECOND CHANCES

"I know." She reached for a packet of sugar and then ripped it open and dumped it in the coffee the server had placed before her.

"I think you should know he has...well...an unhealthy obsession for Danielle Boatman. Do you know who that is?"

"Danielle Boatman? Umm, she owns Marlow House, it's a bed and breakfast in Frederickport. I don't even think Chet knows her."

"He knows her. In fact, he's got quite a thing for her. Convinced he could get her to marry him." Macbeth picked up his coffee and took a sip.

"Marry? Chet?" Laverne frowned.

Macbeth shrugged. "According to your brother, he met Boatman in some bar, and when they were talking, he told her she would look better with short hair. The next day, she cut her hair."

"So?"

"I guess for Chet that was a sign she was nuts for him. Wanted to please him."

"Maybe she does have a thing for him," Laverne suggested.

"Here is the problem—and I want you to promise not to tell anyone I told you any of this—no one. And considering the secrets I've kept for you, you can keep this one for me."

"Go on," Laverne choked out.

"I overheard all this at my cousins' the other night. And frankly, if it were anyone else, I wouldn't bother saying anything. But you and I—well—we do have a history, and I know how much your brother means to you. But I really don't want my cousins to find out I was repeating conversations I heard at their house."

"What kind of conversation?" Laverne asked.

"Apparently, Boatman is showing interest in the guest currently staying at Marlow House. Your brother is jealous. I'm afraid he might do something stupid."

"Something stupid, how?"

"Shoot him, maybe. Run him over in his car. I don't know. I just know he was talking about getting rid of him."

Laverne laughed. "I love my brother, but he's all talk. Oh, he's done stupid things in his past to get himself arrested, but go after some guy over a woman? No way."

TWENTY

It was late Friday afternoon, and Walt sat in the library, the sleeve to his left shirt rolled up while he examined his left wrist. He and Danielle were once again alone in Marlow House save for Max, who napped next to Walt on the sofa.

Before leaving Marlow House earlier, the chief had agreed to have Clint's belongings tentatively delivered on Monday morning. However, before making it official, he wanted to make sure Walt or Danielle had been able to contact Eva or Marie. He didn't want Macbeth picking up the portraits without being assured at least one of the spirits would be able to keep an eye on the man in order to determine his reaction after discovering the paintings were not the original Bonnets.

"What are you looking at?" Danielle asked when she entered the library and found Walt staring at his left wrist while he ran the tip of his right index finger over it.

Walt glanced up at Danielle. "I want you to see this."

Danielle walked to the sofa, scooped up the sleeping cat, and sat down next to Walt. Just as she set the cat on her lap, Max, who was now awake and annoyed, jumped down and strolled from the room.

Giving Max a shrug, Danielle turned her attention to Walt, who extended his left wrist for her to examine. "You see this scar?"

Taking hold of Walt's wrist, she pulled it gently to her and looked closely. "I wonder how Clint got it. Looks like a horseshoe."

"Clint didn't get it," Walt said as he took back his wrist and started buttoning up his sleeve.

"What do you mean?" Danielle frowned.

"When I first woke up in Clint's body, it wasn't there."

"I'm sure it was. You just didn't notice."

"Danielle, look at my forehead." Walt leaned toward Danielle.

She examined his forehead and frowned. "What am I looking at?"

"The stitches. Remember, Clint didn't just break his leg, he had stitches in his forehead."

"Oh! That's right!" Danielle leaned closer for a moment. "Wow, I can't even see where it was stitched. It didn't scar at all."

"The accident happened a little over a week ago. Don't you think it's rather odd it's healed so quickly?"

Danielle shrugged. "I suppose. But aren't you happy about it?"

"When I was a child, I cut my left wrist and had stitches. It was a horseshoe scar. I had it until the day I died."

"I guess Clint's body heals quicker."

Again unbuttoning his left wrist, he once again showed the horseshoe scar to Danielle. "After I woke up in Clint's body, I…well…I inspected it."

Danielle chuckled. "Yeah, I can see doing that. I can't even imagine what it would be like to wake up in another person's body."

"I remember looking at his left wrist and thinking *I finally got rid of that scar*."

"Are you saying the scar wasn't there when you first came to?"

"Exactly."

"When did you first notice it?"

"The day you picked me up from the hospital, but it was just a faint scar. At first, I thought I was imagining things. But it seemed as the horseshoe scar became more prominent, the one on my forehead faded. In fact, when they removed the stitches, the nurse remarked on how quickly it had healed. She actually seemed surprised."

"What does this mean?" Danielle asked.

"It means he's settling into his body and making it his," Eva answered when she appeared the next moment in a hail of glitter. Unfortunately for Marie, when she arrived in the library several seconds later, it was in the midst of a glitter cloud. While some might argue that Eva's glitter was nothing more than an illusion, one would not know by the way Marie sputtered, her nose scrunched up, as she furiously waved her right hand in front of her face, trying to brush away Eva's sparkly trademark.

"Please, Eva. Can't you be more careful with that stuff?" Marie spit several times, as if some of it had gotten into her mouth, while her gray hair sparkled with glitter.

"Sorry, Marie," Eva said with a laugh. The next moment the glitter—even what had fallen in Marie's hair—vanished.

"What do you mean, making it his?" Danielle asked Eva.

"It's just an assumption on my part," Eva explained. "But I suspect our spirit selves have more control over our bodies than we understand. Walt's spirit is settling into his new body, making it his, mimicking his last one."

"I don't recall that happening with Kent's body," Danielle said.

"That was different. Kent never relinquished his body as Clint did. It makes all the difference in the world," Eva told her.

"What about my broken leg?" Walt asked.

"What do you mean?" Eva asked.

"Is it possible the leg is no longer broken?" Walt asked. "That it's healed already, like my forehead?"

Eva shrugged. "I wouldn't be surprised."

Marie laughed. "If it really has, I doubt you'll be able to convince your doctor to remove your cast early. And if you could talk him into doing something like an X-ray to check on the leg, can you imagine what a hullabaloo that might cause if it had healed already?"

Walt absently gave his injured leg a pat. "No. I don't need that kind of attention. And, just because the forehead healed, I can't believe the leg has."

"I wouldn't be surprised." Eva took a seat on a chair facing Walt and Danielle.

"Eva and I stopped by to see how you were doing," Marie explained when she took the chair next to Eva. "But if what Eva says is true, then I suppose you're settling in nicely."

"I'm really glad you both stopped in. I have a favor to ask you," Walt began.

Eva arched her brows. "Favor?"

Walt then went on to tell them about Macbeth's visit and what they needed them to do for him.

"Sounds rather exciting," Marie said.

Danielle smiled at Marie. "I appreciate the enthusiasm. I know you became a little weary standing guard over the paintings when Clint and Macbeth were staying here."

Marie shrugged. "That was different, stuck in one place for hours on end. This time Eva and I will be able to venture into the thieves' den, so to speak."

"When will Macbeth be picking up the paintings?" Eva asked.

"We haven't arranged that with him yet."

"I need to call the chief and let him know Monday will work. And then we have to wait for Macbeth to contact Walt and arrange a pickup."

"It would probably be best if Marie and I show up first thing Monday morning before the paintings arrive. Just in case your Macbeth decides to come early."

Walt nodded. "It would also be a good idea if you check in every day. I'd hate for Macbeth to arrange for a pickup without us being able to get that information to one of you."

Danielle stood up. "I'm going to go call the chief and tell him to go ahead and have the paintings delivered."

After Danielle left the room to get her cellphone, Eva said, "You know, I still can't get over this scoundrel's name. Didn't you say his mother was an actress?"

Walt looked to Eva. "That's what Ian told us. But he goes by Mac."

"But still, for an actress to name her only child Macbeth? Was she trying to keep him from pursuing a life in the theater?"

"What do you mean?" Marie asked.

"Being on this side, I've put aside some of my previous superstitions," Eva explained.

"I remember now," Walt said. "Odd, I didn't even think about that."

With a frown, Marie looked from Eva to Walt. "Think about what?"

"Shakespeare's play *Macbeth* is said to be cursed, so actors avoid uttering the play's name in the theater."

"You mean they never say Macbeth?" Marie asked.

"Instead, they refer to it as the *Scottish Play*," Eva explained. "I know now it's all very silly, but I confess I once avoided the word. So for an actress to name her child something that her fellow actors would be reluctant to say makes me wonder, why?"

"Perhaps the father named him," Walt suggested. "After all, Macbeth followed his father's line of work and became an artist. Maybe that's what the father wanted."

"Considering the little performance he gave, pawning himself off as Jim Hill, I suspect the man has some actor in him," Marie said.

MARIE AND EVA had left Marlow House, promising to check in on Saturday. Once again, Walt and Danielle were alone in the library. The landline sitting on the computer desk began to ring.

"I wonder if that's someone calling for a reservation," Danielle said when she stood up to answer the phone.

"When you called the chief, why didn't you just use the library phone?" Walt asked. "Instead of going to the kitchen to find your cellphone."

Poised to pick up the landline, Danielle turned to Walt and smiled. "I have the chief's number saved in my cellphone."

"Is it that hard to dial a number?" Walt asked.

"It is if you haven't memorized it." Danielle picked up the phone. "Hello, Marlow House. How can I help you?"

"Is this Danielle Boatman?" a familiar voice asked.

"Yes, it is. Who is this?"

"Hello, Danielle. This is Jim Hill."

Danielle looked to Walt and mouthed, *It's Macbeth*.

"Umm...hello, Jim. How are you doing?" Danielle asked. Holding the phone's receiver to her ear, she looked at Walt, who stared at her, listening in on her phone conversation.

"I'm fine. I heard Clint was released from the hospital and is staying with you. I just wanted to see how he's doing."

"He's doing fine. But he still has amnesia."

"Yes, I heard that. I was hoping I could talk to him."

Danielle swallowed nervously. "He won't know you."

"I understand that. But I assume you've told him about me?"

"Umm...yeah..." Nervously biting her lower lip, she looked at Walt and shrugged.

"I just wanted to tell him how sorry I am about Stephanie. And maybe hearing a familiar voice will help him regain his memory."

"Sure...umm...in fact, he's right here. Let me give him the phone."

Danielle picked up the phone and carried it to the sofa, stretching its cord as far as it would go. She handed the phone to Walt and said in a loud voice, "It's your friend Jim Hill. I told you about him. He's the artist."

Walt nodded at her and accepted the phone.

"Hello?"

"I assume Danielle is standing right there?" Jim said.

Walt looked up to Danielle. "Yes." She stood quietly and listened.

"Did you do what I told you to do? Are you having the paintings delivered?" Jim asked.

"Danielle told me about you and how you copied her paintings. She said you're a talented artist. But I'll be honest, I have no use for the portraits, and I wondered if perhaps you would like them, since you painted them."

Macbeth laughed. "Good man, Clint. Pleased you're seeing things my way. When can I pick them up?"

"I already spoke to the police department and asked if they could deliver my personal belongings here. Apparently, they have everything in storage. They're delivering my things, including the portraits, on Monday morning. Would you like to pick up the portraits Monday afternoon?"

"Perfect. I'll call again Monday afternoon and arrange an exact time. I'm glad we had this conversation, especially with Danielle standing there listening. She is still standing there, isn't she?"

Walt looked at Danielle. "Yes. She is."

"Then make sure she knows you've given me the portraits. I don't want any misunderstandings."

When Walt got off the phone, Danielle said, "You handled that brilliantly."

Walt shrugged. "I learned from the best."

Danielle frowned. "What do you mean?"

"You." Walt laughed.

Danielle flashed Walt a smirk-like smile as she carried the phone back to the desk. After she set the phone back down, she turned to Walt and said, "I suppose this means we'll be able to enjoy our weekend. We won't have to worry about Macbeth and his crew until Monday."

TWENTY-ONE

Saturday arrived with a clear blue sky and temperatures in the low forties. The brief warm spell had ended, yet Danielle was grateful the cold didn't include rain. She asked Walt if he wanted to get away from Marlow House for the day, perhaps take a drive or try one of the local restaurants. It wasn't that he didn't want to take her up on her offer. Fact was, he would love to get out and see the world again. However, he was just simply too tired. It seemed that every few hours all he wanted to do was take a nap.

"Your body is healing," Danielle told him.

When Eva and Marie stopped in Saturday morning to see if there was an update on the portraits' arrival, Eva agreed with Danielle's rationale on why Walt was so tired. The spirits visited a while and then left again, promising to return early Monday morning.

Danielle and Walt had other visitors on Saturday. The chief was heading out of town that evening to take his boys to Portland to attend a birthday party for their maternal grandmother. But first, the chief found time to stop by Marlow House with Evan, who was excited to see Walt in the flesh. Right after they left, Ian and Lily came over for about an hour, bringing Sadie with them. Heather dropped in twice, once bringing some cinnamon rolls she had picked up at Old Salts Bakery and once to drop off a mixture of essential oils she said would help Walt relax. Danielle wasn't sure why Walt needed anything to help him relax, considering he kept dozing off every few hours, but she didn't mention that to Heather.

The last visitor they had was Chris, who played a game of chess with Walt. They might have finished had Max not jumped on the board, scattering the pieces. Walt swore he had nothing to do with the cat's leap, but Chris didn't quite believe him.

"Fess up, did you get Max to jump up on the chessboard?" Danielle asked when she and Walt were alone again. The cat in question had retreated upstairs to the attic and was currently napping on the sofa bed up there. Outside the sun had already set.

Walt yawned. He sat with Danielle at the kitchen table. "I'll confess; I just can't focus. I get so tired."

"Does that mean you did or didn't get Max to break up your game?" Danielle asked as she ripped apart one of the cinnamon rolls Heather had brought. Before she could taste the pastry, Walt reached across the table and snatched it. "Hey!"

Taking a bite of the roll, Walt moaned. "I'd apologize, but these really are amazing."

Danielle chuckled and began nibbling the remaining half. "You still didn't answer my question."

Outside, a dark figure moved by the window, yet neither person in the kitchen noticed. When they eventually left the room, they forgot to lock the back door. Later, when Danielle remembered the door and returned to lock it, the person who had been lurking on her back patio had already slipped into the house and down the hallway and was now hiding in the hall closet.

"BELLA!" Heather called for her calico cat. The feline was nowhere to be found. Heather checked all the rooms in her house before deciding the cat must have slipped outside when she had returned from Marlow House.

Grabbing her cellphone from the kitchen counter, intending to use it as a flashlight if needed, she slipped the phone in her jacket pocket and headed outside. Once in her front yard, she discovered there was sufficient moonlight, and there would be no need for a flashlight. However, had she needed the phone, she would not have found it in her pocket. It had already slipped through a tear in the pocket lining.

Heather spied her cat under a bush by the front sidewalk.

"Bella!" Heather scolded as she scooped the wandering feline into her arms. "Naughty kitty!"

What sounded like a gunshot jolted Heather. Still holding Bella, she looked up and spied a car slowly driving down the street. It was then she realized it had been a car backfire, not a gunshot.

Stepping up to the sidewalk, she glanced down the street. She stood in the shadows and watched as the car stopped a moment in front of Marlow House and then made a U-turn and drove back up the street, passing her house again. Because of where she stood, it was impossible for her to tell if anyone had gotten out of the car when it had stopped by Marlow House.

Bella let out a loud meow and began to squirm. Reminded of the cat in her arms, Heather quickly forgot about the car and returned to her house.

HIDING in the downstairs closet behind several jackets and raincoats, the intruder stood frozen. Glancing down, the person focused on the light streaming in from under the door. There were voices, but it was impossible to hear what was being said. Finally, it grew dark. Someone had turned off the hall light.

The intruder grabbed hold of the doorknob and gingerly turned it while easing the door open just a few inches. Peering out into the darkened hall, the intruder spied Danielle Boatman making her way down the hallway toward the staircase. Light coming from several nightlights plugged into random sockets along the hallway made it possible to see.

There was light coming from under the downstairs bedroom's closed door. The intruder assumed Clint was behind that door. A moment later the sound of footsteps going up the stairs were heard and then, after a few minutes, the sound of a door on the second floor closing. Glancing back to the door leading to the downstairs bedroom, the intruder noticed light was no longer coming from under the door. Clint had turned off the bedroom light.

MACBETH SAT in the bushes in front of the empty house next to

THE GHOST OF SECOND CHANCES

where Ian and Lily lived and watched Marlow House. When he had first arrived, he saw Clint and Danielle sitting in the living room. Considering there were no cars parked across the street and only Danielle's car was in the driveway, he was certain they were alone.

He had been sitting in front of Marlow House for about fifteen minutes when the living room window had gone dark. A few minutes later lights went on in the front bedroom. Unfortunately, the blinds were drawn, so he could only see silhouettes. First one, then two, and then one again, and then nothing. Eventually a light went on in one of the upstairs bedrooms. The light in the downstairs bedroom then went out.

Macbeth continued to sit and wait in the bushes, shivering under his jacket that was not sufficient to ward off the evening chill, yet telling himself it would only be a few more minutes. He wanted to give them both time to settle in their beds before he went inside.

STILL STANDING IN THE CLOSET, the door ajar, the intruder heard someone fiddling with the front door. A moment later, it started to open. A few moments later the intruder stepped out of the closet.

Macbeth had already closed the front door and was heading for the downstairs bedroom before he noticed a person standing in the shadows. Startled, he clutched the gun and aimed it at the unexpected figure.

"Mac, it's me. Don't shoot," came a whispered voice.

Macbeth lowered his gun and took several steps forward, careful to be as quiet as possible. "What in the hell are you doing here?" he asked in a whisper while taking a quick look down the hall at the closed bedroom door to Clint's room.

"You need to know something," the person whispered and then pointed down the hallway in another direction. "This way."

"I'm going to kill you if you wake anyone up," Macbeth grumbled as he followed the person down the darkened hall.

The person opened a door and then stepped aside and pointed in the doorway. "It's in there. I thought you should see this for yourself."

"How did you get in the house?" Macbeth asked.

"Please, just look," the intruder urged. "You'll understand if you just look."

Macbeth walked to the now open door, trying to remember where it led. When he had stayed at Marlow House, he had never thought to open the door and always assumed it was another closet. Yet, when he stepped inside the dimly lit space, he realized it was not a closet. A nightlight plugged into a socket just inside the doorway provided just enough lighting for him to make out the steps a few feet from where he stood. *This leads to the basement*, he thought.

Macbeth turned quickly to the person, who now stood blocking the doorway, facing him.

But now, it was not Macbeth aiming a gun; someone was aiming a gun at him. Before Macbeth could utter a single word, the gun in the person's hand went off, sending a bullet straight through Macbeth's heart. The next moment, Macbeth tumbled down the stairs, landing on the concrete floor of the basement.

The shooter turned abruptly, shut the basement door, and ran down the hallway toward the front door, tossing the gun into the powder room along the way.

HEATHER WANTED to put her cellphone on the charger before going to bed. The only problem, she couldn't find it anywhere. It wasn't until she found Bella sleeping on the middle of her bed did she remember she had put it in her jacket before going out to search for the cat earlier.

Unfortunately, when Heather searched the pockets of her jacket a few minutes later, she didn't find her cellphone. However, there was a nice big hole in one of the pockets. With a groan, Heather slipped on the jacket and headed outside to see if she could find where she had dropped the phone.

Heather had worked her way to the sidewalk when she heard an engine rev down the street. Glancing down the dark street, lit only by the moonlight, she noticed a car stopping in front of Marlow House. The next moment, it raced up the street in her direction.

Heather quickly stepped behind a bush to conceal herself. She watched as the car sped by. It was the same car she had seen earlier —the one that had backfired.

"What's going on down there?" Heather muttered, wondering if she should call Danielle and see if everything was okay.

TWENTY-TWO

Cursing, Macbeth stumbled to his feet. Glancing behind him, he noted the basement was virtually black. He could only make out vague shadows. Turning back to the narrow staircase, he looked up to the now closed door leading to the hallway on the first floor. The nightlight's glow cast dim lighting on the walls surrounding the stairwell. He wondered briefly if the door was now locked.

Clutching his right hand, he looked down and was relieved to see the gun still gripped in his gloved hand. He had managed not to drop it during his unfortunate fall. Determined, he made his way up the stairs, trying to decide who to kill first.

ABOUT THE SAME time as Heather started looking for her cellphone, Walt heard what sounded like a gunshot. He had only been asleep for a few minutes when it jolted him awake. Moonlight lit the room. At first, he wondered if he had been dreaming. But then he heard the footsteps. Someone was running down the hallway, and then in the next moment he heard the front door slam.

Walt's first thought was Danielle. *Is she all right?* He reached for the cellphone on his bedside table. In his haste, he shoved the cellphone off the nightstand. It fell to the floor and slid under the bed.

Grumbling under his breath, Walt, now sitting up on the

mattress, awkwardly turned and set his feet on the floor. Headlights from the front window caught his attention. Standing on his right foot while bracing his hands on the edge of the mattress to balance himself, he managed to push off the bed and hop over to the window. Just as he got there, he pulled the blinds open and looked outside. He could see a car parked in front of the house. He then saw someone running out from the bushes in front of Marlow House. Whoever it was got into the vehicle. It was only a shadow of a person. Walt couldn't tell if it was a man or woman. In the next moment the car raced off down the street.

Walt turned back to his bed, determined to retrieve the cellphone. He needed to check on Danielle. He just wasn't quite sure how he was going to get down on the floor to reach it. Before he made his first hop, the closed door to his bedroom took on a peculiar glow. Walt paused and stared. In the next moment the glow swirled and morphed until what appeared to be a man came into full view.

Walt's eyes widened. "Macbeth?"

Macbeth laughed as he pointed the gun at Walt. "I've come to kill you, Clint Marlow."

Reality dawning, Walt arched his brows. "Oh, really?"

"I'm serious," Macbeth snapped, unnerved by the man's apparent lack of fear.

"I'm sure you are." Walt's gaze moved from the gun held in Macbeth's gloved hand to the bloodstain on the center of his shirt. "Can I ask you a couple of questions first?"

"Trying to buy yourself a little time?" Macbeth sneered.

"No, I'm just curious." If it hadn't been for the bloodstain on Macbeth's shirt, Walt would be more than curious about Danielle's current safety. However, he was certain the gunshot he had heard was the cause of Macbeth's gruesome chest wound. He was even more certain that the killer had just driven off a few moments ago. Walt nodded toward Macbeth and asked, "So what happened?"

His right hand now shaking, Macbeth held the gun tighter while pointing it at Walt and said, "You double-crossed me!"

Walt shook his head and waved his hand dismissively. "No, not that. I can understand why you might want to kill me. I was just curious what happened to you." Walt pointed to the shirt. When Macbeth failed to look down, Walt pointed to it again. "Your shirt. The blood. I assume someone shot you."

Macbeth frowned and looked down. With his free hand, he touched the red spot.

"Looks like it went straight through the heart." Walt cringed. "Did it hurt much?"

Macbeth glared up from his shirt, aimed the gun at Walt's chest, and pulled the trigger. Nothing happened.

Macbeth pulled the trigger again. Again, nothing happened.

"I'll give you a hint," Walt whispered. "It's not a real gun. It's only an illusion."

His expression going blank, Macbeth dropped the gun. It vanished before it hit the floor.

Macbeth looked back to Walt. "What just happened?"

"My guess, someone killed you. It would probably be a good idea if you told me who."

"No...this can't be happening..." Macbeth shook his head.

"That's what they all say," Walt said with a shrug. "So tell me, who killed you? Did you see your killer? I'm sure whoever it was ran out of here just a few minutes ago before you came in my room."

Macbeth stood paralyzed for a few moments, unable or unwilling to respond. Finally, he shouted, "No!" and then ran from the house, moving through the front wall and heading to the street.

"I really should have gotten the name of his killer," Walt grumbled under his breath. "I don't think I'm as good at this as Danielle is."

THE GUNSHOT HAD ALSO WOKEN Danielle. Like Walt, she sat up in her bed, wondering briefly if it had been a dream. Snatching the cellphone off her nightstand, she debated calling or texting Walt to make sure everything was okay downstairs. If he was asleep and it was only a dream, a call would wake him, and Walt seemed to need his sleep. She decided a text message would be the better option.

Walt, is everything okay down there?

After sending the text message, she sat and waited for an answer. After a few minutes with no response, she thought, *He's probably sleeping...but maybe he's not...maybe he can't answer...*

Still looking at her phone, it began to ring. But it wasn't Walt calling.

"Heather?" Danielle answered.

"I hope I didn't wake you, but I wanted to make sure everything is okay over there."

Still holding her cellphone to her ear, Danielle looked over to the closed bedroom door. "I thought I heard a gunshot. It woke me up."

"It was probably just the car," Heather said.

"What car?" Danielle asked.

"That's why I'm calling. I saw this car I've never seen before drive up our street twice tonight. Both times it parked in front of your house. It backfired when it drove by. That's probably what you heard. The car is kind of a wreck."

"Why was it parked in front of my house?" Danielle asked.

"That's why I was calling, to make sure everything is okay," Heather told her.

"I tried texting Walt, but I think he's asleep. He didn't answer my text. I suppose I should go down there and see if everything is okay."

"If it makes you feel any better, the car's not there anymore," Heather told her.

LAVERNE TOLD them to let her out of the car. At first, they didn't want to. But she insisted. They dropped her off by the pier and drove away. Instead of starting for home, she strolled down the pier while listening to the waves crashing against the weathered structure.

When she reached the end of the pier, she leaned against the railing and looked out to the ocean. The moon overhead cast a golden light across the dark water.

"I'm going to have to tell them my part in all this..." she said aloud. There was no one to hear her; the pier was empty save for a few diners coming and going from the café on the opposite end of the wooden walkway. "Will they understand? Would they admit they'd do the same?"

After ten more minutes of reflecting, she turned and started walking toward the café.

"Isn't it freezing out there?" Carla asked Laverne when she walked into the restaurant a few minutes later.

Laverne pulled the knit hat off her head and shoved it into one pocket of her down parka. "It's not bad, not if you're dressed warm." She then pulled the gloves off her hands and shoved them with the hat and took a seat.

"You alone?" Carla asked as she stepped up to the table, menu in hand.

"Yes. It's just me. Have any apple pie?"

"Sure," Carla said. "You want it hot?"

"Sounds good. With vanilla ice cream?"

"How else?" Carla laughed. "Coffee?"

Laverne shook her head. "No. I'm having problems sleeping as it is. I don't need any caffeine this late. Maybe a glass of milk."

Carla nodded and then headed off to get Laverne's order.

When Carla returned to the table, she set Laverne's pie and ice cream, along with a glass of milk, on the table. Instead of asking if she could join her, she simply took a seat across from her in the booth. "I haven't seen you in here for a while."

Laverne shrugged and picked up a fork and stabbed the pie. "I don't come to the north end of town much." She stabbed the pie again, capturing a bite on the tip of her fork.

"I see your brother in here from time to time. I think he has a thing for Danielle Boatman. The one who owns Marlow House. It's just down the street."

Laverne was just about to pop the bite in her mouth when she paused and looked at Carla. She studied her a brief moment and then ate the bite. After she swallowed, she said, "My brother does a lot of talking. I don't think they even know each other."

"Oh, they do. Know each other, that is. Of course, I can't really blame Chet for having a thing for her. Danielle is single, good looking, and has a crap load of money. If I didn't like men, I would consider her." Carla laughed.

"Even if my brother likes her, I doubt he has a chance."

"I have to agree with you," Carla said in a whisper. With one finger she absently twisted a lock of her pink and purple hair. "I know Chris Johnson likes her, and he is way hot. I don't think he has any money, but with his looks, I don't even care about the money."

Laverne reserved comment and took another bite of pie.

Carla released hold of her hair and leaned over the table toward Laverne. In a hushed voice she said, "Now Clint Marlow is staying over there. Just the two of them. I heard she isn't taking any other guests. I don't really care for the guy; he's a little full of himself, if you ask me. But he's got some amazing blue eyes." Carla paused a moment and considered what she had just said. She then added, "Now that I think about it, both him and Chris have incredible blue eyes. Bedroom eyes, my grandma used to call them." Carla sat back in the booth and sighed.

"I've heard around town that Clint Marlow is kind of a jerk. I don't imagine Danielle Boatman is actually interested in him."

Carla shrugged. "Maybe not. But I heard from Marjory over at the Mercantile that Danielle went in there a few days ago and bought a bunch of men's clothes. Even slippers. When Marjory asked Danielle who they were for, she said they were for Walt Marlow."

Laverne frowned. "You mean Clint Marlow?"

"Apparently he wants to be called Walt now. I guess that's his real name. He's named after the guy who was killed in Marlow House."

"Which one?" Laverne muttered.

"Obviously, Walt Marlow," Carla said with a giggle.

Laverne shrugged. "He probably asked her to buy them, since he was planning to stay at Marlow House after he got out of the hospital. He probably lost everything he had with him in the car accident."

"Perhaps," Carla shrugged.

TWENTY-THREE

Laverne was still walking on the pier and had not yet stopped for her pie and ice cream when Danielle was huddled on her bed, talking to Heather on the cellphone.

"I'm going to check on Walt," Danielle finally told Heather.

"I want you to call me in ten minutes and let me know everything is okay. You got that? If I don't hear from you, I'm calling Chris, and we're coming over there."

"I'm sure everything is okay," Danielle told her. "Like you said, it was just a backfire I heard."

"Okay. But still, they were stopped in front of your house twice. Just call me. Promise?"

"Fine. I will."

When Danielle ended her call with Heather, she tossed her phone back on the nightstand and climbed out of bed. After slipping on her robe, she went to her bedroom door and eased it open a few inches. Peeking out into the upstairs hallway, she glanced around. Like downstairs, nightlights provided dim lighting. All was quiet.

She hadn't seen Max since he had jumped up on the chessboard earlier that evening, ending Walt and Chris's game. Danielle wondered if the cat was sleeping downstairs with Walt.

She stepped out of her bedroom into the hallway and tiptoed to the railing and looked to the first floor. No lights were on downstairs save for the nightlights. With a deep breath, Danielle started down the stairs, holding onto the railing as she went. There was no sound aside from the ticking of a nearby wall clock and the light touch of her feet as they went down the wooden steps.

When she reached the first-floor landing, she paused a moment and glanced around. Nothing appeared to be amiss. She then headed for Walt's room. There was no light coming from under his closed door. Standing a moment in front of his room, she briefly considered knocking, but if he was sleeping, it would just wake him up, and she saw no reason to disrupt his sleep, especially if the source of her anxiety was nothing more than a car backfiring. Why the car had stopped twice in front of her house was another matter, yet not necessarily an ominous one.

Instead of knocking, Danielle eased the door open and peeked inside. Moonlight spilled in through the partially open window blind, casting a golden glow over Walt's bed—*Walt's empty bed.*

"Walt?" Danielle quickly turned on the room light.

To her surprise she heard him call out, "Down here."

Hurrying around the bed, Danielle came to an abrupt stop when she found Walt sprawled awkwardly on the floor while he shoved one crutch under the bed.

"What are you doing down there?" Danielle asked as she knelt down beside him and helped him to his feet.

"I dropped my cellphone," he explained. "It went under the bed."

"That's why you didn't answer my text," Danielle said as she got him situated on the edge of the bed and then dropped back down to retrieve his phone.

"Did the gunshot wake you too?" Walt asked a moment later when Danielle stood up and handed him his cellphone.

"It wasn't a gunshot. It was a car backfiring," Danielle explained.

Walt shook his head. "No, it wasn't."

"I just spoke to Heather on the phone, and she said it was a backfire."

Walt set the cellphone on his bed and reached out and grabbed Danielle's wrists. He gently pulled her closer then maneuvered her to his left. They sat side by side on the mattress. "Listen to me. Remember when I saw Marie and Eva, and we wondered if I would be able to see all spirits, or just them?" He released hold of her wrists and sat back, studying her reaction.

Danielle nodded. "Sure, but what does that have to do with a car backfiring?"

"I believe I fall into the *can see all ghosts* category," he told her.

Danielle frowned. "Why do you think that?"

"Because I saw Macbeth tonight. He was in my bedroom less than fifteen minutes ago."

Danielle jumped up and ran to the open door. She slammed it shut, locked it, and then started dragging the dresser to block the doorway.

"What are you doing?" Walt asked.

"Making sure Macbeth doesn't get in here again before I call the police!"

"I seriously doubt that dresser is going to stop him."

Danielle frowned at Walt, perplexed at his relaxed demeanor. She wondered if perhaps he forgot he was no longer a ghost—no longer able to wield his spiritual powers. "I just want to slow him down until I call the police!" She reached into her pocket for her cellphone and then realized she had left it upstairs. Silently cursing, she reached for Walt's cellphone, but he snatched it out of her hands.

"Listen to me," Walt insisted.

"We need to call the police."

"The police can't help. Macbeth is dead."

Danielle froze a moment, digesting Walt's words. Finally, she asked, "What do you mean he's dead?"

"Dead. You know, like I used to be."

Danielle frowned. "What makes you think he's dead?"

"I suppose my first clue was the fact he didn't use the door. And then there was the bullet hole in his chest and all the blood."

Danielle swallowed nervously. "Are you saying…"

Walt nodded. "Yes. Although I suppose he did use the door when he came in, but he went through it instead of opening it. And when leaving, he left through the wall." Walt pointed to the west wall of his bedroom.

"Where do you think he was killed?" Danielle asked.

"I suspect somewhere on the first floor, considering the gunshot I heard and the fact I saw someone running from the house and getting into a car right afterwards."

Danielle groaned and sat back down on the side of the bed with Walt. "That means there's a dead body in this house."

"That's what I'm thinking."

Danielle glanced nervously at the closed door. "Are you sure the killer is gone?"

Walt nodded. "Yes. I'm pretty sure that's who hopped in that car and sped off. When I heard the gunshot and it woke me up, the first thing I thought about was calling you, but I inadvertently knocked the phone on the floor, and it slid under the bed. Before I had a chance to retrieve it, Macbeth showed up."

"Who killed him?"

"I tried to get him to tell me. But I don't think he really understood he was dead."

"That's pretty typical."

Walt nodded. "I suspect you would have been more successful than me at getting information from him. You're rather good at that."

"Do you know why he was here?" Danielle asked.

"That I know. He said he came to kill me."

Danielle gasped. "Why?"

"He said because I double-crossed him, which is what I figured when he showed up waving that gun at me."

"But you were going to give him the paintings Monday! Why kill you today?"

Walt shrugged. "I have no idea. But I suspect had you woken up this morning and found me dead, he would have shown up to collect the portraits on Monday."

"After killing you? That would be a little nervy."

Walt chuckled. "Nervy? More along the lines that he would look like a man without a motive—after all, like you said, I had promised to give him the portraits on Monday, something he knew you were witness to hearing me tell him."

"So even though you were going to give him the paintings, and he would not have to share the money with you—since he still believed they were the originals—he still was going to kill you?" Danielle asked indignantly.

Walt shrugged. "Some people just hold a grudge."

"I guess," Danielle grumbled.

"We should probably go look for the body," Walt suggested.

THE GHOST OF SECOND CHANCES

With a groan, Danielle stood, picked up Walt's crutches from the floor, and waited for him to get on his feet—or more accurately his right foot. She handed him his crutches, and together they made their way to the bedroom door. After shoving the dresser back to its original location, she opened the door, and Walt hobbled out first. The moment Danielle stepped into the dimly lit hallway with him, Walt froze.

"Someone's at the door," he said in a loud whisper.

Danielle's first instinct was to run back into the bedroom and lock the door behind her, but she couldn't leave Walt standing alone in the hallway, and he wasn't able to move that fast.

Whoever was at the front door managed to get it unlocked. Panicked, Danielle looked around for something to use as a weapon. The door opened. She snatched a heavy vase from a nearby hall table and was preparing to hurl it when a man stepped inside, aiming a handgun in their direction.

Seeing the gun first, Danielle gasped, but in the next breath she cried in relief, "Chris?" while almost dropping the vase. Behind Chris was Heather, who flipped on the entry switch as she walked into the house, flooding the hallway with bright light.

"Why were you two standing in the dark?" Heather asked, closing the door behind her.

"And what were you planning to do with that vase," Chris asked as he tucked the handgun back in his shoulder holster.

"Since when did you start carrying a gun?" Danielle asked as she set the vase back on the table.

"You know I've been toying with the idea ever since the kidnapping," Chris told her.

"He got it last week," Heather interjected. "I told him he'd better be careful not to shoot himself."

"I thought you got Hunny for protection," Danielle asked.

Walt chuckled. "Hunny is the equivalent of carrying an unloaded gun."

"I don't know about that," Heather said. "I suspect if necessary, she would surprise us all."

Chris looked to Heather. "So I guess this means you dragged me over here for nothing? Aren't you glad I didn't let you call Lily and Ian?"

Walt and Danielle exchanged glances, and then Danielle asked, "Lily and Ian?"

"Heather wanted me to call in all the troops. But I told her there's no reason for us to drag them out of bed for nothing."

"Well...not exactly nothing," Danielle said.

Heather glanced around the entry hall. "Did something happen?"

"I think we have a dead body in the house," Walt announced.

BEFORE THEY COULD EXPLAIN what had happened that evening, Danielle suggested they move to the nearby living room so Walt could sit down. She held her breath when entering the room and turning on its light, fearful of finding Macbeth's lifeless body. But he wasn't there.

The four sat in the living room, the doors to the hallway wide open, while Walt recounted the evening's events. When he finished, they sat in silence, each mustering the courage to do what needed to be done—go on a macabre search to find Macbeth's body.

The silence was broken when footsteps were heard coming down the hall. Whoever it was, they were not coming from the direction of the front door. Chris stood and placed a finger over his lips to signal silence while removing the gun from his holster with his free hand. He turned to the doorway, gun ready, when Lily came bursting into the room. She came to an abrupt stop when finding a gun aimed at her.

"Holy crap, Chris, don't shoot!" Lily called out.

Chris quickly lowered the gun and returned it to the holster as Ian entered the room next.

"What is going on over here?" Ian asked.

"Chris has a gun!" Lily told him.

"Yes, I saw that." Ian looked from Chris to the other three people in the room.

"Why are you guys here?" Danielle finally asked.

"We were watching a movie, and I heard a car backfire. I looked outside and saw a car sitting in front of your house, its motor running. And then someone came running out from your front bushes and jumped in the car and drove away," Lily explained. "I tried calling you, but there was no answer. Then we saw Chris and Heather creeping up your front walk—but I didn't know it was them."

"I was not creeping," Chris insisted.

Lily shrugged. "Walt's bedroom lights were already on, and then I saw more lights go on downstairs. And then I saw the lights go on in here and all of you walking in."

"She insisted we come over to check on you," Ian told them.

"I confess, I wondered why you were having a party without us. But after having Chris draw a gun on me, I suspect this isn't a social call," Lily said. "What's up?"

"Not a party. More a scavenger hunt," Chris told them.

"Scavenger hunt?" Lily asked. "What are we looking for?"

"A dead body," Danielle blurted.

TWENTY-FOUR

"Shouldn't we just call the chief?" Lily suggested after Walt and Danielle explained what had happened that evening. "Dead bodies, well, that's sort of his thing."

"I'm afraid the chief isn't in town," Danielle told her. "He took the boys to Portland. They had some family thing going on tomorrow."

"Which is technically today," Chris reminded them. He sat with the rest of his friends in the living room, where they had all been since Walt and Danielle had begun telling the story of Macbeth's ghost.

Ian stood. "Chris, let's go look for him. Lily, you can stay here." He looked to Danielle and Heather. "No reason for you two to go; Chris and I can do it." He turned to Walt. "With that leg, you should probably just stay here with the girls."

Danielle stood. "This girl is going to help look. I'm not a stranger to death—and who knows, maybe Macbeth's spirit went back to be with his body. If so, I need to talk to him, find out who killed him."

Heather stood. "Me too. It won't be my first dead body. That seems to be the one thing I'm good at. Tripping over dead bodies."

"Okay," Lily grumbled. "I can help look. I don't imagine it's going to take long, anyhow."

Walt pushed himself up on one foot while picking up the

crutches leaning against the sofa. "I'm not staying here. Let's go find the body."

"This will go faster if we split up. But I think Chris should go with Lily, and Heather with Ian," Danielle suggested.

"Why can't I search with Ian?" Lily asked.

"Because when we find the body, it's always possible Macbeth's spirit will be nearby. If so, we need to find out who killed him. You and Ian can't see spirits," Danielle explained.

"You have a point," Lily conceded. "Plus, I'd rather be with the guy who has a gun."

"SO DO you know how to use that thing?" Lily asked as she and Chris walked through the parlor.

"I took a class. I've been going to the range, doing a little target practice."

"I've always wanted to learn how to shoot. Now Dani, she's got a bit of a gun phobia."

"Yeah, I know. Although, she held it together when I walked in her front door tonight pointing the gun at her and Walt."

"So I'm not the only one you've pointed that thing at?" Lily asked. "Don't those classes say something about not aiming guns at friends?"

Chris flashed Lily a smile. "At the time, I thought you were an intruder."

"Just glad you aren't trigger-happy." Lily headed to the door. "Where to now?"

"The bathroom," Chris told her.

When they reached the downstairs powder room, the door was partially closed. Before opening it all the way, Chris stuck his hand inside and turned on the overhead light. When they opened the door, there was no body—but there was something on the floor that shouldn't be there.

"A gun!" Lily gasped, looking down at the handgun lying just inside the room.

"Don't touch it!" Chris warned.

JUST BEFORE CHRIS and Lily found the gun in the bathroom, Walt and Danielle were in the kitchen, and Ian and Heather had just walked through the dining room, finding nothing out of order.

"No one's screamed. I guess they haven't found him yet," Heather grumbled after they left the dining room.

"Let's check the basement."

"But it's creepy down there." Heather cringed.

"Creepier if we find the body," Ian reminded her.

Now standing at the entrance to the basement, Ian took a deep breath and opened the door. It was dark save for the dim glow from a nightlight. Heather reached around Ian and flipped on the overhead light switch. In the next moment light flooded the stairwell.

Ian spied the body first, but it was Heather who let out a blood-chilling scream moments after Chris and Lily found the gun.

OFFICER BRIAN HENDERSON felt as if he had stepped into the movie *Clue*. It wasn't the first time he had had that sensation in this house, considering this wasn't his first dead body at Marlow House. It wasn't even the first murdered one.

It had started to rain right after he got the call. When he had pulled up to Marlow House, lightning streaked over the mansard roofline, giving the scene an ominous feel—*something quite* Clue-*ish*, he thought.

When he had arrived after Peter Morris had been murdered in the house over a year ago, it hadn't surprised him that the witnesses on the scene that evening wore nightclothes; after all, they were guests staying at the bed and breakfast. He wondered why all his witnesses tonight were wearing nightclothes, considering only two of the six were staying at Marlow House. *Were they having some sort of slumber party?* he wondered.

Standing in the center of the library, notebook in hand, Brian quietly took inventory of the witnesses. Chris sat on the sofa, between Heather and Danielle. When Morris had been murdered, Brian remembered Heather had accused Chris of the crime. She had been wrong, and it was obvious to Brian, Chris did not hold a grudge, considering he knew Heather now worked for the man. Sitting across from the sofa was Clint Marlow. Brian found it difficult to think of the man by any other name. In the chair next to

THE GHOST OF SECOND CHANCES

Clint, Ian sat with Lily sitting on his knee. Beyond the closed doors of the library, the crime scene was being processed and Macbeth's body taken away.

Danielle broke the silence. "Don't you want to hear what happened?"

"I'm waiting for Joe," Brian explained. "I'd prefer to talk to you separately, in the parlor. I was hoping to avoid having you all come down to the station to do this."

"Why do you have to talk to us separately?" Heather asked.

"You don't think we're responsible for that man's death, do you?" Lily blurted.

Brian looked to Walt. "I suspect someone in this room is."

"THIS IS REALLY SILLY, Brian. You're just wasting time," Danielle said when she went into the parlor with him ten minutes later while Joe stayed with her friends. "We could have told you everything in the library."

"Why don't you just tell me what happened, so we can speed it up?" Brian told her.

Danielle took a seat on the sofa while Brian sat down on the chair facing her.

"I heard what sounded like a gunshot. At first, I wasn't sure if it was just a dream. I sent Walt a text message to see if he was okay."

"You mean Clint?"

Danielle rolled her eyes. "Please, Brian, don't go there. His legal name is Walter Clint Marlow. What is the big deal? He wants to go by his first name now."

Brian shrugged. "Just seems a little…well, creepy…considering another Walt Marlow lived here."

"There is nothing creepy about it. Do you want to hear what happened tonight or not?"

Brian nodded. "Go on."

"Walt didn't answer the text message. What I didn't know, he had heard the sound too, and when he reached for his cellphone from the nightstand, he had knocked it on the floor, and it went under his bed."

"So why was everyone here?" Brian asked.

"I'm getting to that. Right after I sent Walt the text message,

Heather called me. Earlier, she had been looking for Bella—her cat—when she heard a car backfire. She looked down the street and noticed the car had stopped in front of my house. She didn't really think much about it at the time, but later, when she went back out to look for something she had dropped, she saw the car again. And once again, it was parked in front of my house. She called me a few minutes later to make sure everything was all right."

WHEN BRIAN SPOKE TO HEATHER, she corroborated Danielle's story, explaining how she had called Chris to meet her there when Danielle failed to call her back. Had it been anyone else, Brian might have wondered why a car stopping in the middle of the street—even twice—would merit such notice, yet knowing Heather, he didn't doubt her story.

"What kind of vehicle was it?" Brian asked her. The two sat alone in the parlor at Marlow House.

"A car."

Brian gritted his teeth. He knew Heather wasn't intentionally being obtuse. "Do you know if it was a Ford or Chevy? A specific model?"

Heather shrugged. "I'm not really into cars. I just know it was a jalopy. Kind of a mess."

"What color was it?"

"Kind of hard to tell. It was dark out. Maybe black—or dark green." Heather shrugged again. "Could have been dark gray or maybe navy blue?"

"But you know it was *kind of a mess*?"

"Well, yeah. It was backfiring."

Brian resisted the temptation to roll his eyes. "Was it like a station wagon, or sports car, maybe an SUV?"

"No. It was just a regular car, like the kind my mother used to drive."

Brian perked up. "So what kind of car did your mother drive?"

Heather frowned at Brian. "I told you, I don't know cars. I couldn't tell you if Mom drove a Chevy or Ford. But it would have been an American car. Mom was big on that. Are Chevys and Fords American cars?"

Again Brian gritted his teeth and forced a smile. "The car last night—not your mother's car—do you remember if it had four doors or two doors?"

Heather scrunched up her face while considering the question. Finally, she blurted, "It was a two-door! And it had a trunk, not a hatchback." Heather grinned, proud of herself for remembering that much.

AS HE BROUGHT each witness in, they all painted the same picture: a suspicious vehicle stopping twice in front of Marlow House, hearing a car backfiring. The only inconsistency came when Brian asked why Lily was looking through the house with Chris and not Ian.

"So after you came over to check on Danielle, you decided to look through all the rooms before going home?" Brian asked Lily.

Lily nodded. "Yes. I had seen someone running out from the bushes and getting in the car. And Walt told us that when the gunshot woke him up, he heard someone running down the hallway and out the front door. Of course, we wanted to go through the house, make sure nothing had been disturbed and the windows were all locked."

"Why did you go through the house with Chris and not Ian?"

Lily frowned at Brian. "I'm not sure I understand your question."

"Danielle mentioned you all decided it would be faster to pair up and each check out specific rooms in the house. Why didn't you search the house with Ian?"

Lily stared at Brian. She finally shrugged and said, "Because Chris had a gun?" No one else had provided that answer when asked. In fact, they all gave different ones. What Brian didn't know, before calling the police, they had agreed it would be best to stick to the truth. They would tell the police exactly what had happened—minus the part where Walt saw Macbeth's ghost. But they hadn't anticipated the question on how they'd decided to pair up.

BRIAN WAITED to interview Walt last. Instead of making him hobble to the parlor, the five friends retreated to the living room.

"Did you know Jim Hill's real name was Macbeth Bandoni?" Brian asked Walt.

"Danielle told me," Walt answered.

"So you never knew before that?"

Walt smiled at Brian, who remained standing, notebook and pen in hands.

Walt shook his head. "I'm afraid I can't remember anything prior to my accident. Sorry. If I ever knew, I don't remember."

"Have you seen or heard from Macbeth since the accident?"

Walt stared at Brian a moment before answering. He and Danielle knew he would be asked this question. Finally, Walt said, "He called me and asked how I was doing. I didn't remember who he was, but Danielle had told me everything she knew about him."

"So he just asked how you were and said goodbye?"

"Not exactly." Walt shifted in his chair, trying to better position his cast.

"Then what?"

"I told him he could have the portraits he painted if he wanted them."

"Why would you give him the portraits?" Brian asked.

Walt shrugged. "They really are nothing to me—it's not like I even remember the paintings. Danielle showed me pictures she had taken of them. They are huge. I certainly don't have a place to display something like that. And I figured, since he painted them, maybe he'd want them."

"But they are part of your family history. The man you are named after. I'm surprised you would be so willing to give them away."

Walt smiled again at Brian. "I did ask Danielle first if she wanted the portraits. I knew she'd sold hers. She told me she didn't feel comfortable having something that valuable in her house. She has been so kind, helping me deal with everything, I thought she might like my portraits to replace the ones she sold."

"And she didn't want them?"

Walt shook his head. "No. She said once they took the portraits out of the library, she realized how much room they had taken up. I don't blame her. It's not like Walt Marlow and his wife are anything to her."

TWENTY-FIVE

Danielle wasn't surprised when Brian and Joe gathered fingerprints before leaving Marlow House. The crime lab needed to exclude their prints from any unidentified fingerprints found at the scene—or perhaps try matching one of their fingerprints to those found on one of the two guns.

Two handguns had been found in Marlow House that night—one in the bathroom and the second was found under the body of Macbeth, still clutched in his gloved hand. Danielle and her friends hadn't seen Macbeth's gun when they had initially found the body, because they were careful not to disturb the evidence.

Not everyone had their fingerprints taken, such as Danielle. Hers were already on file with the local police department. But when Brian finished up the fingerprinting, the body was removed, and the scene processed, she expected the police to leave and she and her friends could turn in for the night.

"I need Mr. Marlow to go down to the station with us for more questioning," Brian announced as he closed his notepad and slipped it back into his pocket.

"Why?" Danielle asked. "You already questioned him."

"Mr. Marlow had a prior relationship with our victim, and we have some more questions. I believe it will be best if we wrapped this up down at the station," Brian told her.

"But he doesn't even remember anything," Lily blurted.

Brian looked at her yet did not respond.

"Can't we just come down in the morning after we all get a good night's sleep?" Danielle asked.

"I'm afraid not." Brian's tone reminded Danielle of his attitude when investigating her for Cheryl's murder. It made her uncomfortable.

"It's okay, Danielle." Walt spoke up. "It would probably be better if we get this out of the way now."

Danielle stood up. "Fine. Let me go change my clothes."

"There's no reason for you to go with us," Joe told Danielle. "We'll take him with us, and I'll bring him back after we're finished."

"No." Danielle shook her head. "I don't think that's a good idea."

"We'll take him," Brian told her. "If you want to drive down to the station and wait for him, that's your prerogative." He then looked at Walt and asked, "Mr. Marlow, would you like to change your clothes before we go?"

Walt glanced down at his nightclothes. "I suppose that would be a good idea."

BRIAN WALKED Walt into the interrogation room and showed him to the table. He then glanced at his watch and said, "I'll be right back. Would you like a cup of coffee?"

"Yes. I'll probably need some caffeine to keep my eyes open. Thank you."

"Do you want anything in it?"

"Black is fine," Walt told him.

Instead of going directly to the break room to pour two cups of coffee, Brian slipped into the office next to the interrogation room. There he found Joe standing alone in the dimly lit room, looking through the two-way mirror at Walt Marlow.

"I'm glad you took my advice and insisted on bringing him down here without Danielle," Joe said when he walked into the room.

"I intended to do that anyway," Brian said as he stepped up to the glass window and stood next to Joe while they observed Walt.

THE GHOST OF SECOND CHANCES

Joe glanced briefly at Brian. "Really?"

Brian shrugged. "Just a gut feeling I had. Something didn't quite feel right back there."

"Certainly, you don't think any of them—aside from Marlow—had anything to do with the murder?" Joe asked.

Brian turned to Joe and was about to answer his question when a voice said, "What are you doing here?" It was Walt Marlow's voice coming through the speakers in the interrogation room. Both Brian and Joe turned back quickly to the window and watched as Walt directed his conversation to a chair sitting on the other side of the table.

"So she sent you to check on me?" Walt asked his imaginary friend. He then laughed.

"Insanity defense?" Joe suggested.

"That would be my guess. Does this mean we'll find his fingerprints on the murder weapon?" Brian asked.

"You didn't happen to see Macbeth, did you?" Walt asked aloud. "We looked for him, but we couldn't find him anywhere."

"What is he talking about?" Joe frowned.

"It would help if one of us could find him. Convince Macbeth to tell us who killed him," Walt said.

"I have to say, he is a good actor. He's got me believing he's a nutcase." Brian snorted.

"Why?" Walt asked. "He said he was going to kill me. He tried shooting me—twice. But imaginary guns don't work very well."

"He's doing this for our benefit," Joe snarled. "He wants us to think he's a whack job."

"WALT, stop talking to Eva! Don't say another word!" Marie shouted seconds after she appeared in the interrogation room. Walt sat at the table with Eva. The two looked at Marie, startled at her outburst.

"Goodness, Marie, what is your problem?" Eva asked.

Marie pointed to the mirror. "That! It's a two-way mirror. They're probably in there right now watching and listening to you!"

"Don't be silly, Marie," Eva said as she waved her hand, sending a flurry of glitter over the table. "They can't see or hear me."

"No, but they can certainly hear and see Walt, and about now are probably deciding if he is just a little crazy and likes talking to himself—or maybe dangerous and needs a straightjacket."

Walt looked from Marie to the mirror on the far wall.

Marie looked back at Walt. "Certainly Danielle has told you about the two-way mirror they have in here?" She had, but he had forgotten about it—until now.

The three sat in silence for a few minutes when Marie finally said, "This is silly. I said Walt needs to stop talking, I didn't mean Eva and I should remain quiet."

"If I had known they were spying on this room, I certainly wouldn't have engaged Walt in conversation," Eva muttered.

Marie turned her attention to Walt. "I'm sure Eva already told you we heard a rumor about new paranormal activity on your street, so we wanted to see if everything was okay at Marlow House. Eva arrived before I did, and Danielle asked her to check on you. But as soon as Eva left, Danielle realized she had not warned Eva about this room—and she was afraid if they brought you in here, you might not remember what she had told you about the mirror, which would mean when Eva showed up, you'd probably talk to her. Which you did."

Walt grimaced.

A few minutes later Brian Henderson entered the room carrying two cups of coffee, and a notepad tucked under one arm. He walked over to the table and set one cup in front of Walt and another in front of Eva.

"I don't think that coffee is for me," Eva grumbled as she quickly moved from the seat. The next moment, Brian sat down in the chair she had been using.

"Are you ready to answer a few more questions?" Brian asked.

"Yes." Walt took a sip of the coffee.

Brian picked up his notepad and looked at it a moment. He then looked up at Walt and asked, "What did you mean when you said, 'So she sent you to check on me'?"

Walt stared blankly at Brian.

Brian pointed to the mirror and started to say, "You see, that—"

"Is a two-way mirror," Walt finished for him.

"You knew?" Brian asked.

"I wasn't certain," Walt lied. "Suspected someone was watching me."

"Why were you talking to yourself in here if you knew we might be watching?" Brian asked.

Walt shrugged. "It's late. I'm tired. Probably a little sleep deprived."

"Do you always talk to yourself when you're tired and sleep deprived?"

"Only when I've been unnecessarily dragged down to the police station in the middle of the night, and I think the ones responsible might be in the next room watching."

Marie gasped. "I'm not sure that's the best approach to take with Brian."

"Hush, Marie," Eva said with a chuckle. "Let Walt be. Everyone thought Clint was a jerk, and better for Walt to be perceived as the jerk they already believe him to be than someone who's slipped off his rocker."

"So you don't think we should have asked you to come down here?"

"I just don't know what it is you needed to ask me that you couldn't have asked at Marlow House."

"You are the only one who had a relationship with Macbeth Bandoni."

"I also don't remember anything about that time in my life," Walt told him.

Brian glanced down at his notes then looked back up at Walt. "When you were talking to yourself in here—apparently to amuse yourself at our expense—you said—I'm afraid I didn't get it down exactly—something like, *he said he wanted to kill me—he tried shooting me, but imaginary guns don't work.* Or something to that effect. Why did you say that? It's an odd thing to say, especially considering what happened tonight."

"Those aren't my words," Walt said.

Eva cringed. "You did say something like that."

"Not exactly. But close enough," Brian said.

"Maybe if you played the tape for me, it would jog my memory," Walt suggested.

Brian frowned. "Tape? What tape?"

"I assumed you were recording me when I was in here alone."

Brian stared at Walt a moment. Finally, he shook his head. "No, we hadn't started recording yet."

Walt smiled at Brian and shrugged. "Then I'm sorry, I don't think I can answer your question. I believe you misheard what I said."

"I DIDN'T MISHEAR ANYTHING," Brian grumbled when he walked into Joe's office thirty minutes later.

"I guess he's not planning to use that little show as an insanity defense," Joe said as he set the pen he had been holding on his desktop. He leaned back in the office chair and watched as Brian took a seat across from him.

"He was just messing with us. I was hoping there was some way to connect Marlow to that gun found in the bathroom," Brian grumbled. Before he had released Walt, Joe had popped in the interrogation room for a few moments and had slipped Brian a note, telling him they had nothing to hold Walt on.

"Most of the prints were wiped off the gun," Joe explained.

"I wouldn't expect him to ditch the gun where it could be found without wiping it off. I was just hoping he missed something."

"We did find some partial prints. They're running them now, but they said they definitely weren't Marlow's," Joe told him. "But there is something odd about his fingerprints."

"Odd how?" Brian asked.

"I went ahead and ran his prints through the system."

"You wanted to see if he had something out there?" Brian snickered. "You still have a thing for Boatman, don't you?"

"Oh, shut up. I'm with Kelly now. This has nothing to do with Danielle."

"Yeah, right," Brian mumbled under his breath.

"Don't you want to know what I found?" Joe asked.

"He's a wanted criminal?" Brian suggested.

"There was nothing—absolutely nothing."

Brian shrugged. "So? Just means he has a clean record, wasn't in the military, never worked for the government…"

"The guy was a real estate agent. To get a license you have to be fingerprinted."

"Are you sure it's in the database you used?"

"Clint Marlow's fingerprints were there. He was fingerprinted when he got his California real estate license."

Brian frowned. "I don't understand what you're saying?"

"When I ran Marlow's fingerprints, nothing came up. I thought that was strange. So I searched by name and found his fingerprints. Only thing, they don't match the fingerprints of the man you just interviewed."

TWENTY-SIX

Walt didn't need one of the officers to drive him back to Marlow House after Brian finished the interview and told him he could go. Danielle was already at the police station, sitting in the waiting area. On their ride home, Walt told her all that had happened since he had last seen her.

"I'm sorry about sending Eva over there to check on you without first thinking it through," Danielle said when they returned home. She helped Walt out of the car, and together they made their way to the kitchen door. Before leaving to get Walt, Danielle had turned on the back-porch light. It broke the darkness of the side yard.

"I should have remembered what you told me about the two-way mirror. I was tired. Too much going on," Walt explained as he hobbled into the house.

"I just figured Eva would get there before me. I don't know what I was thinking."

Walt chuckled. "Neither of us was thinking clearly. It was a long night."

Danielle locked the back door and turned off the porch light. "We should both try to get some sleep."

"I'm just hoping I don't regret drinking coffee at the station. I'm still learning how this body reacts to things like caffeine."

"My problem is not caffeine. I'm exhausted, but not sure I'll be able to fall asleep. After all, there was a killer in this house."

"That's why I'm here," Marie said as she appeared in the kitchen the next moment.

"Marie? What are you doing back here?" Danielle asked.

"I just thought, if it were me, I'd be terrified to go back home and try to sleep knowing such a grizzly event had happened under my roof just a few hours earlier. So I thought I'd come keep an eye on things so you two can get some sleep. If someone tries to break in, I'll wake you up. And of course, if necessary, I can raise Chris or Heather for additional help."

Danielle grinned at Marie and found it endearing how this image of a petite silver-haired elderly woman was their security guard. "If I could, I'd hug you right now!"

BRIAN WAS STILL SITTING in Joe's office with him when the call came in. He knew it was about the fingerprints found on the gun, but by hearing just Joe's side of the conversation, he couldn't tell who the fingerprints belonged to—yet they had obviously been identified.

"Well? Is it someone we know?" Brian asked when Joe hung up the phone.

"I know her—but not well," Joe told him.

"Her?" Brian frowned.

"Laverne Morrison."

"Laverne Morrison?" Brian repeated.

Joe nodded his reply. "You know her, don't you?"

Brian let out a low whistle and leaned back in the chair. "I worked on the arson case when her family's house burned down. That was years ago. I see her around town once in a while, but don't really know her."

"Arson? I remember hearing what happened, but I thought it was some electrical fire, not arson."

Brian shrugged. "In the beginning we suspected arson. I guess I always think of that case as arson, but yes, you're right, they eventually ruled it was caused by faulty wiring from a space heater."

"I don't know her well, but murder? And how does she even know our victim?" Joe asked.

"Danielle told us his cousins live in Astoria. And she mentioned Adam knew them in high school. The name is familiar to me, but I can't really place them. I do remember Laverne's brother used to hang out with Adam back then. Maybe there is some connection there."

"I need to get someone over to Astoria and talk to the cousins," Joe said.

"I'll bring Morrison in for questioning." Brian glanced at his watch and groaned. "Why do murders happen at the most inconvenient times? I should be getting off in about an hour."

CONSIDERING sunrise was at least two hours away, Brian had expected Laverne Morrison's house to be dark. It wasn't. The light in the living room was on, and he could see someone was inside watching television. Moments after ringing the doorbell, the light and television went off. When she didn't answer the door, he rang the doorbell again—then again. It wasn't until he knocked and said, "Ms. Morrison, it's the police," did she open the door.

OFFICER BRIAN HENDERSON sat with Laverne Morrison in the interrogation room. Unlike Walt Marlow, she hadn't needed to change her clothes before coming to the station. She was already dressed in street clothes when Brian had arrived.

"Why did it take you so long to answer your door?" Brian asked as he shuffled through the papers in the file folder before him.

Laverne shrugged. "I'm a woman living alone. It's frightening to have someone ring your bell in the middle of the night. Why am I here?"

"I have some questions I need to ask you," he told her.

"In the middle of the night?"

He looked up from the papers. "You certainly weren't dressed as if it were the middle of the night. Do you always stay up so late?"

She shrugged again. "I went out with friends. When I got home, I couldn't sleep."

"Where did you go tonight?"

She frowned. "Why is that important?"

"Could you please just answer my question."

"Went to see a show with friends. They picked me up around seven. The show started at seven thirty." She then mentioned her friends' names and the movie they had seen.

"One of your friends drove?" he asked.

"Yes."

"And she brought you home?"

"Umm…no. I asked her to drop me off so I could get something to eat."

"Then how did you get home?" he asked.

"I called a taxi." She chuckled and added, "I guess they don't really call them taxis anymore. One of those independent services in town."

"Which one?"

"I don't remember. I got the number off a flyer at the restaurant."

"What restaurant did you stop at?" he asked.

"Pier Café. I had pie and ice cream. I'm sure Carla will remember. She's a waitress there."

Brian stared blankly at Laverne. "Yes, I know who Carla is. So why didn't your friends want to join you at Pier Café?"

"I'm not sure why you're asking all these questions. What is this about?" she asked impatiently.

"Please answer my question."

Laverne released a sigh born of exasperation and said, "Because they all wanted to go to another bar and have more to drink."

"Another bar?"

"Yes. After the movie, we stopped to get something to drink. I'm not much of a drinker, and after the third bar, I wanted to go home. But there were several bars between where we were and my house, so I asked them to just drop me off at the pier. I had some pie, called a driver, and then went home. Now please, what is this about?"

Brian removed a photograph from the file and slid it across the tabletop to Laverne.

Laverne glanced down at the photograph and froze. Her eyes widened. With a squeaky voice she asked, "Is he dead?"

"Do you know who he is?" Brian asked, his eyes focused on Laverne's reaction.

She cleared her throat and nodded. "It's Mac. Mac Bandoni. What happened to him?"

"How do you know him?" Brian asked, noting how she continued to stare at the photograph.

"I...I dated Mac for a few months one summer. A couple of years after I graduated from high school."

"When was the last time you saw him?"

Still studying the photograph, she tilted her head slightly. A single tear slipped down her face. "Friday. But before then, I hadn't seen him since we stopped seeing each other. If you would have shown me this picture last week, I would never have recognized him. He changed, you know. Was actually quite attractive back then," she said, her voice almost a whisper.

"You say you saw him Friday. How did that come about?"

Several more tears began sliding down her cheeks. She looked up at Brian and wiped away the tears with the back of her hand. "I ran into him when I was in Astoria making a delivery for work."

"Where was this at?"

Laverne sat up straighter in her chair, attempting to regain her composure. "I...I had stopped to get something to eat. I saw him at the restaurant where I had lunch."

"How did that meeting go?"

Laverne shrugged. "Nothing I remember worth noting. What do you really say to someone you haven't seen for years?"

"You said you two once dated—which one of you broke it off?"

She stared at him a moment as if collecting her thoughts. Finally, she said, "I suppose it was me. That was a difficult year. That was the summer my parents were killed."

"You broke up and never kept in touch? Never saw him again until Friday?"

"Mac didn't live in Oregon. I met him when he was visiting his grandmother; she lived in Astoria. So I suppose even if I hadn't been the one to break up, we wouldn't have dated long. Too much going on in my life back then. Mac loved to travel. He was an artist, really very talented. I believe he lived in Europe after that summer."

"I thought you didn't keep in contact with him?"

She shrugged again. "We didn't. But I'd run into his grandmother sometimes when I was in Astoria. She'd tell me things. But she died a while back."

Brian pulled a second photo from the file and slid it across the table to Laverne. It was of a handgun. "Do you recognize this?"

Laverne stared at the photo. "It's a gun."

"Have you ever seen this gun before?"

"I don't know. I've seen guns before, but not sure I could tell one gun from another." She looked up at Brian. "Is this the one that killed Mac?"

"How do you know Mac was shot?"

"I don't know. But you just showed me a picture of him, and he looks dead in the photograph. I asked you if he was dead, but you never said. But I'm thinking he must be, or I wouldn't be in here. And now you show me a picture of a gun and ask me if I recognize it. So I figure it must be what killed him."

"You say you can't really tell one gun from another. Can you tell me when was the last time you saw any gun?"

Laverne looked back at the photo and absently licked her lips. She shook her head. "I don't remember."

"Then can you tell me why your fingerprints are on the gun that killed the man you used to date?"

Laverne looked up at Brian. "I want to talk to an attorney."

TWENTY-SEVEN

On Sunday morning Laverne remained in custody. Brian and Joe managed to each go home to catch a few hours of sleep while officers on duty ran down some leads for them and interviewed potential witnesses.

Joe arrived back at the station first and was briefed by the officers on duty regarding what they had learned thus far. Brian arrived thirty minutes later, shortly after noon, with take-out food he had picked up to share with Joe. The two sat in the break room eating while Joe updated Brian.

"They talked to the friends Laverne said she went to the show with. That part of the story checks out. But it doesn't necessarily let Laverne off the hook. The time frame from when they dropped her off at the pier and Carla said she was at the café gives her enough time to shoot Bandoni."

"What about the car Heather saw?" Brian asked.

Joe shook his head. "It wasn't the car that took the women to the show and dropped off Laverne. That was a white Suburban."

"So who was driving the car Heather saw, and is Laverne the person Marlow heard leaving the house and getting into that vehicle?"

"The car Heather saw wasn't Laverne's. She drives a four-door. But it does match the description the neighbors gave of the brother's car."

"Chet Morrison?" Brian asked.

Joe nodded. "According to one of the neighbors, he drives a beat-up two-door gray sedan. And the neighbor claims he's heard it backfire a few times."

Narrowing his eyes in contemplation, Brian sipped the soda through his straw and considered the information. Finally, he said, "So maybe Chet and Laverne are in on this together? She goes out with her friends to establish an alibi, knows they will go bar hopping afterwards, and then has them drop her off at the pier. Her brother picks her up there, drops her at Marlow House, then picks her up after she kills Bandoni and then takes her back to the pier so she can be seen having pie by Carla, therefore supporting her motive for having them drop her off on Danielle's street."

"And how do Laverne and her brother know Bandoni is going to be at Marlow House?" Joe asked. "What's their motive? And is Clint Marlow tangled up in all this?"

"I think we need to talk to the cousins and find Chet Morrison."

"Unfortunately, still no one at the cousins' house. But there is a car parked there. According to the registration, it belongs to Macbeth," Joe told him. "The neighbors claim they haven't seen anyone there since yesterday afternoon, but one remembers seeing someone matching Macbeth's description working on the car that's still parked there. He was under the impression it was broken down. And another claimed a car matching the description of Chet's was seen parked at the house."

"You haven't been able to track down Chet?" Brian asked.

"No. And according to one of Laverne's neighbors, when she kicked him out the other night, there was some shouting going on. Chet kept banging on her door, demanding she let him in, but he finally left after the neighbor threatened to call the police," Joe explained.

Brian set his soda on the table and frowned. "If Chet and Laverne were at odds, what are the chances they'd conspire to kill someone just hours after she kicks him out?"

Joe shrugged. "Maybe it was an act? Throw us off? Yet, even if it was an act, what's the motive?"

"We need to find the cousins and Chet. And keep a close eye on Clint Marlow. He's involved in this someway, I'm sure of it."

"What I can't understand," Joe began, "why did the killer dump the murder weapon in the bathroom? At first, I assumed Marlow tossed it there in a panic. Not like he had the time to get rid of it, especially being on crutches. It didn't surprise me his prints weren't on it. I'd expect him to wipe down the handle before dumping it so close to the crime scene. But if Laverne was the shooter, then why didn't she take the gun with her? Hell, she went to the pier afterwards. Why not dump the gun in the ocean while she was there?"

"If we can't find the Bandoni brothers and Chet, we need to talk to someone who knows all of them." Brian stood up and tossed his now empty soda cup in the trash can.

MELONY CARMICHAEL LOOKED MORE fashion model than criminal attorney, with her silky blond hair, perfect features, manicured nails, and designer clothes. She was having Sunday brunch with Adam Nichols when Officer Brian Henderson found them at Pearl Cove. Brian wasn't looking for Melony, he wanted to talk to Adam.

Some of the newer Frederickport residents found Adam and Melony an unlikely couple. For years Adam had played the field, and as far as they knew, he had only entered into one long-term relationship, and that had been with quirky Isabella Strickland. His most notable one-night stand had been with Danielle Boatman's flamboyant cousin, Cheryl. Although, that hadn't worked out for Adam—or for Cheryl—who had been murdered that night.

Melony was different—she was classy and bright. Not exactly the type of woman Adam normally dated. However, Brian understood the connection. He could remember a much younger Melony Carmichael, an unruly teenager who had defied her parents when she and Adam had run away together. Brian always suspected Melony had been the primary instigator in that rebellion.

After her parents had brought her home, she was sent out of the country to a boarding school, only returning to Frederickport after her mother's murder.

"I've been looking all over town for you," Brian told Adam when he walked up to their booth at Pearl Cove. "Don't you ever answer your cellphone?"

"Not when I don't want to be bothered," Adam told him.

Without asking permission, Brian sat down in the booth, forcing Adam to move over to the other side of the bench.

"Hello to you too, Brian," Melony said with a chuckle as she sipped her mimosa.

"What is so important that you had to interrupt our romantic rendezvous?" Adam asked.

"Ahh, Adam, is that what this is? A romantic rendezvous?" Melony teased. "I thought it's because you lost that bet."

"Oh, shut up, Mel," Adam countered, his tone playful.

"This is serious," Brian told him, his expression severe.

"I hope so, since you barged in on us," Adam quipped.

Melony chuckled and took another sip of her mimosa.

"Someone was murdered at Marlow House," Brian announced.

The smiles disappeared from Melony's and Adam's faces.

Melony set her drink on the table. "Is Danielle okay?"

"Yes. It was Macbeth Bandoni. You might have known him as Jim Hill. He was the artist Clint Marlow hired to reproduce the Marlow portraits."

Adam let out a low whistle and sat back in the bench. "Danielle and I were just talking about him."

"How so?" Brian asked.

Ever the attorney, Melony shot Adam a look that said *be careful what you say*. He understood.

Adam shrugged. "I just mentioned Chet Morrison was going to see the Bandoni cousins. She was surprised I knew them. She told me their cousin had been the artist who'd painted the reproductions. I was surprised, because I'd met Mac Bandoni years ago, and when I saw him at Marlow House and was told his name was Jim Hill, I didn't recognize him."

"Why would Danielle care if Chet was going to see the Bandoni cousins?" Brian asked.

Adam frowned. "I don't think she cared."

"I think what Brian is asking, why were you even discussing Chet with Danielle, am I right, Brian?" Melony asked.

Brian nodded. "That's part of it."

"Maybe I can help here." Melony flashed Brian a dazzling smile showing off straight white teeth. "About a month ago, we had a girls' night out, Danielle, Lily, Heather, and myself. We met here. Danielle arrived first and went to the bar to wait for us. Chet was there and tried to hit on Danielle. He used some asinine pickup technique called negging. Danielle got away from him as fast as she could and told us about it. I was curious to see who this joker was, so

I went back to the bar. I recognized him. We had gone to high school together."

Brian frowned. "Negging?"

"It's when a guy tries picking up a woman he thinks is out of his league. Basically, he starts with a compliment, then an insult, trying to undermine her self-confidence. The theory being she will eventually do anything to gain his approval," Melony explained.

"And that works?" Brian asked.

Adam chuckled. "It sure didn't with Danielle; she thinks he's a jerk. But he's convinced she has a thing for him."

"Why does he think that?" Brian asked.

"It's silly, really. Danielle had been thinking of cutting her hair for a while; in fact, I gave her the name of a hairdresser that night. But coincidentally Chet made some crack to her when he tried picking her up about how she might be good looking if she cut her hair," Melony explained.

"And now Chet is convinced she has a thing for him," Adam interjected. "That's why we were talking about him. When Chet's sister was tired of his freeloading, he thought he could get Danielle to rent him a room—at a reduced rate. Of course, she wouldn't even give him a room at the full rate."

"Do you know where Chet is now?"

"Last I heard, he was crashing at the Bandoni brothers' in Astoria. I ran into Laverne the other day, and she told me he was doing some work with the brothers. You could ask her about it."

"Laverne's in jail right now," Brian told them.

TWENTY-EIGHT

When Police Chief MacDonald drove up to Marlow House Monday morning, he found the locksmith van parked in the street and its owner in the process of changing out the hardware on the front door. MacDonald greeted the locksmith and entered the house without knocking.

He made his way to the kitchen and found Danielle and Walt sitting at the table, finishing breakfast.

"Morning, Chief," Walt greeted him, lifting his cup in mock salute.

"Good morning, Chief," Danielle said without standing up. With her mug, she pointed to the coffee maker on the counter. "Help yourself."

"Thanks. I see you're getting new locks." MacDonald grabbed a cup from the overhead cabinet and poured himself some coffee.

"The way people have been coming and going the last few days, I thought we needed to do something. I'm also thinking of having security cameras installed around the exterior of the property."

"I'm surprised you didn't call me yesterday." The chief walked to the table with his coffee.

"I figured Joe or Brian had already done that," Danielle said. "And what was the point? There really wasn't anything you could do from Portland, and I didn't want you racing back to Frederickport."

The chief sipped his coffee and then asked, "Is there anything I need to know that you couldn't tell Joe and Brian?"

"I saw Macbeth's spirit," Walt told him. "That's the real reason we searched through the house."

"Looking for his body?" the chief asked.

Walt nodded.

"I don't suppose he mentioned who killed him?"

"I asked, but I'm afraid he took off without telling me."

Danielle interrupted by asking, "Chief, can I get you anything to eat?"

He shook his head. "No, thanks. I grabbed a breakfast sandwich before I came over here; coffee is fine."

"Brian told me Chet's sister, Laverne, was arrested for the murder. I certainly didn't see that one coming," Danielle said.

"She was released this morning," the chief said.

"You don't think she did it?" Walt asked.

"I don't know. We had to charge her or let her go. I didn't think we had enough to make anything stick. What's her motive? I know they once dated, but that was over twenty years ago, and there's no sign she'd had any contact with him aside from running into him in Astoria the other day."

"Weren't her fingerprints on the murder weapon?" Danielle asked.

"Yes. But not on the grip. And they tested her hands and clothes, and there was no gunshot residue, which wouldn't surprise me if she wore gloves and if the clothes they tested weren't what she was wearing at the time of the murder."

"They tested all our hands," Danielle told him.

"Why would her fingerprints be on the gun if she wore gloves?" Walt asked.

"That's what I'm wondering," the chief said.

"A sloppy killer?" Danielle suggested with a shrug.

"And why have her friends drop her off by the pier? If she had a reason to kill Macbeth, why would she go out of her way to make sure someone saw her in the neighborhood? Especially Carla," the chief said. "And if she killed him before she went to the pier, why wouldn't she have taken the gun with her and tossed it into the ocean?"

"Unless she panicked," Danielle suggested.

"Perhaps." The chief shrugged.

"Sounds like you don't think she's guilty," Walt noted.

"Like I said, I don't know. But Joe and Brian aren't convinced. In fact, they believe you're in some way involved in all this."

Walt arched his brows. "Me?"

"More accurately, Clint. In fact, when I spoke to Brian on the phone yesterday about the case, he was planning to come over here to interview you again. I told him not to. Said I would do it. I don't think Brian was thrilled with me, but he didn't argue."

"I don't imagine he was," Danielle said.

"There was one strange thing that popped up," the chief said.

"What was that?" Danielle asked.

"Joe ran Walt's fingerprints."

Danielle frowned. "I thought he only collected our prints to see if they matched the ones on the guns. Why run them?"

The chief arched his brow. "What do you think?"

"He's hoping to find something on Walt?" Danielle grumbled.

"What was the strange thing that popped up?" Walt asked.

"Clint had his fingerprints on file for his California real estate license. And those fingerprints don't match the ones they took from Walt."

"How can they not match?" Danielle asked.

Walt glanced down at the scar on his wrist. He then looked to the chief. "What does this mean?"

"I told Joe and Brian it was obviously some screw up with the California real estate department and said it wasn't our problem. I know you aren't involved in this, but I can't really tell that to my officers."

"What do you know about Laverne?" Danielle asked.

"I don't really know her. I know who she is. She grew up in Frederickport. A year or so after she was out of high school, her parents were killed in a house fire, and she took care of her younger brother.

"According to what she told Brian, she once dated Macbeth. But that was over twenty years ago. She claims she was the one who'd broken up and that she hadn't seen Macbeth since the breakup—not until Friday when she made a delivery for work and ran into him in Astoria. Brian checked with her boss, Ray Fuller, and he corroborated her story. He sent her to Astoria for a delivery, and Ray claimed she didn't know she would be going until a few minutes before she left. So it sounds like running into Macbeth wasn't something she planned."

"According to Adam, her brother was staying with Macbeth's cousins," Danielle said.

MacDonald nodded. "Brian already talked to Adam about Chet."

Danielle smiled. "Yes, I know. Melony called me. Told me what was said."

"Have you tracked down the annoying brother yet?" Walt asked.

"No. And Laverne refuses to help us find him. In fact, she refuses to say much about anything. The moment they asked her why her fingerprints were on the murder weapon, she stopped talking and asked to see an attorney. Later, before her release, when asked why she had thrown Chet out of the house, she insisted her neighbors had exaggerated, that it was nothing more than a typical sibling spat. No big deal. Claimed he left because he wanted to travel. But when asked where he might be traveling, she said she had no idea and stopped talking again."

"Traveling? But she told Adam he was staying with Macbeth's cousins," Danielle said.

"I know. And when reminded of that, she clammed up again."

"And the cousins? What do they say about all this?" Danielle asked.

"They still haven't shown up," MacDonald told her. "We have someone watching their house, but it looks like they might be traveling with Chet."

THE FIRST THING Laverne did when she got home from the police station on Monday was to take a shower. After getting dressed, she went to her bedroom, pulled her phone from her purse, and called her brother's cell number.

After the second ring she heard, "Laverne? Is that you?"

"Chet, where are you?"

"Listen to me, Laverne..." came his raspy whisper.

"Chet, you have to talk louder. I can barely hear you. Where are you?"

"I can't talk louder; someone might hear me," he whispered.

"What did you do, Chet?" Laverne asked.

"I had to do it. I did it for you, Laverne," he told her.

"You did what for me?" Laverne asked in a wavering voice.

"Mac. I killed him. I had to. Your secret's safe now."

"Oh no! Chet, say you didn't," she sobbed.

"I love you, Laverne. I'm sorry I was such a loser brother," his voice cracked.

"You are not a loser. But, Chet, they have your gun. I recognized it. I didn't tell them it was yours. But if they trace it back to you, you're going to jail again. And this time…you could get the death penalty."

"I don't care. I had to protect you."

"Listen, Chet, please listen to me. All I ever wanted was to take care of you. I'm sorry I kicked you out of the house. I don't know what I was thinking. But I can fix this."

"What are you talking about?"

"You have to promise me you'll disappear. Don't come back. Not until I say it's okay."

"What are you going to do?"

"You'll see. Listen to the news. But whatever you do, stay away. I'll get a message to you some way, I promise. But for now, stay away."

When the phone call ended, Laverne lay on her bed and began to sob. After more than an hour, she pulled herself together, washed her face, and changed her clothes.

"I DIDN'T THINK I would see you again so soon," Chief MacDonald said when he returned to the police station late Monday morning and found Laverne Morrison waiting for him.

Laverne stood up and faced the chief. "I have something to tell you."

"Have you come to tell me where your brother is?" the chief asked.

Laverne shook her head. "No. I've come to confess to Mac's murder."

The chief didn't respond immediately. It was the last thing he had expected her to say.

THE CHIEF SAT in the interrogation room with Laverne while Joe and Brian listened and watched from the next office. Laverne had told the chief she would only give him her confession. After formally waiving her right to an attorney, he asked the first question.

"Why did you kill him?"

Sitting primly in the chair, her back straight and her hands folded on the table before her, Laverne said, "He broke my heart. And when I saw him again, I just snapped."

"Where did you get the gun?" he asked.

"I stole it," she said.

"You stole it? Who did you steal it from?" he asked.

Licking her lips nervously, she said, "I don't know. From some tourist who came into the hardware store. She left her purse open. I saw it. And when she wasn't looking, I took it."

The chief arched his brow. "Do you often steal from your customers?"

She shrugged. "No. But I saw the gun, and something told me to take it. So I did."

"Okay...how did you know where to find Macbeth?" he asked.

She frowned a moment and then looked at the chief. "He hated that name. I only knew his real name was Macbeth because I saw his driver's license once. He was always Mac to me."

"How did you know Mac was going to be at Marlow House?" the chief asked.

"I didn't. But I saw him when I was with my friends. So I asked them to let me out of the car. I followed him." She paused and then asked, "That means it's not premeditated, doesn't it? It's not like I planned it."

"Did another car drop you off and pick you up in front of Marlow House?" he asked.

She frowned. "What do you mean?"

"After your friends dropped you off by the pier, did someone else pick you up and drop you off in front of Marlow House? And then later pick you up in front of the house after you shot him?"

She shook her head. "No. I was walking. I went back to the pier, had the pie, and then called a driver."

"So on a whim, spur of the moment, you decide to kill a boyfriend you hadn't seen in over twenty years?"

"I told you, I saw him on Friday. It...it opened old wounds. I snapped."

"And you just happened to have the gun with you? The gun you stole?"

"Yes. I'm a woman living alone; it's dangerous out there. I feel safer having a loaded gun in my purse."

"What did you do with the gloves?" he asked.

She frowned again. "What gloves?"

"You didn't have any residue on your hands; you must have worn gloves. What did you do with them?"

"I washed my hands really well when I got home, before your men tested them. I must have washed all the residue off."

"Then why weren't your fingerprints on the gun?"

"My fingerprints were on the gun."

"Not on the grip," he told her.

"I wiped the gun off. I guess I didn't do a very good job."

"Okay, I'd like to know exactly what happened."

She frowned at him. "I already told you."

"Where were you when you shot him? Where was he?"

Laverne stared at the chief a moment. Finally, she said, "I don't want to talk about this anymore; it's too painful. All you need to know is that I did it. I wish I hadn't, but I did."

"SHE'S LYING," the chief said when he walked into the office next to the interrogation room fifteen minutes later.

"Which means she's protecting someone, likely her brother," Brian said. "Although I think she's involved."

"We need to talk to Clint Marlow again," Joe said. "He's tangled up in this someway."

TWENTY-NINE

Chris had given Heather Monday off. After their stressful weekend, he had insisted they both needed an extra day of rest and relaxation. She wasn't going to argue with him, considering it was a day off with pay. Because of the unexpected holiday, she took her morning jog later than usual. It was early afternoon before she got on the beach, grateful there was no rain to dampen her run.

She had just jogged under the pier and was heading toward Ian and Lily's house when she spied a man ahead, walking in the same direction she was going. He wasn't very tall, maybe five feet two, with dark thinning hair. Getting closer, she could see his bald spot. She was just a few feet behind him when she came to an abrupt stop. She hadn't seen it before. Heather simply stared. In his right hand, dangling at his side, she spied a handgun.

Standing on the beach, she glanced around. There were other people nearby, yet no one seemed to notice the determined stride of the man walking down the beach, gun in hand. She wasn't sure what to do—*call the police maybe?*

To her horror, he stopped walking, raised his gun, and pointed it at a child nearby. A moment later, he pulled the trigger, and Heather let out a loud shrill scream. Everyone on the beach—including the child and the man with the gun—turned to face her.

"What's wrong?" the child's mother asked Heather.

Heather stood mute, unable to utter a sound. She looked from the confused woman to the man with the gun. Their gazes locked. He raised the pistol, pointed it at Heather, and pulled the trigger. In the next moment he disappeared.

"THAT WAS THE CHIEF," Danielle told Chris and Walt, who were sitting in the library, playing another game of chess. Before starting the game, Walt had promised he would keep Max away.

About to move his knight, Chris paused and looked up to Danielle. "And?"

"Laverne Morrison, she's in custody again for Macbeth's murder," she told them.

"I thought the chief said they didn't have enough to arrest her?" Walt asked.

"She confessed."

"Confessed?" Walt and Chris said in unison.

"Yes. After the chief left here and went back to his office, she was waiting for him. Insisted she had to talk to him—and only him. She told him she killed Macbeth."

"Why?" Chris asked. "I thought you said they hadn't seen each other for years."

"She claimed he had broken her heart and then said she snapped when she ran into him in Astoria."

"Considering how long ago they broke up, that's some delayed reaction, I'd say," Chris muttered.

Danielle pulled up a chair to Walt and Chris and sat down. "The chief doesn't think she did it."

Before either Walt or Chris could respond, they heard frantic knocking at the library window. Looking up, they found Heather knocking on the glass pane and pointing in the direction of the kitchen door.

Through the window they could hear her shout, "Unlock the kitchen door!"

HEATHER RUSHED into the library ahead of Danielle. "I saw Macbeth!" she announced for the second time. The first time had been moments earlier, when Danielle had unlocked the kitchen door and let her into the house.

"Where was he?" Chris asked.

"Walking along the beach, shooting kids." Heather flopped down on the sofa and let out a grunt.

"Excuse me?" Chris frowned.

Walt stood up, using the chair's arm for balance. He then hopped to the nearby recliner. "I don't think we're going to finish our game today."

Chris turned in his chair and faced Heather. "What do you mean shooting kids?"

"Just that. I was jogging down the beach. I see what I assume is a man. And then I see he's carrying a gun in his hand. Next thing I know, he raises the gun and shoots a little kid. You have no idea how freaked I was!" Heather dramatically shivered.

"What happened to the kid?" Walt asked.

Heather gave Walt her most disgusted glare and said, "Well, obviously nothing. Macbeth's a freaking ghost and a nasty one at that. He shot me next, and then he disappeared."

"That's kind of a weird thing for him to do," Danielle said.

Chris shrugged. "I don't know. There's been a few times I've considered shooting Heather."

Heather turned another glare on Chris. "Shut up."

Chris chuckled. "Okay, seriously, why is Macbeth's spirit walking down the beach, using kids as target practice?"

"He seemed angry," Heather said.

"Getting murdered can have that effect," Walt suggested.

"If they didn't already have his killer in custody, I'd suggest we go find him," Danielle said. "But if we're lucky, after he shot Heather and disappeared—well, maybe he disappeared for good."

OVERSIZED SUNGLASSES COVERED a good portion of Sonya Kozlov's face, along with the floppy straw hat, its brim pulled downward, concealing the blond hair tucked up out of sight. She sat behind the steering wheel of the van parked three doors down from Marlow House. In her hands she held an open road map; it rested against the steering wheel. She wasn't reading the map—it would be impossible to do through the dark glasses. But it didn't matter. The map was only a prop, should someone drive by and wonder what she was doing just sitting there in a parked vehicle.

She glanced at her watch. That morning, she had spent hours sitting on a bench at the pier, pretending to read a book. From that venue she could keep track of cars coming and going on Beach Drive. When she first spied the locksmith van, she thought that was what she had been waiting for. But it wasn't.

Just as she decided it was time to move again, she spied someone crossing the street to Marlow House. It was a petite redhead and a tall man wearing a Cub's baseball cap. Walking alongside them was a golden retriever. Sonya decided to wait a few more minutes to move, after they had reached their destination and hopefully went inside.

Instead of going to the front door of Marlow House, Sonya watched as the couple and their dog made their way up the driveway and entered the side yard of Marlow House through the gate. When they were no longer in sight, she started to turn the key in the ignition when a white van came driving in her direction. She watched as it passed her and then made a U-turn and parked in front of Marlow House. Sonya smiled. *This is it,* she thought.

"WE REALLY SHOULD HAVE CANCELLED this delivery," Danielle muttered under her breath to Walt. She stood in the hallway with Walt, Lily and Heather as they watched Chris and Ian help the two delivery men bring in the crate holding Macbeth's paintings.

"Can't really keep them in storage indefinitely," Walt reminded her.

"What are we going to do with them?" Danielle asked.

"You could always put them in the library where the originals were," Lily suggested.

"Walt and I already discussed that," Danielle told her.

"I don't really need to look at a life-size painting of myself every day," Walt said.

"Didn't seem to bother you before," Heather reminded him.

"In all fairness to Walt, he couldn't really look into a mirror back then," Lily said in a low voice so the delivery men couldn't hear. "Who knows, maybe without the portrait he would have forgotten what he looked like. And I certainly can understand why he doesn't want Angela's portrait here anymore."

"Angela I can understand," Heather agreed.

"Are you sure you want us to put the crate in the hallway?" Ian asked as they set it down next to the basement door.

"Not unless you want to take them all the way down to the basement," Danielle teased.

"You don't want to keep the paintings in the basement," Lily said. "They'll get all moldy."

Danielle shrugged. "I guess you're right."

The two deliverymen paid little notice to Danielle's lack of enthusiasm over receiving the delivery and went back to the van, returning a few minutes later with the suitcases that had been removed from Clint's rental van after the car accident. They set the suitcases on the crate. A few minutes later, they handed a clipboard to Walt and asked him to sign for the delivery.

After the deliverymen left Marlow House, Walt hobbled to the living room while his friends helped bring the suitcases into the room with him.

"Are you sure you want us to help you go through these?" Lily asked. "I thought that might be something you'd want to do by yourself."

"Why?" Walt asked. "They belonged to Clint, not me. To be honest, I don't want to keep any of it, but I think I should at least sort through it before I donate it to some charity. But if you don't feel comfortable—"

"Oh no, Walt, it isn't that," Lily assured him.

"Let's just hope we don't find anything we don't want to find," Chris said as he opened the first suitcase.

"Like what?" Heather asked.

"Like maybe Clint was a smuggler?" Ian suggested.

"Or a drug runner?" Lily added.

Danielle chuckled. "I don't think we'll find anything illegal. I suspect the police department already inventoried what was in the suitcases. I know they opened the crate and checked on the paintings."

"Well, pooh," Lily grumbled as she opened the second suitcase. "Does that mean all we're going to find is stuff like dirty underwear?"

With reluctant fingers, Chris gingerly lifted a pair of wrinkled

THE GHOST OF SECOND CHANCES

boxers from the suitcase he had just opened. "I suspect so." Chris cringed and dropped the garment on the floor.

NO LONGER PARKED at Beach Drive, Sonya pulled into the parking lot of the Sea Horse Motel. Before getting out of her vehicle, she pulled her cellphone from her purse and made the call.

"Hello?" came a male voice.

"It's me," she said. "Are you sure you can pull this off?"

"Did it arrive?" he asked.

"Yes. They took it in the house. I think you should get it as soon as possible. We can't waste any more time. But you need to do it at night, when just the two of them are there. People have been coming and going from the house all day. Right now there's about six of them there," Sonya explained.

"We'll do it tonight if we can," he promised.

"I guess I have to trust you on this," she said.

"Do you have the money?" he asked.

"You bring the paintings to the designated site, and if they are what you say they are, you'll get your money."

"If you don't have the money, all of it, we aren't leaving the paintings."

"You'll get your money. Just bring me my paintings." Without another word, Sonya ended the call and then tossed her cellphone back in her purse. Looking up into the rearview mirror, she removed her sunglasses and flashed her reflection a smile.

THIRTY

"I don't believe Marlow has amnesia." It wasn't the first time Joe had expressed this opinion. He and Brian sat with the chief in his office.

"I have no reason to believe he's lying," the chief said. They had been discussing his recent visit to Marlow House. "And what would his motive be?"

"To get close to Danielle, for one," Joe said. "He knows she's worth a fortune."

"The man just lost his fiancée," the chief reminded him. "Danielle believes he was genuinely in love with her. Who knows, maybe he simply can't deal with her loss, and this is his subconscious's way of coping."

Good lord, man, you are getting as adept as Danielle at coming up with this BS at a moment's notice, MacDonald told himself.

"I still think he's in some way involved with Bandoni's murder," Brian insisted.

"Again, I can't see a motive," the chief said. "Although, I have to say, I don't believe Laverne's story. I don't believe she killed him."

"At least not for the reason she's giving," Joe said.

"Why do you think she's lying?" Brian asked.

"Her story doesn't make sense," the chief explained. "For one thing, Heather claims she saw a car that matches the description of Chet's stopping in front of Marlow House twice. And Marlow heard someone running out of the house and saw them jump into that car and drive away."

"So he says," Joe grumbled. "I wouldn't be surprised if he lied about hearing someone running out of the house and seeing them get into that car."

"You forget Lily saw the same thing," the chief reminded him.

"Maybe Laverne is covering for her brother," Brian suggested.

MacDonald gave Brian a nod. "That's what I'm thinking."

"Maybe Laverne and Chet are wrapped up in this, but I still think they're working with Marlow. After all, Marlow would need an accomplice, considering he can't get around very well in a cast," Joe insisted.

"And just what is his motive?" the chief again asked.

Joe shook his head. "I don't know. But if we dig a little deeper, I'll bet we'll find it."

A knock at the door interrupted their discussion. The three looked to the open doorway and saw Special Agent Thomas and Special Agent Wilson from the FBI.

Thomas and Wilson were not strangers to the Frederickport lawmen. They had worked in conjunction with them on several cases in the past. In their mid-forties, both agents were clean-cut, had shortly cropped hair, and each wore a tailored dark suit. MacDonald thought all they needed were dark sunglasses and boater hats to fit the description of the stereotypical FBI agent he had seen in the movies.

"Your person in the front said we could just come back," Wilson said as he entered the office followed by Thomas.

The three Frederickport officers stood, each extending hands in greetings. After a brief exchange of handshakes and hellos, the chief asked, "So what do we owe this visit to?"

"We'll let you have some privacy," Brian said before the agents could respond. "Nice seeing you both again."

Special Agent Thomas stopped Brian and Joe from leaving the office by saying, "No. We'd like to talk to all of you. We understand you two were the ones who responded to the Bandoni murder scene."

"Perhaps we should all sit down," the chief suggested, pointing to the two chairs sitting in front of his desk. He then looked up at Joe and asked, "Can you grab two more chairs?"

Joe gave him a nod and left the office for a moment and then returned with two more chairs. When they were all seated, the chief asked, "So what is this about?"

"We were hoping to talk to the woman you have in custody, Laverne Morrison," Thomas explained.

The chief arched his brows. "How does our murder case involve the FBI?"

Wilson reached into his jacket pocket and pulled out a woman's photograph. He set it on the desk and slid it to the chief. "We've had Sonya Kozlov and her boyfriend on our radar for some time now."

The chief picked up the photograph and looked at it. Not recognizing the woman, he shrugged and handed it to Brian, who looked at it and then handed it to Joe.

"Who is she?" Joe asked as he looked at the photograph.

"She's a Russian who has been living in Portland with her boyfriend. She has money—a lot of it. We believe she and her boyfriend, Maurice Beaufort, are behind a number of valuable paintings disappearing. Currently, she's staying at your Sea Horse Motel, and earlier today, she was parked in front of Marlow House, watching the place."

"What does she have to do with Bandoni's murder?" the chief asked.

"When she first arrived in Frederickport, we intercepted one of her phone calls after she visited the local museum here. She was calling Macbeth Bandoni, and by what they were saying…" Thomas paused a moment and pulled a folded piece of paper from his jacket's inside pocket. He stood up and handed it to the chief. "Rather than me explaining the phone call we intercepted, this is its transcript."

The chief accepted the paper and unfolded it. He read it quickly and then asked, "Can I read this out loud for Joe and Brian to hear?"

Thomas nodded. "Certainly."

MACBETH BANDONI: *Why are you calling me? I told you not to call me again. We have nothing to talk about.*

Sonya Kozlov: *If you wonder why you haven't heard anything about the paintings being fake, it's because the expert hasn't seen them yet.*

Macbeth Bandoni: *I don't know what you're talking about. Sonya, please. It's over, and thank you for calling. It just reminds me I need to get another phone.*

Sonya Kozlov: *No. But it's not over, Mac. You can still get the paintings and get the money. Don't you want the money?*

Macbeth Bandoni: *What are you talking about? I explained it. Any day now they're going to come looking for me, and I need to disappear for a while.*

Sonya Kozlov: *No, Mac. You have until May. We've been given a reprieve. You're back in business. We're back in business. And I want my paintings.*

Macbeth Bandoni: *Where are you?*

Sonya Kozlov: *I'm in Frederickport. I'm going to stay until you get my paintings for me. Can I count on you?*

Macbeth Bandoni: *If what you say is true, yes. I'll get back with you.*

AFTER THE CHIEF finished reading the transcript, he folded it up again, stood, and handed it back to Thomas before sitting back down behind his desk.

"The Bonnets," Joe blurted. "That's what they're talking about."

Thomas nodded. "According to the docent in the museum who talked to her, she was there to see the Bonnets."

The chief shook his head and said, "The Bonnets—the originals—are all in Portland, locked up in some museum."

Joe shook his head and said, "That's what they want us to think, Chief. They obviously switched Danielle's paintings with the fake Bonnets Bandoni painted."

"I don't see how," the chief said. "I helped them load the paintings into the crate before it was locked and put into the van."

"How do you know the paintings you put in the crate weren't the originals?" Thomas asked.

Before the chief could answer, Brian said, "Sorry, Chief, even if you did load the reproductions in the crate, it would have been possible for them to switch the paintings that night. From what I know, the crate wasn't loaded into Marlow's van until the next morning, right before they left."

"Don't forget, Chief," Joe reminded him, "Bandoni showed up here and tried to get you to turn over the paintings after the accident. Now we know why he was so intent on getting them—they were the real Bonnets, and if you ask me, Clint Marlow was in on this. He would have had to have been. Bandoni would need someone's help to switch out the portraits, and Marlow is the one who arranged everything."

The chief sat speechless, unable to come up with a believable retort. He knew Clint Marlow had been involved in the attempted theft, and he knew the paintings had been switched. Of course, they had been switched back, Walt Marlow had seen to that.

"When we leave here, we plan to interview Walt Marlow. In fact…" Wilson glanced at his watch. "Our art expert should be here within the hour."

"Art expert?" the chief asked.

"Like Joe and Brian, we believe Bandoni switched the paintings before he left Marlow House. Our art expert will be able to prove that. The only question, was Marlow involved?" Wilson asked. "Not only in the art theft, but the murder."

"Of course he was," Joe said.

"I agree," Brian chimed in.

"You said something about wanting to talk to Laverne Morrison?" the chief asked.

THEY BROUGHT Laverne into the interrogation room first and left her there. She sat alone at the table, her hands folded on the tabletop in front of her as her fingers fidgeted. Watching her from the other room through the two-way mirror were the Chief, Brian, Joe and Special Agent Wilson.

"Who are you?" Laverne asked when Thomas entered the room and closed the door behind him.

"Hello, Ms. Morrison. I'm Special Agent Thomas, with the FBI."

"FBI?" she squeaked.

He took a seat across from her at the table and said, "I understand you have confessed to the murder of Macbeth Bandoni."

"What does this have to do with the FBI?"

"What do you know of Bandoni dealing in stolen art?"

Laverne frowned. "I know Mac was an artist. I don't know anything about stolen art."

"Do you know what his relationship was with Clint Marlow?" he asked.

She shrugged. "Just what I've heard around town."

"Which is?"

"Mr. Marlow hired him to reproduce some paintings at Marlow House," she said.

"Have you ever met Clint Marlow?"

She shook her head. "No."

"Are you sure? Wasn't he at Marlow House when you shot Bandoni?"

Laverne shrugged. "I don't know. I didn't see him."

"Where were you when you shot Bandoni?"

"I don't want to talk about this." She looked down. "I want to go now. I already confessed. I just want to go back to my cell."

"Since you already confessed to the crime, what harm would it do to talk to me about what happened?" he asked gently. "I heard Bandoni's body was found in the library. Were you two looking for the paintings there?"

Staring down at her folded hands, she refused to look up. "I don't know anything about paintings."

"Did you go to the library because that's where they used to be displayed?" he asked.

"That's where I found him. I don't know what he was looking for. But when he saw I was there, he got upset with me. I was afraid. I didn't mean to shoot him. It was an accident."

In the next room, Wilson looked at the chief and said, "I think you're right. She didn't kill him."

THIRTY-ONE

It wasn't the first time Chet had slept on the beach. He stared up at the sky, trying to determine the time by the sun's position. If he hadn't dropped his watch and broken it—or left his cellphone in his car, he wouldn't be playing this guessing game—one he wasn't very good at.

Taking a deep breath, he took in the salty cool scent and closed his eyes, listening to the waves break along the shoreline. He wasn't exactly sure where he was; there was no one else on the beach with him. When he had woken up, his brain was muddled. It must have been all that booze he'd had to drink the night before. At least, he assumed it was the night before. He wasn't exactly sure.

He needed to find where he had parked his car, but first, he just wanted to rest a little longer and clear his head. Everything was jumbled up, and it felt as if he had been crashed on the beach for hours, yet sleep eluded him.

With his eyes still closed, Chet tried to recall his last memory. He and Angelo had been throwing back some beers when Mac asked them for a lift somewhere because his car wasn't working, and Angelo's other two brothers had taken off in their car. Chet had plenty of reasons to hate Mac, but there was fifty bucks in it for him. Chet couldn't remember much after that. But he had experienced blackouts before when drinking, so he wasn't overly concerned. He was just grateful he didn't have a massive hangover. However, he did wonder why he was on the beach.

While trying to piece together the fragments of the last day, Chet heard a loud sniffing sound. Abruptly opening his eyes, he found himself looking into the muzzle of a drooling Rottweiler. The dog's snout was only inches away from his nose.

Startled, Chet shouted, "Oh crap!" at the same time the dog started barking. Jumping up in fear, Chet resisted the temptation to start running, certain the dog would be on his back before he took his first step. At the moment the dog was not lunging, yet he stood his ground, barking incessantly. Chet almost felt as if the dog was asking him what he was doing here on the beach, but that was an insane thought, so he put it aside and instead wondered if perhaps animals were after him. First Danielle's cat had sunk his claws into his thighs, and now this dog appeared out of nowhere in a most unfriendly manner.

"Rex, come!" Chet heard a woman shout. He glanced in the direction of the shout and spied a woman holding a leash some distance away.

The dog hesitated a moment and then turned abruptly and ran to his human.

Regaining his composure, Chet stared at the woman now looking in his direction, waiting for her dog to reach her.

"You need to keep that animal on a leash!" he shouted angrily.

She glared and offered no apology. However, when the dog reached her, she did clip on the leash before heading off in the opposite direction.

"I didn't need that," Chet grumbled. He stood there a moment and watched as the woman and dog disappeared from sight. Alone again on the beach, he took a deep breath and considered what to do next.

"I might as well forget about catching a little more sleep. I better figure out where I parked my damn car," Chet grumbled as he started down the beach in the opposite direction from where the woman and dog had gone.

Chet walked along the shore for a while, trying to get his bearings, when he started recognizing the landmarks. He used to come down here when he was in high school. Just up ahead, beyond the massive rocks jetting out beyond the breakers, was a path leading to one of the beach parking lots. He was fairly certain that was where he would find his car.

Before making his way up to the pathway, something in the mountain-like rocks beyond the breakers caught his eye. Turning to look out to the ocean, Chet froze.

"My car!' he shouted, running toward the water. He stopped just where the wave had rolled over the sand before retreating back to the sea.

"No!" He stomped his foot. Out in the water, crashing repeatedly against one of the enormous rocks, was his car, only its roof visible, while the rest was submerged under water. He knew all of his worldly belongings were shoved in the car's trunk.

Flopping down on the sand, Chet buried his face in his arms as they rested against his bent knees. He groaned and cursed his bad luck. However, he knew luck had nothing to do with it. It was probably his stupidity. Lifting his head, he looked back out to his floundering vehicle.

As teenagers, they had sometimes played a game of chicken. Late at night after getting drunk, they would drive their cars down on the beach and race toward the ocean. The winner was the one who drove the farthest. Of course, sometimes the winner would also be the loser because that person's car would be swept out to sea.

Chet remembered that before Mac asked for a ride, Angelo had suggested they play the game again when his brothers returned. *Is that what happened?* he wondered. After dropping Mac off, had they met Angelo's brothers down at the beach and decided to act like stupid teenagers?

He stood up abruptly and dusted off his jeans. "That damn Angelo, he just left me here!"

Turning from the ocean, Chet stomped up to the walkway. He didn't have his cellphone on him, so he couldn't call anyone to pick him up. Without checking, he knew he didn't have any money in his wallet. He would do the only thing he could, he would walk to Angelo's house and make him and his brothers help him get his car before it was swept out to sea.

When Chet finally reached the Bandoni house, he congratulated himself for not being out of breath. Chet wasn't much of a walker, but he credited his lack of exhaustion to his adrenaline, fueled by his anger at Angelo for ditching him after their night of drinking had gone off the rails. Unfortunately, there didn't seem to be anyone at the Bandoni house. The only car parked in the driveway was Mac's, and nothing was parked in the garage.

Chet camped out in the front yard for a while, waiting for one of the brothers to come home. Yet thinking of his car still bobbing around out there like a piece of trash tossed in the ocean, he grew antsy and realized the only thing left to do was to seek help from his sister. Chet stood up and started for the sidewalk. He then noticed a car parked two doors down with someone sitting in the driver's seat. Whoever it was, they seemed to be watching the Bandoni house. Picking up his step, he moved quickly down the sidewalk in the opposite direction of the parked car while glancing over his shoulder. Whoever was staking out the house didn't seem interested in him.

He had no intention of walking all the way to Frederickport. All he had to do was borrow a phone, call his sister, and wait for her to arrange for someone to pull his car out of the ocean and take them both back to her house. Not for a moment did Chet doubt Laverne would help him in spite of the fact she had just locked him out of her house.

Making his way back toward the beach, Chet spied two young women walking in his direction. With a grin, he sprinted up to them.

"Excuse me," he began.

The two women ignored him and continued walking.

With a frown, Chet turned around and looked at the women, who had just walked past him.

"I said excuse me!" he shouted.

Neither woman responded.

Cursing under his breath and calling the women an unflattering name, he spied an older man just coming out of a gift shop.

"Excuse me, sir," Chet called out as he ran up to the man.

Like the women before him, the man refused to acknowledge Chet.

Not ready to give up, Chet approached a half a dozen more people—some young, some old—asking to make a call from their cellphone. They all ignored him.

"I never realized how rude people are here!" he grumbled. Frustrated, he decided to hitchhike back to Frederickport.

Standing along the roadside, he stuck out his right thumb. He wondered briefly about Oregon hitchhiking laws. He hadn't lived in the state for years, but he knew in some places it was frowned on and sometimes against the law. But seeing he had no other choice, he tried flagging down a ride while slowly making his way toward Frederickport. Cars whizzed by without slowing.

Chet continued to walk backwards and hitchhike. Eventually he made it out of Astoria. So far, not a single car had even slowed down. Realizing he was wasting precious time and fearing his car would be gone when he returned, he decided to take a more assertive approach to hitchhiking.

No longer standing out of the way of incoming traffic, he boldly stood along the edge of the highway, his right thumb shoved out so far that a car would have to swerve to avoid hitting it. Which didn't happen. The next car that sped past Chet looked as if it were aiming at his thumb. If Chet hadn't made a last-minute jump to the side of the highway, he was certain he would have been plowed down by the vehicle.

Deciding assertive hitchhiking was going to get him killed, Chet picked up his step and walked faster, out of the way of traffic, while extending a thumb.

Cursing the world, Chet spied a scenic pullout up ahead. Parked there was a tour bus he recognized. It was from Frederickport, and considering the direction it was headed, it was on its way back to Frederickport.

Breaking into a jog, he headed toward the bus. When he reached it, he saw the driver was inside, the door open. Its passengers were all outside, enjoying the scenic view while the driver waited patiently, reading something on his cellphone. Doing a quick head count, Chet figured there were plenty of empty seats on the bus.

Chet considered asking the driver if he could get a lift back to Frederickport, but his luck so far had been crappy; he didn't hold out any hope for the driver's generosity. He then realized the driver hadn't seen him walk up.

When his passengers start to get back onto the bus, will he even notice one more person? Chet wondered.

Ten minutes later, as passengers started lining up to get back onto the bus, Chet managed to blend into the small crowd. No one seemed to notice as he walked onto the bus with the rest of the passengers. He headed to the rear of the vehicle and sat down in a seat next to the window.

THE GHOST OF SECOND CHANCES

Confident he was finally on his way to his sister's house, he took a deep breath and leaned back in the bench seat and looked out the window, waiting for the bus to be on its way.

"You want to sit by the window this time?" a woman's voice asked.

Chet glanced over to the aisle and found two elderly people eyeing his seat.

"If you don't mind, I'd like to sit by the window," the man said.

"Are you sure?"

"Yes. Go ahead, you take it," the woman urged, pointing to Chet.

"Excuse me, I'm already sitting here," Chet told them.

Ignoring Chet, the man moved toward the window seat and started to sit down.

Chet did not scream because the man sat on his lap. He screamed because the man sat through his lap—it was as if Chet was not even there. But he was.

THIRTY-TWO

Danielle felt a bit like a voyeur. Walt's long dark lashes fluttered, his eyes closed in sleep. With each breath his chest raised, only to lower again, continuing the cycle. She had never seen him like this before. Life coursed through Walt, and she couldn't stop watching him as he napped on the library sofa. While he looked practically identical to the illusion of the man his spirit had created, there was something different, and it wasn't the fact he was using Clint's body. It was the healthy glow of his complexion—something vibrant in his carriage. She resisted the temptation to brush his hair from his forehead, while also surprised his hair had grown out enough since the accident to make that actually possible.

She wanted to drop kisses on his forehead and crawl up on the sofa with him and just snuggle. Danielle missed their evenings when he had joined her in bed for their nightly chats. Of course, they had never snuggled. That was impossible to do without a body. But now…now he had a body and…

Danielle blushed at the thoughts racing through her mind. Sitting in the chair across from the sofa, she opened the book on her lap and told herself to stop gawking at Walt.

A few minutes later her cellphone rang, and she cursed herself for not turning off the ringer. Snatching the phone off the table next to her, she stood up to leave the room to answer the call and then heard Walt say, "You don't have to leave the room. I'm awake."

THE GHOST OF SECOND CHANCES

Flashing an apologetic smile to Walt, Danielle sat back down on the chair and answered the phone. Across from her, on the sofa, Walt stretched groggily and sat up, placing his feet on the floor. He listened to her side of the conversation.

"That was the chief," Danielle said when she got off the phone.

"I sort of figured that." Walt yawned and stretched again.

"We're going to have company in a few minutes."

"I hope they're bringing food. I'm starved," Walt said with a mischievous grin.

"I seriously doubt they're going to bring food. It's Agents Thomas and Wilson."

Walt frowned at Danielle. "The G-men?"

Danielle nodded. "They want to question you about Macbeth. The chief asked if he could call and tell me to expect them, and they said okay. But they told him they would appreciate it if I didn't tell you they were coming."

Walt made a tsk-tsk sound and said, "Shame on you."

"To be fair, they asked me not to say anything to Clint. And I didn't." She grinned. Standing back up, she said, "You want me to get you something to eat?"

"Do I have time?"

Danielle shrugged. "What do you care? You don't even know they're coming."

"You're right!" Walt beamed. "Any more of that chocolate cake?"

"You already ate it all. You know, Walt, I had no idea you had such a big appetite. You're always hungry!"

"Don't blame me. A person gets hungry after ninety years without eating. Anyway, I like your cooking. I don't remember being this hungry in the hospital."

"Thanks, but I suspect even mediocre cooking looks good after hospital food—not to mention that ninety-year thing. If you just want a snack, how about a slice of carrot cake? I froze half of the last one I baked, and it'll only take a minute in the microwave to thaw out."

WALT WAS JUST FINISHING up the piece of carrot cake Danielle had prepared for him when the FBI agents arrived. He sat in the library, the leg with the cast propped up on the coffee table.

"Walt, there is someone here who would like to talk to you," Danielle said as she led Special Agent Wilson and Special Agent Thomas into the room.

Walt glanced up from the sofa at the men and smiled. "I hope you don't mind if I don't stand up."

Thomas started to pull his ID from his jacket's inside pocket to introduce himself to Walt. But before either agent or Danielle could make any introductions, Walt asked, "Do I know you?"

"I don't believe you do," Danielle told him.

Thomas and Wilson then showed Walt their IDs while making their formal introductions. After they were finished, Wilson asked, "Just how well did you know Macbeth Bandoni?"

Walt set the empty plate he had been holding, now covered with cake crumbs and a used fork, onto the table next to his foot. "I'm not sure if he was simply a casual business acquaintance or a close friend. You see, gentlemen, I was recently in a car accident and now have amnesia. So unfortunately, I can't remember anything prior to the accident."

"That's rather convenient," Wilson sneered.

Walt's smile vanished, and he narrowed his eyes, glowering at the agent. "It wasn't convenient for the young lady who died in that accident."

"I understand she was your fiancée," Thomas said.

Walt turned to Thomas and nodded. In a serious tone he said, "That's what I've been told. Her father visited me in the hospital. He seemed like a very nice man and was devastated to lose his only daughter. One couldn't help but feel sorry for the man. But I simply don't remember anything about her. Of course, that doesn't mean I can't appreciate the fact a young woman lost her life. It's tragic, nothing convenient about it, and to make light of that is reprehensible, in my opinion. Life is precious. I'm quite grateful for my second chance at life."

"Mr. Marlow, if you committed a crime prior to your accident, do you believe you won't be held accountable as long as the world believes you have amnesia?" Wilson asked.

Walt looked Wilson in the eyes. "Special Agent Wilson, what crime do you believe I have committed?"

"There seems to be an inordinate amount of attention being paid to the paintings you had commissioned," Wilson noted.

Walt arched his brows. "Has there?"

"We understand the paintings are here," Thomas said, glancing from Walt to Danielle.

"Yes, they arrived earlier today. They've been in storage. After the accident, the police put them there while Walt was in the hospital."

"What do you plan to do with those paintings now?" Wilson asked Walt.

"I'm not really sure. When Mr. Bandoni called to see how I was, I told him he could have the paintings. After all, he painted them."

"You were planning to give them to Bandoni?" Wilson asked.

Walt smiled at Wilson. "As I have told you both, I really don't remember anything prior to my accident. But what I do know, I no longer have a home, nowhere to display the paintings, and quite frankly, I don't really want them. Not sure why I ever did. I have asked Danielle if she would like them, since she sold hers to the museum. Which I can't say I blame her, considering what they're worth."

"But now Bandoni is dead; then I suppose you'll just have to keep them," Wilson sneered.

Walt's smile brightened. "Unless you want them, Special Agent Wilson. Would you like a couple of life-size portraits?"

"We would like your permission to inspect them," Thomas said.

"Inspect them?" Walt asked.

Thomas glanced at his watch. "There's an art expert who should be arriving any minute now. We believe the portraits you have may in fact be the originals, not the reproductions painted by Bandoni."

"How in the world can that be?" Danielle asked. "The chief himself helped load the reproductions in the crate, and I saw it locked and later put into the van before the accident."

"I'm not sure how he did it, exactly. But it's what we suspect," Wilson said.

"Then by all means, have your art expert look at my paintings," Walt said.

"You have no objections?" Wilson asked.

Walt shrugged. "Not sure why I would."

The agents asked Walt a few more questions, but each time he reminded them of his loss of memory. Danielle then asked if they would like something to drink while they waited for the art expert to arrive.

Walt sat alone with the agents while Danielle went to prepare a tray of iced tea.

"What do you think of this house?" Walt asked impulsively.

Thomas and Wilson exchanged glances and shrugged. "It's a house," Wilson muttered.

"When I was in the hospital, my roommate asked me about my stay here—of course, I didn't remember anything. He told me I shouldn't return, insisted the place was haunted."

"Well...have you seen any ghosts?" Thomas asked.

Walt shrugged. "Only two or three."

"Funny," Wilson grumbled.

"Do you believe in ghosts, Agent Wilson?" Walt asked.

"I don't want to talk about ghosts," Wilson snapped.

"Really? I find the subject fascinating." Walt beamed. "Have you ever been at Marlow House before today?"

Thomas glanced at Wilson and then back to Walt. "Yes, a few times."

"Ever smell that cigar? Joanne the housekeeper told me about it. Says it comes and goes. I haven't noticed it yet. Well, at least, not since the accident." Walt laughed.

"What are you talking about?" Danielle asked as she walked into the room carrying a tray with glasses of iced tea and a plate of cookies.

"Your guest was wondering if your house is haunted," Wilson grumbled.

Danielle glanced at Walt and arched her brows in a silent question. He returned with a shrug and guilty smile.

"I know some people say this place is haunted. But if it is, I promise we only have friendly ghosts." Danielle set the tray on the table after Walt put both of his feet on the floor.

She picked up two glasses of tea from the tray and started handing them to the agents when Walt said, "Friendly and mischievous." He stared across the room at the bookshelf, remembering when Marlow House had been visited by a more than mischievous ghost who had sent books flying across the room. He had been quite angry at the time, annoyed at the harsh treatment of his precious books. But he couldn't help but think about how he himself had

THE GHOST OF SECOND CHANCES

once harnessed his energy as a spirit. Focusing his attention on the books, he imagined what it might have once felt like as a spirit to send the books flying.

In the next moment—to the utter surprise of everyone in the room, including Walt—a first edition Mark Twain came flying off the shelf. The glass Wilson had just accepted from Danielle slipped from his fingers, fell to the hardwood floor, and shattered into countless pieces.

"WHAT IN THE world just happened a few minutes ago?" Danielle asked Walt after the art expert had arrived and was now in the hallway removing the paintings from the crate while she and Walt remained in the library alone.

"I have absolutely no idea," Walt stammered.

"I didn't see any ghosts around," Danielle said.

"I don't think there was." Walt cringed. "I think I did that."

"How could you do that? You aren't a ghost anymore!"

"All I know, I was focusing on the bookshelf, imagining how I would have done it when I was still a spirit—and then—well, then the book flew off the shelf."

"I'm not sure what surprises me more, the fact the book flew off the shelf, or that you would throw a first edition Mark Twain on the floor!"

"It's not like I actually thought it would work," Walt snapped.

"I WOULD HAVE STAKED my career on those paintings being the originals," Wilson grumbled when he and Thomas climbed back into their vehicle several hours later. Once in the car, Wilson angrily slammed the door shut and put on his seatbelt.

"Are we just going to ignore that other thing?" Thomas asked as he fastened his seatbelt.

"I've thought a lot about Marlow House since the last time we were here," Wilson said. "She has that house rigged. I know it. That's the only logical explanation. It's nothing more than a promotional stunt. A lot of people want to stay in a haunted house, and we both know she once owned a marketing firm. She knows what she's doing. I just don't appreciate being the butt of her joke."

"I have to say, you looked as if you had seen a ghost in there when that book went flying." Thomas chuckled.

"You were a few shades lighter yourself." Wilson shoved the key into the ignition.

Ignoring Wilson's comment, Thomas shifted the conversation back to their reason for coming to Marlow House. "We don't really have anything on Marlow. He obviously didn't switch the portraits, so he wasn't trying to steal the originals."

"Doesn't mean he didn't kill Bandoni," Wilson said as he turned on the engine.

THIRTY-THREE

Three police officers stood on the shore and watched as the tow truck pulled the gray sedan from the beach to the nearby road, seawater spilling from its hull. The dead body had already been removed from the vehicle and loaded into the medical van, while other police and fire vehicles parked nearby on the beach. Curious onlookers stood off in the distance, speculating on how the car had gotten into the ocean.

A police officer sprinted from one of the police cars parked by the van to the three officers watching from the shoreline. When he reached them, slightly out of breath, he said, directing his words to his supervisor, "You're right. That ID matches up with one of the guys they've been looking for in Frederickport."

"We'd better give MacDonald a call," the supervisor said.

POLICE CHIEF MACDONALD called his babysitter up to let her know he would be running late and could she please give his sons dinner. It was already prepared and in the slow cooker. Since his kidnapping, he had begun relying less and less on his sister to help with the boys. They seemed happier when able to stay home after school with a babysitter instead of going to their aunt and uncle's house until their father came home.

He tried not to stay after hours at work, yet today it was unavoidable. He needed to tell Laverne about her brother, and he didn't feel right leaving that task to one of his people.

Instead of talking to Laverne in the interrogation room, the chief had someone bring her to his office.

"What's this about?" she asked when the female officer showed her in.

Instead of answering the question, he pointed to one of the chairs facing his desk and asked her to sit down. When she reluctantly complied, he looked up at the officer and said, "Please leave us alone, and close the door. But wait in the hall in case we need you."

Without a word, she nodded at the chief and then did as he instructed.

"What's going on?" Laverne asked when she and the chief were alone.

"I'm very sorry to have to tell you this, Laverne. But I'm afraid there has been an accident. It's your brother."

"Chet? Is he okay?"

"I'm sorry. He's dead."

Laverne let out a gasp, her eyes wide as she stared at the chief, her hands now over her mouth. She shook her head in denial. "No, that can't be. I just talked to him today."

The chief frowned. "That's impossible."

Vigorously shaking her head, she said, "No. He can't be dead."

"I'm sorry, but it's Chet. They matched his fingerprints. Why did you say you talked to him today?"

Laverne looked down guiltily and wiped away the tears now sliding down her face. "Because I talked to him on the phone."

"Laverne, you couldn't have talked to your brother today. According to the coroner, he's been dead for over twenty-four hours."

Laverne's head snapped up, her gaze meeting the chief's. "That's impossible. I called Chet's cellphone after I left here the first time. He answered. We talked."

"I don't know who answered your brother's phone. But it wasn't Chet."

Speechless, Laverne stared at the chief.

"Laverne, did it sound like your brother?"

Staring blankly, Laverne blinked several times. "Well, it was kind of hard to hear him. He said he had to whisper. He sounded afraid, like he was hiding."

"Afraid of what? Who was he hiding from?"

Laverne shrugged. "He didn't say." She blinked again and asked, "Are you sure it was Chet they found?"

The chief nodded.

"Where...how?"

"They found his car in the ocean, about twenty feet from shore; it was stuck on some rocks. He was inside. The coroner hasn't yet determined the cause of death, but by the condition of the body, he believes he has been dead for at least twenty-four hours—if not more."

Looking downward, Laverne closed her eyes and tried processing what she had just learned. Finally, she looked up at the chief and said, "He told me he killed Mac. That's why I confessed. But if it wasn't Chet I talked to, then Chet didn't kill him."

"Why would you confess to a murder that you believed your brother committed?" he asked.

Once again, her tears began to fall. "Because I was supposed to protect Chet. He's my little brother. It's my fault that Chet has had such a rough time of it."

"Why is it your fault?" he asked.

"It's my fault he's dead. I shouldn't have thrown him out." Burying her face in her hands, she began to sob.

"WHAT ARE YOU GOING TO DO?" Brian asked the chief. They stood in the hallway while the female officer sat in the chief's office with Laverne, trying to comfort her.

"I never thought Laverne killed Bandoni," the chief said. "I was hoping after a few nights here, she would come to her senses and tell us what was really going on."

"Are you going to let her go?" Brian asked.

"I don't see how I can keep her locked up. Without her confession, we could never make the charges stick, not to mention her confession was full of holes. But someone obviously wanted her to believe her brother was the shooter."

"Maybe he was," Brian suggested.

The chief, who had been watching the door to his office, turned to Brian. "Why do you say that?"

"Just because Chet was already dead when someone took that phone call doesn't mean he was dead when Bandoni was murdered. And Chet's car matches the description of the vehicle Heather and Lily saw in front of Marlow House."

"True." The chief let out a sigh.

"Laverne might have wanted to protect her brother, but she thought that caller was him. Which leads me to believe she felt Chet had a motive for the murder and was capable of pulling the trigger."

"Chet was staying with the cousins, and now they've all disappeared. Did one of them pretend to be Chet?" the chief speculated. "And why? What do they know?"

"If one of the cousins knew Chet killed him, why call his sister and tell her? Why not call us?"

"For one thing, she called Chet's phone. They didn't call her," the chief reminded him. "I'd like to know a little more about the relationship between Macbeth and his cousins."

LESLIE HAD ALREADY GONE home for the day, and Adam Nichols had stayed late because a renter was stopping by for a key. There had been a time when more than just Leslie had worked with him at the property rental office. Yet over the last two years, they had begun leaving. It was nothing personal. One had decided to relocate to another state, another had a career change, and another had married and then, shortly thereafter, gotten pregnant and decided to stay home. Instead of replacing those who had left, Adam had decided to streamline his business. Of course, if Leslie decided to bail, he would need to start recruiting.

The renter had already come and gone. Instead of locking up and going home, Adam sat at his desk, staring at his computer monitor. It wasn't that he particularly missed visiting those websites that made other people blush. But recently, just about every time he tried surfing one of the websites, his electricity went out. And it didn't just happen on his office computer, it happened on his computer at home. While it didn't happen every time, it happened enough to freak him out.

Adam wanted to get to the bottom of the mystery, but it wasn't exactly something he felt comfortable discussing with anyone. Bill Jones had tried to figure out what was happening at the office yet couldn't find the source of the problem. Of course, Adam never mentioned to Bill that the only time this happened was when he went to one of *those* websites.

Instead of giving it another try, Adam turned off his computer and stood up from his desk. When he walked out of his office a few moments later, he found Police Chief MacDonald walking in the front door.

"Surprised to find you still here," the chief greeted Adam.

"Evening, Chief. I was just getting ready to go home. What can I do for you?"

"Do you have a little time? I'd like to talk to you. Maybe we can run over to Lucy's Diner and grab some dinner?"

LESS THAN FIFTEEN MINUTES LATER, Adam sat with the chief at Lucy's Diner.

Menu in hand, Adam shook his head and said, "Chet's dead? Wow. He was just in my office the other day, looking for a place to stay."

"His sister's taking it kind of rough. When I took her home, I got one of her neighbors to sit with her."

Adam tossed the menu on the table and let out a deep sigh. "Those two always had an odd relationship. I always thought of Laverne as more a mother figure than a sister to Chet. She practically raised him, even when their parents were alive."

"Why was that?" the chief asked.

"I don't remember what was wrong with them exactly. I just know they were both pretty sick. Each had some sort of debilitating disease, MS or ALS, something like that."

"They had the same disease?" the chief asked.

Adam shook his head. "No. They each had a different disease. I remember my mother once making a crack about the Morrisons and their lousy luck. I mean, it's tragic enough when a disease like that hits a family, but when both parents are each hit with a different one, what are the odds of that? When I was in high school and would go over to Chet's house, his parents were always in bed."

"Did they have any outside help?"

Adam shrugged. "I don't think so. I'm pretty sure Laverne did most of the cooking and cleaning. She was the one who would get on Chet's butt if he didn't finish his homework."

"Must have been rough on her."

"Was Chet's death an accident, or is this another murder?" Adam asked.

Before the chief could respond, the server came and took their orders. After she left, Adam asked the question again.

"At the moment it looks as if he drove off the highway into the ocean. There were empty beer cans in the backseat. But we'll know more when we get the autopsy back."

"Where exactly did they find his car?" Adam asked.

After the chief told him, Adam sat back in the chair, a quizzical expression furrowing his brow.

"What is it?" MacDonald asked.

"When we were in high school, the Bandoni brothers and Chet liked to play chicken in that area. I went once, but I swore, never again."

"Chicken?"

Adam nodded. "They'd drive down to the beach, line their cars up like a drag race, and then head to the ocean. The one who drove the farthest without stopping was the winner."

"Sounds kind of stupid...and dangerous."

"Ya think?" Adam snorted. "When I was there, the youngest cousin—can't remember his name—won the game and about lost his car. It took all of us to get it out of the water. I don't even want to think about what that seawater did to the undercarriage of those vehicles. But then, Chet and those boys weren't the brightest bulbs."

"The Bandoni brothers, what was their relationship to their cousin Mac?"

Adam considered the question a moment and then shrugged. "I only saw Mac a couple of times. That was when Laverne was dating him. To be honest, I think that was the only boy she ever dated back then. Never had time for a social life. Pretty sure she met him through Chet and his friendship with the cousins."

"Do you know what the relationship between the brothers and Mac was?"

"What comes to mind, hero worship."

The chief frowned. "Hero worship?"

Adam nodded. "I used to find it a little odd. I mean, Mac was this short skinny guy, while his cousins, well, they were good-size boys even back then. I think the only reason they didn't play football is because they'd gotten into fights in town and were each kicked off the team. But they idolized that older cousin of theirs. Talked about how he traveled the world. How smart and talented he was."

"Can you think of any reason Chet would want to kill Mac?" the chief asked.

Adam arched his brow. "Chet? Not really. But to be honest, until recently, I hadn't really seen him in years. I have no idea what's been going on with him."

THIRTY-FOUR

It was late Monday evening, and they had finished dinner hours ago. Walt and Danielle sat in the parlor, contemplating turning in for the night.

"I still can't believe Chet's dead," Danielle mused.

"The man was annoying, but it would be a little harsh to wish him dead. The chief doesn't know if it was foul play?"

Danielle shrugged. "I guess not. I assume they'll know more when the autopsy is finished. But according to the chief, Chet is one of the suspects for Macbeth's murder. While I didn't have much use for him, I really didn't see him as a killer."

"If he shows up here, maybe he'll tell us what happened."

Danielle cringed. "Oh, please, Walt, don't even suggest that! I didn't want Chet hanging around when he was alive; I can't even imagine how annoying he would be as a ghost!"

"Tsk-tsk, Danielle. Speaking ill of the dead?" Walt teased.

"You know what I mean. I'm sorry he's dead. But that doesn't mean I'd welcome his ghost."

"Even if he answers some questions?"

Danielle stood up. "Even then. Some things just aren't worth the trouble knowing. And with that, I think I'm calling it a night."

THIRTY MINUTES later Danielle was upstairs in her bathroom, just getting out of the shower. After drying off, she dressed in a pair of plaid pajama bottoms and a pink T-shirt. Sitting on the side of her bed, she combed out her damp hair and thought of Joanne's phone call earlier that evening. She was coming back to work in a couple of days. Danielle had enjoyed having some alone time with Walt and regretted it was about to end.

Standing up, Danielle walked to her dressing table and tossed her brush in one of its drawers. She looked up in the mirror at her reflection.

"It's not like Joanne will be here twenty-four seven," she reminded herself.

Turning to her bed, she paused a moment and just looked at it.

"I miss our evening chats in bed," Danielle mused. She then glanced at her closed door. "Maybe Walt can't make it up here, but I could always go down there. I mean, really, considering all the times he just barged into my room, aren't I entitled?"

Biting her lower lip while considering going back downstairs, she said, "It will all be very respectable. The poor man is wearing a cast."

Looking back to the bed, she realized she was no longer sleepy —and no longer ready to end the day.

SINCE SAYING GOODNIGHT TO DANIELLE, Walt had taken his shower and had slipped on a pair of boxers and a T-shirt. He had left his bedroom door open for Max. But so far, the cat had not shown up.

Walt was just hobbling to bed when he heard a noise coming from the open doorway. With a crutch tucked under each arm, he made his way from the bedroom into the hall. At first, he thought the sound might be Max, who sometimes enjoyed a late-night romp through the house. But when he reached the middle of the hallway, there was no cat, and the source of the sound confused him. It came both from his right—and his left.

The hallway, virtually dark save for the glow from the random nightlights in various electrical sockets along the floorboard, gave no clue as to the source of the sound. Walt heard it again and looked to the front door. A rattling noise came from that direction. But then, behind him, he heard a familiar voice ask, "Walt, what are you doing out here?"

Danielle's unexpected question sent him spinning in her direction, and he almost stumbled, yet with her help, he managed to keep upright.

"Oh, I'm sorry, Walt," Danielle said with a giggle, still holding onto him. "I didn't mean to startle you."

In the next moment it was Danielle who was startled when the front door crashed open, and three large figures quickly entered the house. Without thinking, Danielle let out a gasp, calling attention to herself and Walt.

"Get them!" one of the men shouted.

THE THREE MEN each wore ski masks, concealing their faces, yet both Danielle and Walt had no doubt who they were, considering their size. The intruders had turned on the hall lights while closing all the doors leading to any rooms that faced the street. They obviously did not want any of the neighbors to see what was going on.

One of the three men had pulled two dining room chairs into the hallway, about fifteen feet from where the crate sat near the basement door. The man told Walt to sit in one and Danielle to sit in the other. Another man pulled out a rope and used it to secure the pair to their respective chairs. So far, the intruders had not threatened them with guns or knives. Their size and number were intimidating enough for a man in a cast and a petite woman.

The two prisoners watched as the three men hovered over the crate, trying to figure out how to get it open.

Grateful the intruders hadn't gagged them, Walt asked in a whisper, "Is the crate locked?"

Danielle, whose eyes were on the men, nodded. "We should have just told Wilson and Thomas not to bother relocking it."

"Why don't they just carry the crate out?" Walt asked.

"They probably want to make sure the paintings are there. And maybe they don't have room in their car?" she suggested.

One of the men looked in their direction and shouted, "Where's the key?"

"It's in the parlor, on the desk," Danielle called back.

"Parlor? You have a sissy parlor?" the man asked. The other two men started to laugh.

Danielle nodded in the direction of the closed parlor door. The man went to retrieve the key and returned a moment later. Danielle and Walt watched as he unlocked the crate. With the help of his accomplices, they unloaded the enormous oil paintings and set them by the front door.

One of the men looked to Danielle and Walt and said, "I'm pretty sure they'll fit in here."

Another one glanced down at the crate and said, "Having a lock means we don't have to nail the thing shut." The three men laughed.

"Wait!" Danielle shouted, "You can't lock us in there. We won't fit."

"We'll make you fit," the man told her as the three lumbered ominously in their direction.

"Hold on!" Walt shouted. "Just take the paintings and leave. You can have them. There's no reason to put us in there. We're tied up."

The three men stopped, and for a brief moment, Walt thought they were going to take the suggestion, when the men started laughing again.

"Seriously, Clint, you really think we're going to let you get away with trying to double-cross our cousin?"

"I don't know what you're talking about," Walt told them.

"I don't know who you are," Danielle lied. "But Clint has amnesia. He doesn't remember anything prior to the car accident."

"Even if that is true, which I don't believe for a minute, once he gets his memory back, he'll know who we are, and we can't let that happen. I figure once we lock you in that crate together and get the paintings loaded, we can start a nice little bonfire in here. I don't think it'll take long for this old wooden house to go up like kindling."

"You intend to kill us?" Danielle shrieked.

One of the men said, "Now you're catching on."

"Why? You have masks on. We don't even know who you are," Danielle lied.

"The masks are for your neighbors in case they see us leaving."

The three men stood facing their intended victims, their back to the now empty wooden crate. Instead of pleading for his or Danielle's life, Walt focused all his attention on the crate. In the next moment, the lid slammed shut. The three men jumped in surprise. When they turned and saw what had happened, they laughed nervously, but turned back to Walt and Danielle, determined to carry out their deadly plan.

They had only taken one step when the sound of something heavy sliding across the wooden floor distracted them. Turning back in the direction of the crate, the men were horrified to find it sliding across the floor toward them, picking up speed as it moved along.

Unable to fully comprehend what was happening, the men stood frozen but then at the last moment tried to jump out of the way of the incoming missile. Unfortunately for them, they didn't move fast enough and in the next moment were plowed down like bowling ball pins, sending them each flying in opposite directions.

The crate stopped moving. A few moments later the would-be killers were just getting back on their feet when the front door flew open, and men wearing FBI bulletproof vests came streaming into the house, their guns drawn. One of the men was Special Agent Wilson, and another was his partner, Special Agent Thomas. Wilson holstered his weapon as his men put the three intruders in handcuffs and removed their ski masks. As Danielle and Walt had assumed, it was the Bandoni brothers.

"That damn crate about killed us!" Angelo shouted, looking wild eyed at the now still crate.

"This place is haunted!" Arlo screamed. "Get me out of here!"

THIRTY-FIVE

Sirens coming up the street had woken not just Lily and Ian, but also Heather and Chris, who each lived on opposite ends of Beach Drive. It was past one in the morning on Tuesday, and it seemed that every light on the first floor of Marlow House was on. Lily and Ian had rushed over first, yet it wasn't long before Chris and Heather had shown up. They had each looked out their front doors to see where the police cars were going when they saw the siren lights spinning around and around in front of Marlow House.

Still shaken, Danielle sat on the sofa between Lily and Walt, with Walt's arm around her shoulder, pulling her close. Joe Morelli, who was on duty and had arrived after the FBI agents, stood at the doorway to the living room, trying to process what he was seeing.

He watched as Chris stood in a corner chatting quietly with Ian and Heather instead of comforting Danielle. Joe understood Chris still had feelings for Danielle, yet the man didn't seem fazed that she was currently being comforted by someone like Clint Marlow. Even Lily's expression when looking at Marlow confused Joe.

"I'M GLAD PLAN A WORKED," Walt said as he hugged Danielle tightly to his side.

Leaning against his shoulder while Lily sat next to her, continually patting her knee, Danielle looked up to Walt and asked, "You had a plan B?"

"Of course." Walt smiled down at her.

"What was plan B?" she asked.

"No reason to kill us both. I was going to agree to willingly go into the crate if they would first put you outside out of harm's way."

"I don't think they would have agreed to that, considering their plan was to burn all the evidence," Danielle said.

"Thank God plan A worked!" Lily said. She then frowned and asked, "What was plan A?"

Danielle chuckled and looked over at Joe, who stood by the doorway looking in their direction. "I'll have to tell you later."

"Now that I think about it, we really didn't need a plan A or B, the G-men would have still shown up in the nick of time," Walt said.

Lily glanced over in the direction Danielle had just looked and spied Joe staring at them. She looked back to Danielle and Walt and whispered, "Maybe you two shouldn't be sitting like this."

"After believing I was about to be roasted alive, I don't really care what anyone thinks," Danielle told her.

THEY BROUGHT Franco into the interrogation room first, while they held the brothers separately in other rooms. MacDonald, who was not on duty, yet had been called, had told his officers to give Wilson and Thomas what they needed. At the moment, they needed the interrogation room.

Franco sat facing Special Agents Wilson and Thomas.

"Okay, I confess, we were going to steal the paintings. But they belonged to us, so it's not like it was really stealing."

"How do you figure that?" Wilson asked.

"They were the last things Mac painted. He was our cousin. Actually, more like an older brother. When Mac called Marlow to see how he was doing after the accident, Marlow told him he didn't want the paintings, told Mac he could have them. I guess because of everything that had happened, Marlow just didn't want them anymore. Of course, Mac did. Before he could pick up the paintings, he was murdered. Since we're Mac's next of kin, we figured the paintings really belonged to us now."

"So why didn't you just ask Mr. Marlow for them?" Wilson asked. "If you were so certain he was going to give them to your cousin anyway?"

Franco let out a bitter laugh. "Yeah, right. Like he would just give them to us. But they mean something to me and my brothers. They were painted by our cousin. It's sentimental, you know."

"But you weren't just going to steal those paintings, were you?" Thomas said.

Franco looked up to the agent. "What do you mean?"

"You were planning to kill Marlow and Boatman."

"God no! I confess, one of us made a crack about it, more just to scare them so when we didn't put them in the crate, they'd be relieved and maybe not call the cops when they got out of the ropes."

"So you weren't going to kill them?" Wilson asked.

"No way! Over a couple of paintings? You have to be kidding."

Thomas removed a photograph from a file folder he had been holding and slid it across the table. Franco looked down at it and frowned. "Who's that?"

"You don't know her?" Thomas asked.

Franco picked up the photograph and studied it a moment. He then shook his head and tossed it back on the table. "She doesn't look familiar. Who is she?"

"She was an acquaintance of your cousin's. Her name is Sonya Kozlov. Do you remember Macbeth ever mentioning her?"

Franco chuckled. "Mac hated his name. I called him by it once, and he slapped me into Sunday. Never did it again."

"Did your cousin bully you a lot?" Wilson asked.

Franco glared up at Wilson. "I never said he bullied me. He hated his name. Can't say I blamed him. I deserved that smack."

"Back to the original question, did Mac ever mention her?"

Franco shrugged. "Not that I remember."

The agents asked a few more questions and then announced Officer Joe Morelli would be interviewing him next. A few minutes later, Joe changed places with the FBI agents.

"We've been trying to contact you since your cousin's death, but no one has been at your house. Where have you been?" Joe asked.

"My brothers and I went to Portland. We left Saturday. Checked in about six that evening. I can give you the name of the place we stayed, and I'm sure they can verify that. We checked out yesterday, did some running around in Portland, and then headed home last night."

"But you didn't go home," Joe said. "We've had someone staking out your house since the murder."

"We didn't even know Mac had been killed. We heard about it on the radio on the way home. Didn't go back to our house. We came straight to Frederickport. Decided to get Mac's paintings. After all, they were the last things he painted, and he was like a brother to us," Franco explained.

"What about Chet?" Joe asked.

"Chet? Heard on the radio he was killed in some car accident."

"I thought he was staying at your house. Did he leave when you left for Portland?"

"We told him he could stay at our house. Mac was crashing there too, said he didn't care if Chet stayed. In fact, the day we left, Mac asked Chet if he could drop him off at Marlow House that evening. Mac's car was broken down."

"You and your brothers, you only have one car between you, right?" Joe asked.

Franco frowned. "Yeah, why?"

"I don't know. I'd just think three adult men would have more than one car between them."

"No reason. We get along fine with one car, and it's cheaper."

"So Chet dropped your cousin off at Marlow House?"

Franco shrugged. "I suppose. Last time I talked to either one of them was when we left Saturday afternoon."

"Who do you think killed your cousin?" Joe asked.

"I know that crazy woman killed him. You arrested her, didn't you?"

"She was released after new evidence was discovered." Joe watched closely for his reaction.

"Her brother did it, right?" Franco asked.

"Why do you think Chet Morrison would kill your cousin?"

"It had to be either him or his sister. And I know Mac was going with him that night."

"Why would Chet or Laverne want Mac dead?" Joe asked.

Franco stared at Joe a moment before answering. Finally, he said, "Mac used to date Laverne, years ago. It was just a summer fling. He wasn't that interested. Her parents were invalids, and she was the primary caregiver. Chet was in high school then. Anyway, maybe Mac wasn't that interested in her, but she—well—she was crazy about him. And when I say crazy, I mean crazy. One day there's a house fire at her place, and both her parents are killed. Mac goes to comfort her, and she tells him she set the fire—which means she's now free to go with him when he leaves for Europe. He never asked her to go to Europe with him."

Joe stared blankly at Franco for a moment before asking, "Are you saying Laverne Morrison murdered her parents?"

Franco nodded. "Of course, we didn't know about it back then. But it explained a lot. Like why Mac broke it off with Laverne and then took off to Europe earlier than planned. He just wanted to get as far away from that crazy woman as possible."

"Why didn't he go to the police?" Joe asked.

"He was afraid she'd say he was involved. You know, revenge for turning her in to the cops and not returning her feelings. Anyway, he told us about it the other day, right after he ran into Laverne in some restaurant. It really shook him."

"So why would Chet kill him?" Joe asked. "Was he involved with the fire?"

"Mac didn't think Chet even knew about it. But if Laverne went to her brother with some twisted version of the story, he might have killed Mac to protect his sister. Probably why Chet drove off some cliff."

"What do you mean?" Joe asked.

"Knowing Chet, he panicked after they killed Mac. That's probably why he drove his car off the road."

When Arlo's and Angelo's turns in the interrogation room came, their stories were similar to Franco's. Each swore they never intended to hurt anyone and reminded Wilson and Thomas of the fact that none of them were carrying weapons at the time they had broken into Marlow House. Of course, that didn't include the tool they'd used to literally rip the doorknob off Danielle's front door.

"IT WASN'T ARSON," Brian told Joe when he came in for work early Tuesday morning. The two officers sat alone in the lunchroom.

"That's what I thought, but they all swore that's what Mac had told them," Joe said.

"They're just throwing Laverne under the bus to get the attention off them," Brian said.

"Maybe, but they all told the same story. All claimed Mac had told them about the fire after he ran into Laverne at a restaurant."

"Who's to say Mac wasn't lying to his cousins?" Brian suggested.

Joe shrugged and sipped his coffee.

"So what does Kelly think about you putting in all these extra hours?" Brian asked.

"She understands. She knows I'm trying to build my savings account."

"What, so you can get married?" Brian asked.

Joe smiled and sipped his coffee again.

Brian laughed. "I knew it! But, Joe, you two are already living together. If you want to get married, just do it."

"I'm not going to jump into marriage. First Kelly and I are seeing how things work out with us living together. It's kind of an adjustment living with another person."

"Don't I know it," Brian muttered under his breath. "Did you forget I was married twice?"

"When I get married, I want it to be just once."

"I should've been married just once. After my first one didn't work out, I should've learned my lesson and not tried again," Brian said with a snort.

Joe rolled his eyes and took another drink of coffee.

"So, tell me, why did the FBI do the raid at Marlow House? I heard you were already on the scene."

"They had Marlow House under surveillance, and when they saw the Bandonis break in, they wanted to get all their men in place before they went in."

Brian frowned. "Waiting like that was risky. Who knows what might have happened had they waited a few more minutes."

"According to Danielle, they planned to lock her and Marlow up in that wooden crate where the portraits had been stored and then set the place on fire."

Brian cringed. "Crap. She must have been terrified."

"I guess, considering the way she was all over Marlow afterwards."

Brian arched his brows. "Does this mean she and Chris are no longer a thing?"

"If they are, they have an odd relationship. He saw the cars there last night and came over after they had arrested the Bandonis. Lily and Ian were over there too, and Heather."

"Damn, the entire Beach Drive bunch."

"Pretty much. But it was Marlow Danielle was all over."

"All over how?"

Joe shrugged. "You know, leaning all over him while he comforted her. It was strange. Last thing I heard, no one could stand that guy. Now she's fawning all over him, and frankly, I think the real truth, Marlow about got her killed, and she's too naïve to see it."

"You still think he's mixed up in this?"

"Absolutely. I know the FBI says those paintings of his are the reproductions. But I'd bet anything he planned to switch the paintings for the originals. Maybe the chief being there that night foiled their plans."

"How so?" Brian asked.

"The chief helped them load the paintings in the crate. Maybe that wasn't supposed to happen. We both know Marlow insisted on taking Danielle and the chief out to dinner that night while Bandoni backed out at the last minute and stayed at Marlow House. I bet his cousins were supposed to come over and help him switch the paintings that night, and something happened, and they couldn't do it."

"One flaw in your scenario," Brian said.

"What's that?"

"If they couldn't switch the paintings, then they knew the paintings in the crate were the fakes not the originals. So why all this interest in the fakes?"

Joe looked at Brian and frowned. He scratched his head and said, "Hell, you're right. I'm not thinking straight."

"Maybe you would think a little straighter if you got more sleep. And you aren't going to do that by putting in all these extra hours."

THIRTY-SIX

On Tuesday morning Danielle stood in the entry hall with Adam while Bill Jones examined the damage to her front door. Crouched on his knees to get a closer look, Bill said, "They ripped the knob right off. Screwed the door up good." He glanced over to Danielle. "And you say the Bandonis did this?"

Danielle nodded. "Yep."

Bill stood all the way up while dusting his hands off on the sides of his work pants. "I always liked Arlo; he's the middle brother. But Franco, I thought he was a little off." He tapped the side of his head with one finger. "If you know what I mean."

"So can you fix it?" Adam asked.

"This is a nice old door. Would be a shame to put something else in here. This one has character."

"Oh no, I don't want another door!" Danielle said. "I was hoping you could fix this one."

"I could do it. But I'd have to remove it, take it back to my shop. Can't promise to have it back this week. That would mean I'd have to board up your front door in the meantime," Bill told her.

"How about buying an inexpensive door to temporarily replace this one?" Danielle suggested.

"It would be cheaper to just board it up."

"I really don't want to nail up sheets of plywood; that'll mess up the siding. Not to mention, everyone will have to come in through the side yard," Danielle said.

Bill shrugged. "Okay. It's your money."

Danielle flashed him a smile. "Thanks. When can you start?"

Bill glanced at his watch and then looked back at Danielle. "I can go pick up a door now and then get back here and switch them. I'll have to get some hardware too, that's if you want to be able to lock up the front door."

"That would be wonderful." Danielle beamed.

"Thanks, Bill," Adam told him.

Bill glanced over at Adam and rolled his eyes and then said a brief goodbye to Danielle before leaving out the front entry. As he made his way down the front walkway, heading to his truck, he muttered under his breath, "Surprised you didn't just get the Bandonis to fix the door like you conned me into fixing the library window. That wouldn't have cost you a penny." He chuckled and then added, "But better for me."

DANIELLE LET Adam into the parlor, where Walt was lounging on the sofa, book in hand. He looked up when they entered the room.

"Can he fix it?" Walt asked.

"I think so." Danielle glanced from Walt to Adam, who stood silently at her side.

Walt looked to Adam and smiled. "Hello. Have we met?"

"Walt, this is Adam Nichols. I told you about him."

Walt's smile broadened. "Hello, Adam. I understand you're the one who originally sent me information on Marlow House. You're the Realtor, right?"

Adam nodded, yet said nothing.

"I understand I was a major jerk to you when we met," Walt said cheerfully.

Adam's eyes widened. He glanced to Danielle, who flashed him a smile. He looked back to Walt.

"Umm...well, you were with your fiancée, and I just don't think you wanted to be bothered."

Walt shrugged. "No. I think I was a jerk. At least, that's what Danielle has told me."

Speechless, Adam glanced from Walt to Danielle.

"Would you guys like something to drink? Coffee, iced tea maybe? Lily dropped off some cinnamon rolls from Old Salts. Would you—"

Before Danielle finished her question, both Adam and Walt blurted, "Yes!" to the cinnamon rolls. Danielle chuckled and said she would be right back.

Once Adam was alone in the parlor with Walt, he wandered to one of the chairs facing the sofa and sat down, while Walt held his book open, as if preparing to read again.

"How long are you staying in Frederickport?" Adam asked.

Walt closed the book on his lap. "I'm not sure. At the moment, I'm taking one day at a time."

"Sounds like you've had a lot of excitement since you got out of the hospital. A murder one day, and then someone ties you up and intends to set you on fire."

"Yes, it has been a little more excitement than I need." Walt smiled at Adam.

"You know, Danielle, she's all right," Adam said, his tone serious.

Holding the now closed book on his lap, his left leg propped on the coffee table, Walt nodded. "Yes, I agree."

"My grandmother and Danielle were very close."

"Yes, Danielle has mentioned your grandmother—Marie. She sounded like quite a character. Danielle speaks fondly of her."

"I sort of think of Danielle as my kid sister."

Walt's grin broadened. "That's interesting. She's mentioned she thinks of you as her unruly kid brother."

Unable to suppress his grin at that comment, Adam let out a snort and said, "I'm older than her."

"It's nice you both think so fondly of each other."

Adam's expression grew serious again, and he looked into Walt's eyes. "Here is the thing, Marlow, be careful with Danielle. She has a lot of friends in Frederickport, and none of us want to see her taken advantage of."

Walt arched his brow. "How would I do that?"

"I know she probably feels sorry for you; after all you've been through. But don't wear out your welcome, if you know what I mean. You were kind of a jerk when you were staying here before. Danielle, well, she tends to be a little more forgiving than she should be. But you need to know the rest of us won't be that forgiving."

THE GHOST OF SECOND CHANCES

Walt smiled at Adam and leaned back in the sofa. In a quiet voice he asked, "Is that a warning?"

"You just need to know we're watching, and we won't let you do anything to take advantage of her."

Walt's smile widened. "In spite of everything, I think I like you, Adam. I'm glad you're such a loyal friend to Danielle. She's worthy of that loyalty."

Adam frowned. *In spite of everything?* Adam thought. *What does that even mean?*

Before Adam could press Walt on his meaning, Danielle returned to the parlor with a tray carrying three glasses of iced tea and three cinnamon rolls.

DANIELLE HAD JUST HANDED Walt and Adam each a glass of iced tea when she heard a man scream, "What are you doing here?"

"Who's that?" Danielle asked, looking at the doorway leading into the entry hall.

"Who's what?" Adam held his hand out, eagerly waiting for her to pass him a cinnamon roll.

"What are you doing here?" another man screamed.

Walt glanced to the doorway. He recognized the last voice. "It's nothing," he said, nervously eyeing the door.

Perplexed, Danielle looked to Walt, who had clearly heard something, but then she looked at Adam, who appeared oblivious to the fact two men stood out in the entry hall yelling at each other.

"What's nothing?" Adam asked. He glanced from Danielle to Walt. "What is it? Did you hear something?"

As soon as Adam asked the question, the two men Danielle and Walt had heard started arguing again, their voices louder. Adam continued to be unaware of the shouting coming from the entry hall.

Danielle quickly handed Adam and Walt each a cinnamon roll and then said, "If you will excuse me, I'll be right back."

DANIELLE STEPPED into the hallway and found Chet and Macbeth's spirits facing off by the open doorway to the living room.

Each man's features contorted into an angry mask as virulent accusatory words spilled from their mouths.

She groaned, wishing she had not encouraged Adam to stick around after Bill had taken off. At the time she thought it was a good idea. It was an opportunity for him to meet Walt. But now, now she wished she had Walt to help her deal with the two angry spirits who were in the midst of screaming at each other at the top of their lungs. Which, of course, was only a figure of speech. Neither man possessed a lung.

"I'm dead because of you!" Chet screeched.

"You're dead? You're one to talk. You might as well have been the one who pulled the trigger!" Macbeth screamed back.

"If I could kill you, I would!" Chet yelled.

"You never were very smart, Chet; you already did that!"

"I did not!"

Danielle took a deep breath and then walked to the spirits. Thus far, neither had noticed her standing outside the parlor door. When she got a few feet away from them, she said in a quiet firm voice, "Would you both just shut up."

Both spirits immediately stopped talking and turned to Danielle, each blinking in surprise.

"You can see us?" Chet whispered.

"Unfortunately, I can hear you too."

"I don't understand. No one has been able to see me yet," Macbeth stammered.

"What about me?" Chet asked angrily. "I can obviously see you!"

"Don't be stupid, Chet," Macbeth snapped. "Oh, never mind. Forget I said that. You're all about stupid!"

"I asked you two to be quiet," Danielle hissed. "Now I want you both to go to the library and wait for me. Do you understand?"

"Why do we have to do that?" Chet asked.

"Because Adam is here, and he can't see or hear you. And if you both want me to help you, then you need to let me get Adam to leave so I can come talk to you both."

"Why would you want to help us?" Macbeth asked.

Her first impulse was to tell them the truth. She wanted to help them because she didn't want them hanging around Marlow House. Fortunately, she caught herself before expressing her truthful answer. The last thing she wanted to do was give Chet any ideas and end up with him hanging around. There had to be a better answer.

Finally, Danielle said, "Do you two want to spend eternity together?"

"What do you mean?" Macbeth asked.

"If I don't help you—if you don't listen to what I have to say—then you both risk spending eternity together. Do you really want that?"

Macbeth stared at Danielle, his eyes narrowing under his bushy brows. "Why should we believe you?"

Danielle smiled knowingly. "Has anyone else been able to communicate with you?"

"No," Chet answered.

Danielle shrugged. "Then I suppose that means I know something that you don't. But of course…if you want to…"

"No!" they shouted at the same time.

"I'll meet you in the library," Macbeth grumbled and then disappeared.

Chet frowned and looked around. "Where's the library?"

Danielle pointed down the hallway. "It's the room with all the books."

THIRTY-SEVEN

"Why can't the chief just come here?" Walt asked Danielle. The two stood in the kitchen while Macbeth's and Chet's spirits hovered just inside the back door. Adam had left fifteen minutes earlier, and Danielle had just finished apprising Walt of the situation.

"I called him, and he can't get away from the office. But I'll need you to stay here until Bill comes back. I don't want to leave the house open."

Walt nodded. "I understand."

"You really aren't Clint, are you?" Macbeth asked.

Looking at Macbeth, Walt shook his head. "No, I'm really not." When introductions had been made after Adam's departure, Danielle had explained Walt's true identity.

"That's kind of creepy." Chet cringed. "Stepping into someone else's body."

"Considering some of your actions when you were alive, I don't think you are in any position to judge," Danielle snapped.

Chet frowned at her. "You know, you're sort of an opinionated woman. I don't think we could have ever worked out."

"Now that you're dead, you finally figured that out?" she asked.

Chet's frown deepened. "And you're kind of mean too."

Danielle rolled her eyes, yet Walt said, "Danielle, go easy on poor Chet here. He has a big adjustment to make."

"Whatever," Danielle muttered as she snatched her purse from the counter and headed to the doorway. She stopped when she got to the spirits, who stood blocking her way. "You two need to stay here with Walt."

They both shook their heads. Macbeth said, "No. This is about my eternity, and I'm going with you."

"Me too!" Chet chimed in.

Danielle turned to Walt, looking for support. He only shrugged and said, "I understand how they feel. Plus, how are you going to convince Laverne to believe you without their help?"

Danielle groaned and then pointed for the spirits to get out of her way. They quickly moved through the wall to the back porch. Danielle started to open the door when she paused and looked back to Walt.

"You just didn't want them hanging out here with you," she accused.

Walt smiled sheepishly and said, "Well, that was part of it. But you'll need them to help you with Laverne."

Danielle groaned again and opened the door, hearing Walt chuckle as she left the house.

When she reached her Ford Flex, she found the spirits inside, each fighting for shotgun. They appeared to be wrestling on the passenger seat, yet neither was capable of actually making any sort of contact with the other one aside from visually.

Throwing open the car door, she shouted, "In the backseat, both of you. Or we aren't going anywhere, and you two will be stuck together for eternity!" She doubted it was true, but she had to say something because there was no way she could drive down to the police station with both spirits on the passenger seat poking at each other like two unruly preschoolers. A few moments later she was relieved after they complied and moved to the backseat.

With a deep breath to clear her thoughts, Danielle climbed into her car and tossed her purse on the now empty passenger seat. As she fastened her seatbelt, she glanced over her shoulder and saw the spirits each sitting quietly on the backseat—Macbeth on the left side and Chet on the right.

"Don't forget to buckle up!" she called out.

She waited a moment and watched as the two reached for their seatbelts. When their hands moved through the belts, they each tried several more times to pick it up before realizing the futility of the task.

Danielle chuckled under her breath and muttered, "That never gets old."

Chet glared at Danielle. "You really are mean."

Backing out of her driveway, Danielle said, "I'm sorry, Chet. I guess that was kind of mean." *But still funny*, she thought.

"You know, I was wrong," Macbeth said as Danielle pulled out into the street.

"About what?" Danielle glanced into the rearview mirror, expecting to see her passengers, but saw nothing but the backseat. Feeling momentarily foolish for forgetting ghosts had no reflection she thought, *I suppose that serves me right for telling them to put their seatbelts on.*

"I told you no one had seen me since I died. But someone did. I'm sure of it. A woman on the beach."

"What woman?" Danielle steered her car down Beach Drive.

"I've seen her before; I think at your house when we were staying there. I shot her with my gun and she screamed."

"You shot someone?" Chet asked. "You're going to hell when we're done."

"I didn't really shoot her!" Macbeth argued.

"Ahh…yes…that was Heather. She told us about seeing you. She's like Walt and me. She can see spirits."

"How many people are there like you?" Chet asked.

Danielle shrugged. "I don't know. It's not like they ever include that question in the census."

"What question?" Chet asked.

"You know, can you see ghosts?"

"I don't want to be a ghost," Macbeth grumbled. "But I really don't want to go to hell either."

"I don't even know if there really is a hell," Danielle told him.

"But you don't know if there isn't?" Macbeth asked.

"I know there is something—and I know—well—yeah, I think there is something like a hell. But considering you both are still here and the Universe hasn't sucked you up, then that's a good sign."

"Sucked us up?" Chet squeaked.

"I'm thinking of these two people I knew—not very nice. They weren't even given the opportunity to set things straight after they died, like you two are. I watched as their spirits were literally sucked up." Danielle cringed. "Looked most unpleasant for them."

Furrowing his bushy brows, Macbeth glared at the back of Danielle's head. "You're making this stuff up."

Danielle let out a sigh and said, "No, actually, I'm not. That was a true story." By her tone, both Chet and Macbeth found her claim chillingly believable. They sank back in the seat and looked out the side windows while considering their current circumstances.

After a few minutes of silence, Danielle asked, "Macbeth, can I ask you a question?"

"I hate that name," he grumbled. "Call me Mac."

"Actually, it's about your name," she said.

"What about it?" he asked.

"I understand that in theater circles even saying Macbeth is considered taboo. Something about it being cursed."

"Yeah, so what?" he grumbled.

"Wasn't your mother an actress?" she asked.

"Yeah, what about it?"

"Why would your parents name you Macbeth considering the stigma attached to the name? From what I've heard, some actors even avoid saying it because of the curse."

Macbeth let out a snort. "My mother named me Macbeth because it was her favorite play."

"What about the curse?" Danielle asked.

"My mother was also an atheist. Both my parents were."

"Atheist? What does that have to do with anything?" Danielle asked.

"My parents didn't believe in God or any religion. It also meant they didn't believe in superstitions, like Macbeth being cursed or bad luck. Mom thought that was all silly. When I was a kid, I wished my folks had believed in God. Not because I wanted religion in my life, but then maybe my mother wouldn't have named me something that got my butt kicked every week when I was a kid. Well, that was until I learned to fight back."

"Gee, I'm sorry about that, Mac," Danielle said sincerely.

In the backseat Macbeth shrugged while Chet flashed his spirit companion a glare. Considering all the problems Mac had brought him, Chet wasn't moved by a story on how Mac had been bullied as a kid.

"BEFORE WE BRING Laverne in to question her on this, I want you to go through that case file again," Chief MacDonald told Brian. The two sat alone together in the chief's office.

"Unless there's something they overlooked when investigating the fire or Laverne confesses, I suspect this will go nowhere. It'll be nothing but hearsay on the Bandonis' side. But I'll look and see what I can find," Brian said.

A knock came at the door.

"That's probably Wilson and Thomas. I told the front desk to send them right back to my office when they got here," the chief said as he stood up.

Brian walked over to the door and opened it. As the chief had predicted, it was the two FBI agents.

"I thought you two would be getting some sleep," Brian said when he let them into the office.

"No time for sleep," Thomas told him.

Brian glanced over at the chief and said, "I'll go look for that file."

The chief nodded, and Brian left the office, closing the door behind him.

"Sonya Kozlov checked out of the motel this morning," Wilson told him.

"I don't think your murder has anything to do with our art-theft ring," Thomas announced as he took a seat in one of the chairs facing the desk. The chief sat back down in his chair, while Wilson remained standing.

"Why do you think that?" the chief asked.

"It looks like the woman you originally arrested was probably the killer. You have a motive now, and her brother's car matches the description two witnesses saw by Marlow House at the time of the murder. They were probably in on this together. I imagine she thought you were getting too close, which is why she confessed to save her brother. But when she found out he'd died in a car accident and she realized she didn't have to take the rap for him, she changed her story," Thomas explained.

"You no longer believe Marlow was involved in the murder?" the chief asked.

"We don't think so, but we believe he might be involved in a possible art heist. We suspect that's why Macbeth Bandoni went to see him so late that night. I don't think he wanted anyone else to see him going there. But frankly, we don't really care about the murder; that's your jurisdiction. But what we do care about is getting the goods on Kozlov, and we believe Marlow might be the key," Wilson said.

"Do you have anything to connect Marlow to Kozlov?" the chief asked.

Wilson shook his head. "No. In fact, Bandoni wasn't even on our radar until we intercepted that call Kozlov made to him after she visited your museum. We're planning to dig deeper into Marlow. But first we want to talk again to the Bandoni brothers. We'd also like to have a chat with the Morrison woman."

SPECIAL AGENTS WILSON and Thomas were just leaving the chief's office when Danielle arrived.

"I was afraid they were going to stick around," Danielle said after she and the chief were alone in the office. Alone if you didn't count Macbeth's and Chet's spirits.

"They're convinced Walt is involved in this art-theft ring they're after. They're trying to connect him to Sonya Kozlov."

"Clint knew nothing about Sonya," Macbeth said. "In fact, she didn't even know he was in on the plan."

Danielle looked briefly to Macbeth and then back to the chief. "Mac said Clint didn't know anything about Sonya, and she didn't know he was working with him."

The chief frowned. "Mac?"

"Well, he doesn't really like being called Macbeth," Danielle explained.

"What are you saying, Danielle?" the chief asked.

"I didn't really want to go into this on the phone earlier this morning. Knowing those FBI agents have been intercepting cell-phone calls doesn't make me comfortable."

"What are you saying?" the chief repeated.

"Mac and Chet are with me."

The chief glanced around the room. Danielle pointed to where they were standing. He let out a sigh and then looked back to Danielle. "Did they say who the murderer is?"

"More like murderers. Chet was murdered too. And Laverne wasn't involved. In fact, she didn't kill anyone, in spite of what you told me on the phone this morning."

"So who is it?" he asked.

"That's the easy thing. I can tell you who they are, but we need to figure out a way to prove it."

THIRTY-EIGHT

Danielle had never before noticed how the ticking sound of a clock wasn't much different from a persistent drip from a kitchen faucet. She had also never noticed the wall clock—whose ticking sound now filled her head. It hung on the wall behind her in the chief's office. There was no other sound in the room. Not even the two spirits had made a peep since she had concluded her summation of the recent events, as told to her by the two now silent ghosts. The chief sat silently at his desk, his brows furrowed in a frown. Danielle imagined he was trying to figure out how they were going to prove the killers' identities. She hadn't yet shared with him her idea.

Finally, Danielle broke the silence when she said, "I'm not thrilled with the fact Wilson and Thomas seem hell-bent on dragging Walt into this."

"We all knew this was one of the risks Walt faced when accepting Clint's offer. But the fact this Sonya woman didn't know Clint was involved might be the silver lining."

"Unfortunately, Mac's cousins knew he was involved," Danielle reminded him.

"Which is one reason we need to find some way to prove who is behind the killings," the chief reminded her.

"There's another thing," Danielle began.

"What's that?" the chief asked.

"If the FBI starts looking into Clint's history, aren't they bound to find out about the fingerprints?"

"What about his fingerprints?" Chet asked from the sidelines.

"Shut up. They aren't talking to you," Mac snapped.

The chief winced. "I've been thinking about that. I told Brian and Joe it was probably a mix-up at the California Real Estate Department. But I still don't understand why his fingerprints would change."

Danielle shrugged. "I don't understand either. But Eva says Walt's settling into his body. Making it his own. Whatever that means."

"I still say that's creepy," Chet muttered. "Using someone else's body. Yuck."

"Are you two going to talk forever?" Macbeth grumbled. "We need to get over to Laverne's before those FBI guys show up and talk her into a guilt confession."

Danielle glanced at Macbeth. "You might be right, Mac."

"What, you listen to him and ignore my question?" Chet whined.

"He might be right about what?" the chief asked.

"I need to go talk to Laverne before those agents show up at her house. And before Brian decides to bring her in for more questioning. We don't need another fake confession muddying the waters," Danielle told him. "But first, let me tell you my idea for getting the killers to confess."

DANIELLE PARKED her car in front of Laverne's house. She glanced in the backseat at Mac and Chet. "Okay, do you two understand how this has to go?"

"Yes," Chet practically groaned. "You want us to keep quiet unless you ask a question."

"It's really important you both keep quiet because it can get really confusing if you guys start talking while I'm trying to explain all this to Laverne. She'll only hear me, and if I start talking to you guys too, she won't hear or see you, so it'll make me look nuts. And even if I don't respond to you, it'll be hard for me to focus on what I'm saying. And trust me, she's going to think I'm nuts as it is. The objective is to prove I'm not crazy while trying to convince her to believe my crazy story."

A few minutes later Danielle stood on Laverne Morrison's front doorstep, two anxious spirits by her side. Danielle was fairly certain Laverne was home, considering her car was parked in the driveway. She rang the doorbell and waited.

When no one answered the door, Chet said, "Let me check to see if she's here. It's possible she's at work and drove with someone else." The next moment Chet disappeared into the house. When he returned, he said, "Ring the bell again. She's just sitting in the living room, eating ice cream—straight from the carton. Looks like she's been crying too, considering the stack of used tissues and her red eyes."

Danielle rang the bell again. When Laverne didn't answer, she knocked firmly on the door and yelled, "Laverne, please, answer your door."

A few minutes later the door opened, the security chain preventing it from opening more than a few inches. Laverne peeked out over the chain and asked, "What do you want?"

"Laverne, my name is Danielle Boatman. I was a friend of your brother, Chet. I'd really like to talk to you for a moment, please."

"Now I'm a friend!"

"Shut up, Chet. You know what she said about talking!" Macbeth admonished.

Laverne did not respond, but a few moments later she unchained the door and opened it wider, motioning for Danielle to enter.

"Thank you," Danielle said as she stepped into the darkened living room. There were no lights on. If it wasn't for the sunlight streaming through the edges of the curtain, the room would be pitch black.

"You really were a friend of my brother?" Laverne asked. "I wasn't sure if that was just a story my brother made up."

"Gosh, Laverne, that doesn't make me sound very good," Chet whined.

"Chet and I met a few times, and we had a mutual friend, Adam Nichols."

Laverne nodded. "Yes, I know Adam. He and Chet grew up together."

"Can we sit down, Laverne? I have a few things I need to tell you, and I think we should probably sit down."

Laverne looked uneasily at Danielle. For a moment Danielle wondered if Laverne was regretting letting her into the house. But then she motioned to the sofa while she moved to the chair she had been sitting on when Danielle had first arrived. At least, Danielle assumed it was the chair she had been sitting on, considering the container of ice cream sitting on the end table next to it.

Once Laverne sat down, she looked over at Danielle, who was now sitting on the sofa, and asked, "What did you want to talk to me about?"

"First, I want you to know I'm here to help you. I have your best interest at heart. Honest," Danielle said.

Laverne frowned. "Umm…okay…"

"I am going to tell you something, and your first reaction will probably be to think I'm crazy and to ask me to leave. But I want you to hear me out."

"What is it?"

"I can see ghosts. Your brother and Mac Bandoni are here with me right now."

Laverne bolted from her chair and pointed to the front door. "Out! Get out of my house!"

Macbeth looked to Danielle and said, "Well, you called that one spot on."

Danielle remained seated. "Mac didn't set the fire that killed your parents. He only said that because he was trying to manipulate you."

Laverne froze and stared at Danielle.

"Mac took you on a picnic one night, down on the beach. You had some wine. You told him you had never had alcohol before. He asked you to go to Europe with him, and you said you couldn't because of your responsibility to your parents. But then you had too much to drink, got a little drunk, and said things you later regretted. While you were drunk, you and Mac talked about how it would be better for everyone—even your parents—if they just died. A little more wine and you started talking about ways to kill them so no one would suspect."

Zombielike, Laverne backed up and flopped back down in her chair, still staring at Danielle. "I've never told anyone about that," she whispered.

"You told Chet. After your parents' funeral. You were so guilt ridden," Danielle said in a soft voice.

Laverne shook her head. "This is impossible."

"It's very possible. I've seen and communicated with spirits since I was a child."

"And you're saying they're both here? Chet and Mac?"

Danielle nodded. "They want to set things right so they can move on."

Laverne continue to shake her head. "This is too crazy…you found out somehow. Maybe Mac's cousins told you. I heard they broke into your house and tied you up. I bet Mac told them what happened, and they told you for some reason. And I know Mac set the fire. He told me."

"I can prove I'm telling the truth. Ask me anything…something only Chet or Mac will know," Danielle challenged.

Laverne stared at Danielle. Finally, she asked, "What's Chet's favorite drink?"

"Aw, come on, Laverne, not that." Chet groaned. "Ask something else."

"Well? What is it?" Laverne challenged.

"For some reason he wants you to ask something else," Danielle said.

"I knew it. It's all a lie." Laverne stood up again.

"A Shirley Temple," Chet confessed.

Danielle arched her brows at Chet. "Your favorite drink is a Shirley Temple? You mean like lemon-lime and grenadine?"

"If it's made right, you use ginger ale instead of lemon-lime. And it needs three cherries." Chet told her.

"Ginger ale and three cherries?" Danielle asked.

Laverne let out a gasp.

"Come on, Chet, if you're going to go for a kid's drink, why not a Roy Rogers?" Macbeth asked with a snicker.

"Do you believe me now?" Danielle asked.

"I don't know." Laverne frowned at Danielle. "But why are you telling me all this?"

"Because I don't want anyone to get you to confess to a crime you didn't commit. I'm afraid your guilt might get you to do that, and then the real killers will get off."

"I don't understand."

"What I am about to tell you needs to stay between us," Danielle told her. "Please."

"Go on," Laverne said.

"When the Bandoni brothers were arrested, they told the police that you set the fire that killed your parents."

Laverne gasped. "Why would they say that?"

"I don't want to go into everything that was said. Because in some ways, the less you know, the better it will be for you. When the police interview you again, I don't want you to slip and say something you shouldn't know. I just need you to understand that Mac only said he set that fire because he was trying to manipulate you back then. He thought that would be a way to…well…make sure you went to Europe with him like you promised instead of staying and taking care of your brother. And once there, it would be a way for him to control you. But it backfired when you didn't have the reaction he expected. It didn't quite work out like he planned." Danielle shot Macbeth a reproving glance.

"Okay, okay…I get it," Macbeth grumbled.

"You say killers? Are you saying Chet was murdered too?" Laverne asked.

"Yes."

"Who are they?"

"I can't tell you. Like I said, it will be better for you if you don't know everything. You'll find out soon enough. But for right now, when the police—or maybe someone from the FBI—interviews you, stick to the truth. Tell them what happened that night. Admit that you found your brother's gun in his things before you kicked him out, and that's why your fingerprints were on the gun."

"You know about that?" Laverne whispered.

"Laverne, you were a good sister. You tried to protect me, even when I didn't deserve your loyalty. I love you. And if I see Mom and Dad again, I'll tell them they can be proud of you," Chet said.

Danielle conveyed Chet's words to Laverne. She started to cry.

THIRTY-NINE

After leaving Laverne's house, Danielle returned to the police station with the two ghosts.

"Thomas and Wilson left. They talked to the Bandonis again, but they're sticking to their story," the chief told her.

"I'm not surprised."

"Are you ready to try this?" the chief asked.

"I hope it works." She looked to the spirits. "You know what you have to do."

"And you'll stay here?" Chet asked.

Danielle nodded. "Just listen to what they're saying, and if it's anything we should know, one of you come tell me. But one of you needs to stay with them so you don't miss anything." A moment later Chet and Macbeth vanished.

"Well?" the chief asked.

"They're gone." Danielle sat down in a chair. "If they tell me anything, I'll send you a text message."

"Okay. Let's try this." The chief left Danielle in his office and then went to find Brian. He found him in the break room having a cup of coffee.

"Did you get ahold of the Portland hotel?" the chief asked as he entered the room.

"Yes. The Bandonis checked in a little after six on Saturday and checked out yesterday. Just like they said. They were there the whole time. In fact, the manager said they didn't really go anywhere. Hung out at the indoor swimming pool, had pizza delivered to their room."

"Did they say which brother checked in for them?"

"Arlo's name was on the register. But the manager said it was pretty busy and can't remember if all the brothers were there or not. But he saw them all later. Said they were hard to miss considering their size."

The chief nodded. "Okay, so their alibi checks out."

"You don't really think one of them did it, do you?" Brian asked. "I think it's pretty obvious who the killer is. Chet. And while I'm not buying the arson story, I have to wonder if this has something to do with Laverne and her past relationship with Macbeth. I'll bring her in for more questioning."

"You know, we don't have the coroner report back on Chet's death," the chief reminded him.

"Pretty clear to me what happened. Karma arrived early. Chet must have driven off the road somewhere after killing Bandoni, and his car ended up on those rocks."

"I want you to hold off on bringing Laverne in. First I want to question the brothers again."

Brian frowned. "I don't understand?"

"I know this has been your and Joe's case," the chief began. "But I need to talk to them myself."

"Is there a problem with how we've been handling the case?"

"No. But this morning I received a few anonymous tips," the chief explained.

"What kind of tips?"

"I'd rather not go into that right now. But I want you to monitor the interview. I intend to talk to Franco first."

"You think Franco knows more about his cousin's murder than he's letting on?"

"Just trust me on this, Brian."

BRIAN WAS ALREADY STANDING at the window looking into the interrogation room when Joe walked in. Hearing Joe enter, he glanced over his shoulder. "You should be home sleeping, Joe."

"Yeah, right. You think I was going to stay home after you told me the chief got some tips on our case, and he wasn't ready to share them?"

"If you had been in bed, like you should have been, and not calling me to see how things were going, you wouldn't have felt compelled to come down here," Brian told him.

Ignoring Brian, Joe stepped to the window and looked into the adjoining room. Franco sat alone at the table, his gaze persistently darting up to the two-way mirror. The next moment the chief walked into the interrogation room.

"OUR ATTORNEY IS SEEING about getting us out on bail," Franco said as the chief sat down at the table. "I'm not sure I should be talking to you without him here."

"I don't intend to ask you any questions about the charges you're currently facing. I wanted to ask you a few questions in regard to your cousin's murder."

Franco visibly relaxed. "Oh, that. Sure. I guess that would be okay."

The chief smiled at Franco. "According to the hotel in Portland, your brother Arlo checked you in a little past six on Saturday."

Franco nodded. "Yeah. That's what I told the other cop."

"I just have one problem. The hotel manager didn't remember seeing you when your brother Arlo checked in."

Franco shrugged. "So? I had to use the head."

"You're saying you were using the bathroom when your brother checked in?" the chief asked.

"Yeah, so?"

The chief rested his elbows on the table and leaned forward, studying Franco. "Another problem, I have a witness who saw you down the street from the pier, on Beach Drive, just before sunset on Saturday. That would have been less than two hours after you checked in to the hotel. Not enough time to get back here."

"They're wrong."

"Franco, you tend to stand out in a crowd."

"Wasn't me. I was in Portland."

"Do you have any idea how many houses now have cameras installed around their property? You know, cameras that capture who walks by their house and stamps it with the time and date?"

BOBBI HOLMES

Franco stared at the chief, speechless.

"WHO SAW FRANCO? WHAT CAMERAS?" Joe asked. He stood next to Brian, looking through the two-way mirror at the interrogation room.

Brian shrugged. "I have no idea."

The chief looked up to the mirror and nodded.

Brian glanced to Joe and said, "That's his sign. I need to get Angelo now. The chief wants to make sure the brothers see each other before he questions Angelo."

"What is he doing?" Joe muttered.

"Not a clue."

Ten minutes later, Joe watched as Brian led Angelo into the interrogation room. He then removed a visibly agitated Franco.

"WHAT DID they want to talk to you about?" Arlo asked Franco when Brian returned him to the cell.

"Yeah, you punk. I'd like to slap you both," Macbeth grumbled. He stood with Chet by the window in the cell, unseen to the brothers.

"Someone saw me," Franco said after Brian left. He started pacing.

"What do you mean? Saw you where?" Arlo asked.

"On Beach Drive before sunset on Saturday."

"So? Just tell them they're wrong," Arlo said.

"I think they have pictures. Hell. We need to figure out some way to explain this." Franco continued to pace.

"It looks like Franco did show up on Beach Drive before sunset like we thought," Chet said.

"They didn't see me drop you off, did they?" Arlo asked.

"He didn't say anything, but I doubt they have cameras on that turnoff into Frederickport. Anyway, that was like four hours earlier."

"Go tell Danielle Arlo dropped Franco off at the turnoff into town, around four in the afternoon. Also tell her Franco was on her street before sunset, like we suspected," Macbeth told Chet.

THE GHOST OF SECOND CHANCES

"WHEN WAS the last time you saw Chet Morrison?" the chief asked Angelo.

"Before we left for Portland on Saturday. It was late afternoon."

"And you didn't see him again?" the chief asked.

"No."

"Interesting." The chief leaned back in his chair and studied Angelo. "It seems we have a witness that saw you driving Chet's car on Saturday evening."

"That's impossible. I was in Portland Saturday night. You can ask the hotel. We checked in around six." Angelo leaned back in the chair. "Stayed in the room all night, ordered up pizza."

"According to our witness, you were driving Chet's car, and your cousin Mac was sitting in the passenger seat. Chet was in the backseat."

"Why would he be sitting in the backseat of his own car?" Angelo asked. "Anyway, I was in Portland."

The chief shrugged. "I have no idea. But we have a witness that claims you were driving the car that dropped Mac off at Marlow House. The only thing, when you drove by later, it wasn't Mac you picked up from Marlow House, it was your older brother Franco. He didn't see anyone in the backseat. Where was Chet? Passed out from whatever you put in his beer?"

Angelo stared at the chief. "I'm not saying anything else without my attorney here."

IN THE ADJOINING office Brian and Joe stared dumbfounded at the window.

"He's doing it again," Joe muttered.

"What do you mean?" Brian asked.

"The chief. He seems to know things no one else does. He's done this before."

Later, when Brian returned Angelo to the cell with his brother, he didn't bring Arlo back with him. Instead, the chief had instructed him to leave Angelo and then return fifteen minutes later for Arlo.

"They know!" Angelo wailed when the three were alone.

"Shut up," Franco said. "Maybe they have this cell bugged."

"Oh, that's great," Arlo groaned. "If you thought that, why were you flapping your jaws after you came back?"

"Obviously because the thought hadn't occurred to me at the time!" Franco snapped.

"What are we going to do?" Arlo asked.

"We shut up now and don't say anything to the cops. You hear me? If they question you, Arlo, don't say anything. Wait for our attorney."

TWENTY MINUTES later Arlo was led into the interrogation room. After the chief entered, Arlo said, "I'm pleading the Fifth. I'm not saying anything without my attorney."

The chief smiled and walked to the table and sat down. "That's fine. I'm not going to ask you a thing. I'll do all the talking."

Arlo frowned yet remained quiet.

"We know what happened. You dropped your brother Franco off at the turnoff into Frederickport around four on Saturday. You then went alone to Portland and checked in to the hotel. You ordered several pizzas and let them think your brothers were in the room with you."

Arlo remained quiet and shifted nervously in his chair.

"Franco managed to get into Marlow House and hide. Meanwhile, Chet thought he and Angelo were dropping your cousin Mac off somewhere because Mac's car was broken down. There was nothing wrong with Mac's car, which I'm sure we'll find out as soon as our people look it over."

"I don't know anything about Mac's car. I was in Portland. I have witnesses."

"The only reason Chet agreed to take Mac somewhere was because Mac offered him fifty bucks. Unfortunately, Chet had been drinking all afternoon—something Angelo had made sure of—and he was in no condition to drive. Which is why Angelo offered to take the wheel."

"I don't know, I was in Portland." Arlo looked as if he were about to cry.

"What Chet didn't know, Angelo had drugged the open beer Chet had taken with him. So by the time they reached Frederickport, he was out. The original plan was for Mac to murder Marlow, and then you planned to set up Chet for the crime. After all, the gun Franco used to kill your cousin was the one you had stolen from Chet's car. I imagine you thought Chet's fingerprints were on the gun. But it wasn't his prints, it was his sister's."

"I want to go back to my cell now," Arlo pleaded.

"Here's the deal, Arlo, while you are an accessory to the murders, you weren't there when Franco pulled the trigger or when Angelo picked up Franco and the two of them pushed Chet and his car into the ocean. By the time you got back from Portland to pick up your brothers late that night, they were already dead. You need to cut a deal, Arlo. Or you could be facing the death penalty like your brothers."

JOE AND BRIAN stood speechless in the next room, watching the drama unfold. They looked at each other and shook their heads.

"Where did the chief come up with all this?" Joe stammered.

"I have no idea. But if this is some cockamamie theory on what happened, and he actually thinks Arlo is going to roll on his brothers, he has lost it!'

The next moment Joe and Brian watched as Arlo Bandoni waived the right to an attorney and rolled on his brothers.

FORTY

Frederickport weather had taken a turn for higher temperatures again, and considering all the recent drama, residents on Beach Drive decided it was an opportunity to get together, unwind, and spend a little time on the beach. Because of Walt's cast, actually gathering on the beach was a little difficult, so they decided the next best thing was to get together at Chris's house and relax on his back patio overlooking the ocean.

Walt and Danielle arrived first, and Chris gave Walt a brief tour of his house. What surprised Chris was Walt's interest in his home. He looked closely at every room, every decorating accent.

"It's so different from Marlow House," Walt mused. "So modern."

"This doesn't have the charm of Marlow House," Chris conceded.

Walt shook his head as he hopped from one room into the hallway. "No, I really like your house. So different from what I'm used to."

"Then we have to show you Chris's office," Danielle said brightly. "The old Gusarov estate is about as different from Marlow House as you can get."

"So I've heard." Walt smiled.

When Chris showed Walt and Danielle to the patio, they found Eva and Marie sitting atop the side wall that separated

Chris's house from the neighbor's. Eva wore her hair wrapped in a beige silk scarf, while a floppy straw hat perched on Marie's head.

"Where have you two been?" Danielle asked as Walt hobbled to a chair and sat down.

"We understand we missed all the action!" Marie said.

"And we want to hear all about it!" Eva added.

"We could have used your help." Danielle sat down on a chair next to Walt.

"You didn't need us, Danielle," Eva said with a merry laugh. "I understand you and Walt did just fine yourselves."

"Can I get you a glass of wine?" Chris asked Danielle.

Danielle started to stand up again while saying, "I can get it myself…"

Chris told her to sit back down and said, "I have your favorite in there." He then looked at Walt and asked, "Instead of wine or beer, would you like some brandy?"

Walt's lips formed a slow smile. "Brandy?"

"It was Marie's suggestion. I'm not much of a brandy drinker, but Marie told me what her father's favorite was; I remember you mentioning several times how you used to enjoy an evening brandy with him."

"Thank you, Chris. I haven't had a brandy since…since the night I was murdered. But yes, I would love one."

"Me too," Danielle piped up.

"Not your wine?" Chris asked.

Danielle shook her head. "I haven't had brandy in ages. I'd like to try a little."

Chris was inside getting drinks when Ian and Lily showed up, and a few minutes later, Heather arrived.

When they were all settled on the back patio, Heather asked, "Okay, if I understand correctly, Macbeth's cousins are the ones who murdered him and Chet. But why? The article in the newspaper didn't say much aside from the fact the middle brother turned state evidence on the other ones."

"I'm more curious to find out what happened to Chet's and Macbeth's spirits." Ian glanced around. "Did they move on?"

Danielle looked to Ian, who sat in one of the patio chairs next to Lily, a beer in hand. "Chet and Macbeth moved on. I think they were anxious to deal with whatever penance they have waiting. But I suspect it will go better for them considering how they helped us untangle this mess."

"So why?" Heather asked. "Why did they kill their cousin? Why kill Chet?"

"Originally," Danielle began, "Macbeth's plan was to kill Walt and set up Chet for the murder."

"Why did he want to kill Walt?" Heather asked.

"After talking to his spirit," Walt interjected, "I think the real reason, he was afraid of me."

"Afraid?" Lily frowned.

"When he overheard Danielle and me talking, he thought I was pulling another scam. Thought I didn't have amnesia. At first, he just wanted to blackmail me for the paintings. But then afterwards, he started thinking about it and was worried I might double-cross him and try to get rid of him."

"Why did his cousins kill him?" Heather asked.

"It seems the Bandoni brothers had some serious financial problems," Danielle told her. "They inherited their grandmother's house a few years back, but they're behind on the taxes, and none of them seem capable of holding down a real job. They have just one car they all share. I guess they do handyman jobs around town, but they're not that reliable, so their business isn't doing well.

"They thought Macbeth was going to score a fortune with those portraits, and he was only planning to give them a pittance. When Clint was no longer taking his share from the heist, the cousins thought Macbeth would give them a bigger cut. But he wasn't going to give them much more. They were tired of him pulling rank on them their entire lives. I guess they finally realized they didn't have to let him call the shots anymore."

"Why kill poor Chet?" Heather asked. "I know he was annoying, but I can't help but feel sorry for the guy."

"It was Macbeth's initial plan to kill Chet," Danielle explained. "He wanted to set him up for the murder, establishing jealousy as a motive, since Chet had been telling his friends how he and I were a thing."

Lily wrinkled her nose. "Eww…"

"Macbeth planned to steal Chet's gun, believing it would have his fingerprints on it. Then he had Chet drop him off at Marlow House, hoping someone would see his car in the neighborhood. After killing Walt, he was going to ditch the gun, and by that time

Chet would be passed out from the drugs they had slipped in his beer, and they'd run his car off into the ocean."

"Brutal." Heather cringed. "But I thought Chet's gun killed Macbeth?"

"The cousins got ahold of the gun first. Both Chet and Macbeth thought Laverne had taken it. So Macbeth changed plans. He got another burner gun to kill Walt and planned to put it in Chet's car after driving it off the cliff. Make it look like Chet panicked after he killed Walt. Of course, his cousins changed the plan again. On their way back to Frederickport, they learned about Laverne's fingerprints being on the gun, so they came up with a new motive for the murder."

"Wow," Lily muttered. "What about the paintings? Killing Macbeth or Chet, wouldn't that make it more difficult to get the Bonnets? Or what they thought were the Bonnets."

"They figured the police would assume they had their killer, so everyone's guard would be down. And since Mac was killed when the paintings weren't even in the house, no one would link the two crimes," Walt explained.

"That would have been pretty bad luck had Macbeth been successful. Murdered for a second time," Chris said with a snort.

As Walt sipped his brandy, he said, "Don't I know it."

"One thing that doesn't make sense with Macbeth's plan," Heather began. "Wasn't it risky for him to kill Walt before the paintings were delivered? If he had been successful, why would the police bother delivering his things on Monday? Why not just leave them in storage?"

"To be honest, I don't think Macbeth really considered that possibility," Danielle said.

"This is all very gloomy talk. I think we need to change the subject," Lily suggested.

"To what?" Ian asked.

"I want to know how Walt managed to move that crate without touching it," Lily said.

Danielle set her glass on the table between her and Walt. "I think I may have figured that out."

All eyes turned to her.

"I've been doing some internet searching on the matter," Danielle explained.

"If you've found the answer, then I have to say you really can find anything on the internet." Chris chuckled.

"Telekinesis," Danielle told them.

"Telekinesis?" Marie asked from the sidelines.

"Also called psychokinesis. It's the ability to move objects through mind power," Danielle told her.

"Oh phooey, that is nonsense. I've heard of that before, but those people who say they can do that are charlatans. No one can move objects with their minds," Marie insisted.

In the next moment Walt released hold of his now empty brandy glass and watched as it floated over the patio toward Marie. Everyone froze, their eyes focused on the glass moving through the air seemingly under its own power. Just as the glass moved over Chris, it dropped as if someone had been carrying it, yet suddenly let go. Startled by the abrupt motion of the glass falling, Chris managed to grab it before it hit the patio floor. All eyes turned to Walt.

Walt shrugged. "I've been practicing."

"I don't understand," Marie muttered.

"I don't either, Marie. But when Walt was a spirit, he eventually learned to harness his energy. He didn't do it right away. In fact, he was dead for almost ninety years before he could move much of anything. Oh, maybe a few slammed doors over the years. But it wasn't until after I moved in and he came to terms with his reality did he figure out how to do it. I suspect, whatever he learned—he retained."

"I thought Walt could move things because he was stuck in Marlow House," Heather said.

Danielle looked to Heather. "It's about the energy. Eva and Marie are using their energy to make themselves seen, to move around, and we all assume that if they decided to haunt just one place, they could then refocus that energy to move things like Walt does."

"But Walt's moving around now," Lily said. "Look, he's here. Not stuck in Marlow House."

"But he has a body now," Danielle reminded her. "He doesn't need that energy in the way he did before because he has a physical body. One that burns calories, has its own energy."

"I think I understand where Danielle is going here," Ian said.

"And it is an interesting theory."

"Wow." Heather let out a sigh. "There really is so much we don't understand in this world."

From where Eva perched, the glamorous ghost said with a chuckle, "You have no idea, my dear. No idea at all."

BRIAN AND JOE stood with the chief and FBI Special Agents Thomas and Wilson in the hallway just outside the chief's office.

"So you don't think Marlow was involved in any art theft?" Joe asked, sounding disappointed.

Wilson shook his head. "Not saying we don't believe he was involved, but we don't have any concrete proof."

The death penalty had been taken off the table for the two brothers charged with murder, under the condition they work with the FBI on the current art-heist ring under investigation.

"The Bandoni brothers insist Marlow was in on the plan with their cousin, but they all admit it was nothing but hearsay. None of them ever had any contact with Marlow. It was all based on what Macbeth had told them," Thomas explained. "And considering they admitted Macbeth had told them years ago about how he made up an arson story to try to control his girlfriend, it's obvious the man was capable of telling outrageous lies."

"At least we were able to obtain that search warrant we've been trying to get on Kozlov's boyfriend."

"What I don't understand," Brian said, "after Arlo confessed, he admitted Mac had let him into Marlow House, and they switched the paintings, putting the originals in the crate. But your expert insists the reproductions were in the crate."

"They were obviously switched again—either before they were put in the crate or after," Thomas said. "We'll probably never know what really happened."

AFTER THE AGENTS said their final goodbyes, Joe's shift ended, and he left for home. The chief went to his office to catch up on paperwork, while Brian took the box on the long-ago Morrison arson case back to the evidence room.

Brian was unable to stop thinking of the chief's odd behavior while interrogating the Bandoni brothers. It wasn't the first time he seemed to cite statements from imaginary anonymous witnesses. What made matters even more curious, Brian had later discovered Danielle Boatman had been waiting in the chief's office during the time of the interviews. Had she been the anonymous witness? Or had Marlow been the anonymous witness and had passed that information through Danielle?

Brian then thought about those fingerprints of Walt Marlow and how they didn't match the ones on file with the real estate department. His thoughts shifted again, thinking of how Clint Marlow was now Walt Marlow. From there, his thoughts jumped to the original Walt Marlow.

Walt Marlow, dead for almost a hundred years yet he still dominated Marlow House. His memory had been kept alive by the massive portrait in the house's library and by Danielle's interest in the house's history. However, the portrait was no longer on display in the library. In its place was a houseguest who looked as if he had stepped out of that painting.

Curious about the original Walt, Brian recalled an evidence box he had once come across when reorganizing the evidence room and digitalizing their records. One box had been on Walt Marlow—who apparently had been arrested for moonshining yet had somehow gotten the charges dropped. Returning the arson evidence box back to its original location, he went to look for the box on Marlow's arrest.

His motivation was idle curiosity, nothing more. It didn't take him long to find the box. Opening it, the first thing he spied was a fingerprint card. Brian smiled at the dog-eared card and marveled how far forensic science had progressed in the last century. Removing it from the box, he saw that the fingerprints belonged to Walt Marlow—the original Walt Marlow—the one who had been murdered in the attic of Marlow House.

Brian didn't know why he did it. There was no reason to. Why compare the fingerprint card of a man who had been dead for almost a century with the fingerprints of his namesake, a man who was currently alive? He didn't know what he expected to find. He certainly didn't expect to see what he did.

Brian Henderson looked again. He shook his head and told himself he was imagining things. He held the old fingerprint card under a brighter light and looked closer. It was impossible. Once again, he studied the fingerprints taken of Walt Marlow on the night of Macbeth's murder.

They were the same.

The fingerprints belonging to Walt Marlow—the Walt Marlow who had died almost a hundred years earlier—matched the fingerprints taken of the man he first knew as Clint Marlow—fingerprints taken just days earlier.

THE GHOST WHO DREAM HOPPED

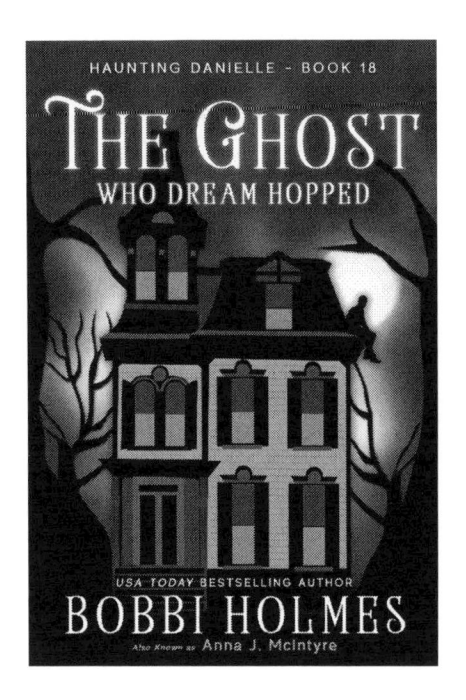

RETURN TO MARLOW HOUSE IN

THE GHOST WHO DREAM HOPPED

HAUNTING DANIELLE, BOOK 18

Officer Brian Henderson knows there is something just not right about Walt Marlow, and he's determined to find out what it is.

Meanwhile, Beverly's dead husband visits Danielle in a dream hop, telling her about his wife's part in his death.

Can Danielle convince Brian to stop worrying about Walt and be a little more concerned about his new girlfriend, Beverly?

NON-FICTION BY

BOBBI ANN JOHNSON HOLMES

Havasu Palms, A Hostile Takeover
Where the Road Ends, Recipes & Remembrances
Motherhood, a book of poetry
The Story of the Christmas Village

BOOKS BY ANNA J. MCINTYRE

COULSON FAMILY SAGA

Coulson's Wife
Coulson's Crucible
Coulson's Lessons
Coulson's Secret
Coulson's Reckoning

UNLOCKED HEARTS

Sundered Hearts
After Sundown
While Snowbound
Sugar Rush

Printed in Great Britain
by Amazon